Theater
of *Karma*

Kooch Daniels

SUSA:
MAY LOVE
GUIDE YOUR
PATH.
♡Kooch

Published by Tarot Media Company,
A Cigno E Gallo, Inc. Company
San Francisco, California USA
www.TarotMediaCompany.com

ISBN 978-0-9833024-6-9

Images from The Incidental Tarot, used with the gracious permission
of Holly DeFount, (c) 2011 by Holly DeFount.
www.TheIncidentalTarot.com
Book and jacket design by Chris Lowrance, www.ChrisLowrance.net
This book is typeset in Minion Pro.

This story is dedicated to my earthly mother, my spiritual mother, and all of you who have filled my inner being with love.

Preface

Many scholarly books about the tarot discuss history, symbolic interpretations, and key thematic ideas to explain the cards. Most however, discuss these magical cards without exploring the unpredictable worlds of potential realities and events that might accompany their underlying meanings. When I couldn't find a book that discussed real-life card scenarios, I was inspired to write this one.

I started to write my true-to-life tarot book after doing thousands of readings. Early on in my card reading profession I understood the meaning of the cards fairly well, but it took some time for me to see how the archetypes of the tarot play out in real life. To help other people easily recognize present day tarot archetypes I planned to create a book that listed different examples of life scenarios. Since so many tarot students have questions about the meanings of reversed cards, I wanted to place a major focus on different dimensions and challenges that these might represent.

Initially, my "how to understand the tarot cards as they relate to real life" book was intended to introduce tarot students to worldly situations that they might encounter while doing readings with the major arcana cards. Each chapter would depict events that a card reader might conceivably hear when giving readings to the public. Each major arcana card's keywords and thematic would be the underlying foundation for each chapter.

After starting this project, I asked my daughter, Lila Welchel, to read my first sample chapters. She said, "Mom, why don't you turn these separate narratives into one story? It will read so much better than if you just list isolated incidents." After thinking about her comment, I embarked on my first novel. If you're reading this page, you're about to discover how my efforts turned out.

Many of the scenarios in this story are snippets taken from actual events, but of course, the names and faces of my characters have been

changed to protect the innocent — or in some cases the guilty. Perhaps you will meet a neighbor or a friend here, as all of my characters are based on real people who have passed into and out of my life (and maybe yours too).

My editor, Nicola Scott, is living proof that you might not believe that some of the characters or their situations are real life events. While reading my material she would sometimes write in the margin "Kooch, you have to keep your characters believable. No one's going to believe this stuff could happen." Oh, how sweet, I thought while reading her comments — life is stranger than fiction.

I'd like to thank Lila and Nicola for giving feedback to my writing. I especially want to thank Lila for her timely writing and mailing me her poem that is presented in chapter 18, The Star. I should also thank the spirit of synchronicity that encouraged her to unknowingly send me this poem just when my story line needed it. Also, I want to thank my husband who critiqued each chapter after I wrote it, and encouraged me to continue my writing. His words gave me strength and encouraged my "knowing how" even when I wasn't sure whether to proceed. Also, I want to thank Jaen Martins and her double-Gemini, mercurial mindfulness for reading my novel and her prepublication insights; Smitty Wermuth for her wisdom about illusions and delusions; Jude Simmons for her life long encouragement to write "our story"; and Tara Daniels for her cups of tea and our walks together to help me stay centered on my path. Also, many thanks to Rob McNutt who generously supplied some juicy details about challenges in the big city that helped give form to one of my characters.

In addition, I want to thank NROOG and my tarot teachers whom I first studied with in San Francisco in the early 70's, and my present day tarot community in the SF Bay Area, which includes the most awesome group of tarot readers you'll ever be lucky enough to meet. Most especially, love and hugs to Anastasia Haysler and The Tarot Media Company for wanting to produce this book. Also, my heartfelt thanks to Holly Defount for allowing me to grace the pages of this book with her beautiful tarot art.

Of course, I don't want to forget to give a big thanks to all of you to whom I have been lucky enough to give readings. You're awesome!

Kooch Daniels
Bodega, California, USA
October 31, 2011

Table of Contents

One: The Magician

I. THE RED KING

Hermes, Be Our Guide

Carmella had won Jerry's attention by flirting ferociously with him the day they first met. Just thinking about his larger than life smile made her grin, but now she resisted reaching for his hand, knowing that he was emotionally involved with someone else. If only she could stop her heart from being attracted to him, she thought, wishing life could be easier. Why do I feel so romantically drawn to him, she wondered. Perhaps it's his coal-colored eyes and penetrating stare that seem to pierce yet nourish some private place in my inner core, she mused silently.

"Would you like to stop driving for a while and take a hike on the beach?" Carmella asked Jerry after they had been traveling the Marin coastal road for nearly an hour searching for a seemingly invisible address.

In all of her twenty-six years she had never said no to an adventure, but she was feeling a bit car sick from Jerry zipping around the zigzagging curves on Highway One. She would be happy to change plans, get out of the car, and spend some time standing on solid ground. Wanting to make a good impression on her new friend, whom she had recently met at a mutual friend's birthday party, she decided not to complain even though her stomach was secretly whining without shame.

"No. It took us too long to get out here. I don't want to give up on finding this place," Jerry said just before he slammed on the brakes and made a sharp right turn onto a dirt driveway that was partially hidden by a decaying fence and overgrown foliage.

Jerry stopped for a minute, pulled his windblown dark hair away from his eyes, and then began to slowly drive down the long, bumpy drive that was lined on both sides with towering eucalyptus trees. At the end of the driveway, Jerry briefly paused to notice Carmella's pretty smile before he parked in front of an old wrought iron fence made with rods twisted into the shapes of raven wings. Standing tall behind it, an old Victorian farmhouse in visible need of repair seductively beckoned. Directing his attention to the patchwork walkway leading to its front door, Jerry invited her to join his venture. "Let's get going before it gets dark," he said, opening his door.

Even though he seemed oblivious to her instinctive hesitation, Carmella was eager to please him, and promptly got out of his time-worn sedan. Following two steps behind him, she gingerly went up the path until she stopped to read a sign barely recognizable in faded letters: Condemned, Do Not Enter. She could barely believe that he was still moving briskly toward the front door. Not wanting to be left behind, she took a deep breath of the cool ocean air, and continued trying to match Jerry's swift stride. Carmella, who had asked him if she could tag along because of her interest in the supernatural, walked ahead bravely even though her common sense was telling her to go in the other direction.

Not wasting any time, within minutes Jerry was at the ivy covered door waiting for her to join him in entering what looked like a dilapidated Grimm's fairy tale cottage in the woods. He appeared to be on a mission to connect with some plausible part of an invisible reality that might exist in this forlorn place where any normal human would fear to go. The locked door with its dirty cracked windowpanes wasn't hard for Jerry to force open.

Noisily it unbolted from its top hinges and almost hit Jerry on the head as it partially disengaged from its rotting frame. Carmella stepped back ready to return to the car when Jerry grabbed her hand. "Come

on. You can't stop now," he said with a look in his dark eyes that made Carmella want to melt. How could she say no?

With only slight hesitation, she let herself trail behind Jerry as he entered the dimly lit old house and began to carefully walk through several empty rooms, all filled with cobwebs, empty beer cans, cigarette butts, and shattered glass. The decaying slanted floorboards creaked loudly in response to their steps as if warning them that they didn't belong here. Carmella could hear her heart fiercely beating as they came to a narrow spiral staircase leading to the second floor.

"So far, I don't feel anything strange down here. Do you see or sense anything weird, Carmella?" Jerry asked without stopping his exploration to wait for an answer.

Besides some broken jewelry in a decrepit chest of drawers filled with the dust of decades, Carmella wasn't having any luck seeing anything extraordinary. Except for Jerry, of course, who was so cute that she would discard her common sense and follow him into this eerie old house. Just as she was ready to move along, she saw something shining within a crack smaller then a keyhole. Pulling her courage from its safe hiding place, she stuck her long fingernails into the hole to force entry into the opening. The aged wood groaned, cracked, and separated to finally reveal a faceted blue stone with cunning geometry. It was so beautiful that Carmella couldn't help but instantly grab it and put it in her pocket. Surely, no one would notice it missing from these ruins, she breathlessly whispered to herself.

As if walking in a haze, Carmella heard, "Ya doin 'okay? Let's go upstairs and see if we can find anything out of the ordinary." In spite of her disapproving facial expression, Jerry boldly jogged up the decaying stairway and disappeared.

Thank God it's late afternoon and not midnight, she thought, taking a deep breath and consciously relaxing the muscles in her legs that seemed to protest moving toward the stairs. Not wanting to disappoint Jerry, she stopped herself from telling him that she preferred to study what it means to truly be alive instead of investigating the shadowy ruins of the departed. Relaxing her breath, she told herself that if she wanted to understand the meaning of the Great Mystery of Life, she shouldn't be afraid to search for its truth, even under the decaying compost of the nature of existence.

Moving slowly, lost in a sense of apprehension, Carmella climbed the stairs nervously toward Jerry. He sure has a cute behind, she thought, trying to distract herself from her growing sense of fear. The first upstairs room they entered was much like the rooms downstairs.

Dirt, cobwebs, dead insects, bat guano, and a few scattered pieces of broken furniture were disturbingly visible in between the corners that seemed to come together without symmetry. But when they entered the most distant room at the end of the dimly lit hall, their relatively benign environment suddenly changed. Seeming to speak without words, it had an otherworldly silence that shouted the pain of a dreary, unnatural heartache, or as Carmella would later say, "It was creepy." Completely empty without any tell-tale signs of any life from the past, even dust, it seemed to express a forlorn agony of someone being left all alone in the dark. A weird symbol that looked like something from a B grade horror movie used to point out the doorway to hell was drawn in red paint on one of the dingy walls.

"Do you hear that?" Jerry questioned with an excited look of anticipation.

"I feel the hair on the back of my head crawling toward the ceiling, but I don't hear anything. Can we leave now?" she inquired, trying to stifle her sense of alarm.

"No." Jerry answered, not paying any attention to Carmella's increasingly visible anxiety. This otherworldly environment had just the right qualities to allow Jerry to step into his invisible cloak of the magician. He looked mesmerized as he hollered incomprehensible words into the vacant room and began to communicate with spirits who roamed the outer edge of waking reality. "Do you see anything in the corner?" he asked, pointing to an area that had unusual marks on the floor and a rusty, large-linked chain hanging from a hook on the wall.

Not wanting him to notice that she was starting to panic, she answered calmly, "Some strange marks. Maybe they're saying 'It's time to exit'." Carmella noticed her hands beginning to tremble as she wiped the sweat of fear from her face.

"Are you kidding? Those marks look like magical symbols to summon the souls living in the spirit realm. This room can be a vortex that forms a pathway between the worlds of the visible and the invisible. It feels so perfect for doing a séance." Jerry said excitedly. "Let's sit down on the floor and try to open communications with spirits who might be using this as their dwelling place."

Carmella, trying not to appear unnerved, took out her cell phone camera to take a picture of the room. Even her tiny camera seemed to shudder with fear as it captured the cryptic images in its lens.

Jerry sat crossed-leg on the floor in the middle of the room. Carmella became more nervous as she saw him become uncharacteristically quiet and go into a meditative, trance like mood. Soon Carmella heard him

talking with some invisible presence that only he perceived. "Where do you come from?" he inquired earnestly. "How old are you?"

A window in the room that had been slightly ajar suddenly slammed shut with a rusty moan. Carmella's adrenaline levels soared, as she perceived an undecipherable stream of words shoot like warring arrows above her head. She strained her imagination to decipher the sounds she was hearing, and then she distinctly heard the demand, "I want my rabbit back!" She was hoping that she was imagining things but the tone of the ghostly childlike voice mixed with an excited rhythm and a sad groaning of a timeless past was undeniable. Carmella started to panic.

"Jerry, I want to leave," she said trying to calm her voice while tugging at his shirt. A hound started barking incessantly from somewhere outside the room. As cold chills covered her arms, Carmella ran to open the door expecting to see a dog, but nothing was there.

"Jerry, please! Can we leave?" she asked, wishing she hadn't decided to spend her afternoon chasing her emotional fantasies while getting to know Jerry better.

As if in a daze, Jerry stood up and quickly went running out of the room with a faint trail of blood noticeably dropping from his wrist. "Something bit me. Let's get out of here," he yelled, dashing down the stairs.

"Wait for me!" Carmella shrieked, her voice releasing the high-intensity panic she was feeling as she rushed out of the house trailing closely behind him.

The unnerved trespassers couldn't leave the dilapidated dwelling fast enough. As Jerry and Carmella ran outside into the normal-appearing world, the sounds of their huge sighs of relief were echoed by the strong coastal breeze. Soon, they returned to Jerry's unlocked car, and the sounds of their car doors closing triggered a returning rational sense of personal safety. Sitting in a familiar haven safe from their previous uncertainties, they turned to look into one another's eyes.

"You're bleeding!" Carmella cried out as she looked at Jerry. He was holding his wrist. She began to search her bag for something to bind Jerry's wound. The only thing she could find was her favorite tie-dye hanky decorated with a peace sign that she used to wrap her tarot cards. "Goddess bless me and my cards!" she murmured as she removed the cloth from her cards and began to bind Jerry's curious injury.

"Ouch! Can't you be easy on me?" Jerry asked in a series of notes sounding an S.O.S. alarm.

"I'm sorry! I'm just trying to help."

"Yes. I know. But, please, can you be little more gentle?" he asked, wincing with noticeable dread.

She relaxed her hold on Jerry's arm and said, "Yes…okay…just tell me how I can do this to help you the most."

"If you really want to help you can start talking to me about the Forty-Niners. Talking about sports always helps me get back into my normal state of mind. Once I'm more grounded I'll be able to drive without my mind flying off the road into another dimension." Jerry replied with a disjointed but purposeful voice that made it obvious his recent adrenal rush hadn't totally removed him from his out-of-the-body trance-like state of the previous moments.

"Okay! Okay!" Carmella replied even though she knew nothing about sports. She still hadn't forgotten the humiliation and embarrassment of always being the last one chosen to play on any team when she was in high school, and she still tried to avoid sports. The only thing she could think of in relation to the Forty-Niners was Joe Montana. Her dad had talked about him all the time when she was growing up. "What do you know about Joe Montana?" she asked awkwardly while trying to catch her breath. She watched Jerry trying desperately to find where to put the key in the ignition. It became obvious that he was partly in this world and somewhere else far away, and that his wrist hadn't sustained serious damage as he no longer appeared to even notice his wound.

"Well, he has a beautiful wife." Jerry muttered almost inaudibly as his key found the starter and the choking ignition made it known that the car was preparing to leave. Jerry put his clutch into reverse, and slowly backed out of the drive, barely missing a ditch before he turned his car around to begin their journey home.

Carmella couldn't get Jerry to talk with her anymore as he fell into complete silence. Feeling frazzled and a bit inept as a ghost buster, she looked at the tarot cards she was holding in her lap. Trying to get a conversation going, she said, "My auntie would give me card readings all the time when I was a teenager. When I got older, before I went to college, she thought I was becoming like her. She taught me how to use these mysterious playing cards. She told me that instead of me calling her all the time to answer my questions, that I should know how to use the cards to find answers for myself."

Carmella might have worried about Jerry's lack of response, but she was well aware of the trauma they had both experienced. Luckily at the present moment, he seemed to be driving with alertness. Fortunately he was navigating the curves slowly and smoothly without the reckless impatience he had shown earlier while driving this same road. Enjoying

the panoramic landscape and thinking about their recent experience, she was happy that she had gotten to witness Jerry acting as a psychic detective, and was even happier that she had mustered the daring to enter the old house.

As if on automatic pilot, she began shuffling her cards. "Jerry, I'm going to pull a card for you," she said, once again trying to engage him in conversation.

She stopped her shuffle and turned over the card that was on top of the tarot deck. "This card represents you," she said looking to see what card had turned up.

Carmella grinned as she saw the image of The Magician with one of his hands pointing toward the heavens and the other aiming to the earth. "As above, so below!" she declared, trying to get Jerry to talk about the connection between the micro and macrocosms. "Do you think the caduceus, the universal, curative wand of the Mercurial Magician heals consciousness directly or does it affect the mental reflections of the subconscious mind? Can there be any physical or emotional cures when restoring health and harmony goes against the law of karma?"

When Jerry didn't respond except to say, "Know thyself," Carmella reflected on his answer and decided that it might be best if she echoed his silence and didn't ask any more questions. Once again she looked at Jerry trying to get his attention, but he mutely ignored her. Obviously, he was mentally preoccupied with other affairs.

Frustrated, she thought about pulling one more card from her tarot deck to ask another question: Why did her heart feel so strongly attracted to this man? A momentary sadness crossed her mind. She needed to put that question out of her mind. Besides, it was a silly feeling that she couldn't afford to entertain.

Trying to be objective about her present lack of communication with Jerry, she looked out the window to put her attention on the natural beauty of the coastline. The sight of glimmering waves crashing over the rocky shore soothed her unsure emotions.

"Did you see any monsters in that strange room?" Carmella asked trying to pull her friend out of his silence.

Jerry acted like he didn't hear her and said nothing. Steadily they made their way back to San Francisco. Making up her mind not to appear upset by the unexpected silence, Carmella tracked the bizarre recent events in the seclusion of her own mind.

Two:
The High Priestess

II. THE HIGH PRIESTESS

A Sacred Circle

A few days later, Carmella was happy to be in the lush Marin countryside again. Hiking the winding trail leading to the top of Mount Tam, she stopped suddenly when the gathering in the large circular meadow came into view. It was hard for Carmella to believe that most of the people she was viewing from a distance were actually sky clad, a word used by pagans to refer to being naked in a magical circle. The light, dancing with shadows, made their bodies look as if they had merged to become one with part of the sacred mountain.

To overcome her mounting anxiety, Carmella rubbed her blue stone that she had put in her pocket while exploring the old house with Jerry. She enjoyed holding it as it felt smooth to her touch and warmed her hand with a subtle electric current. Perhaps it would bring good luck.

Lost in ambivalent thoughts about her recent unexpected career change, she forgot about her stone, and walked nervously to the circle. Right now she needed to focus on her new line of work, and was eager to carry out her freelance assignment of writing a magazine article on the present day practices of witchcraft. She tried to distract herself from her discomfort of taking off her clothes in public by musing about the most probable theme for her writing project. Without showing any signs of unease, she walked curiously into the large ring of thirty or more people all in different stages of undress who were secretly gathering at early dusk to celebrate the full moon.

Trying not to appear out of place, Carmella, bravely climbed out of her clothes, placed them nearby under the branches of a mighty oak, and joined the group of smiling folk who were starting to form a ritualistic circle. Walking in unison, they followed the lead of a priestess and moved into the shape of an unbroken spiral in rhythm to a drumbeat's metric command. Surprisingly, both Carmella's modesty and her writing assignment became meaningless as she moved whole-heartedly into the revolving spiral dance and joined the custom of kissing the cheeks of all the men who skipped by in front of her. "Queen Mother, Isis, Astarte, Diana, Hecate, Demeter, Persephone!" everyone repeated over and over in hypnotic hymn. By the look in everyone's eyes, the flowing line of merry-makers seemed to silently agree that they were celebrating the spirit of something timeless, beyond intellectual measure.

Once the spiral dance was complete, everyone joined hands to form a perfect ring around a nearby table decorated with backyard garden flowers, daggers, wands, and a very ancient-looking silver chalice. Impressive to behold, these altar items played a symbolic role in the ceremony being performed inside the circle by three cantaloupe-breasted women whose large bellies revealed the rippled swells of past pregnancies and indulgence in the good life. The presiding priest of the circle, who looked like a scrawny rag doll with brightly-colored flowers in his braided beard, wore nothing more than a mask, a crown headdress of horns and feathers, and a magnificent sword dangling from his star-studded leather belt. In a visual sense, he appeared to follow behind the priestesses, quickly attending to their needs as their voices mingled in a seductive appeal to become one with the goddess. Carmella couldn't stop looking at the size of his penis, which was larger than any she had previously witnessed. No wonder he's the lord of the circle, she chucked silently to herself.

In accord with ceremonial behavior, Carmella bowed to a priestess who was blessing each person with smoldering sage as she slowly danced

around the circle singing "We all come from the goddess." When the ritual neared its end, it was time for an experience that one of the high priestesses identified as calling down the goddess. Following her noble command, in unison everyone lay on the ground with his or her head toward the center of the circle waiting for Mother Nature's blessing. "She is one, She is all!" the priestesses bellowed. "Beauty and strength. Love is the only law!"

As Carmella became comfortable lying on the cool ground, her entire body began to feel united with the underlying energy of the earth. In her mind, the voices of the priest and priestesses faded away. Effortlessly, she went into a timeless state of consciousness where dreams and reality seemed to merge in a sense of euphoria. Through a repetitive rhythm from which she was not separate, Carmella could recognize a pulsing beat of life, death, and rebirth, constant and transcendent. As she listened, the world around her was being transformed into a resounding melody that included muffled voices of people whispering, women and men shouting, and bodies moving with roused emotion. "What is happening to me?" she asked soundlessly.

Instead of hearing an answer, Carmella felt someone tap her shoulder. "You're going to get stepped on if you don't move. Do you need help getting up?"

Carmella didn't want to respond, but she opened her eyes. It was Jerry.

Reaching for her hand, Jerry continued, "You looked like you were asleep. When you get up, the magic of this place will become even more alive. I know a wondrous spot where you'll be able to see the sun setting over the western waves while the moon is rising in the east. Can I take you there?"

Aroused from her soulful reverie, Carmella lost touch with the subtle voices that had been filling her mind. Smiling, yet overwhelmed by her shyness at sitting completely naked in front of Jerry who was completely dressed, she quickly went from her sublime mystical experience back to being a mainstream tourist in a foreign land. Her sense of embarrassment eased as she reminded herself that she was on a mission, her writing assignment. "Oh! Of course, I'd like to see the moon rising," she said, secretly wondering what the fates had planned for her and Jerry.

Jerry's strong but gentle arms pulled her upright. Looking deeply in her eyes, he dusted some leaves from her hair, and started to speak, but Carmella turned away and ran to retrieve her clothes. Soon she was back by his side, dressed with a modest schoolgirl charm. Without talking

they left the sacred circle that was beginning to look like a nudist camp social hour.

With Jerry taking a slight head start, they began walking toward a jutting cliff adorned with wind-blown junipers bending sideways with the tell-tale signs of time. In her mind's eye, Carmella watched herself move farther away from what seemed like a remarkable and unusually intimate connection to the spirit of the earth. She had just been feeling something otherworldly, and was reluctant to leave the dream-like state of the previous moment. Never before had she felt like she could reach out and touch the infinite mystery of the creation. Now that feeling was gone, and her mind slipped back to her unforeseen meeting with Jerry. Surprisingly, her emotions felt an unexpected longing to hold him in her arms, but since he was presently married, that feeling didn't make any sense. Still, she couldn't help but wonder if their souls had called one another to meet again today.

Even though she became absorbed in the natural beauty of their surroundings as they walked, she couldn't help but notice how handsome Jerry was. Astounded by getting to spend alone time with Jerry, her mind raced to think about what she might say. Perhaps she could confide in him and tell him how devastated she felt about losing her job on the editing staff of Vanity Fair. She moved her shoulders to release the ensuing tension in her neck when she realized that she didn't want to reveal that unresolved inner conflict. Or maybe she should tell him about the rock that she had put in her pocket while they were together in the old house that seemed to warm her hand after holding it for a short time. Instead Carmella said, "I didn't see you in the circle. When did you get here?"

"I arrived late. Everyone was lying on the ground with eyes closed when I got here. Norman must have told you about this open Sabbath, right?" he replied leading her down a well-worn path on a nearby bluff.

"Yes." Carmella responded, recalling her original purpose for attending the ritual. She remembered her long-time friend Norman suggesting that she experience the old religion first hand in order to give the article she was writing more credibility. He had put her in touch with his pagan friend who extended an unexpected invitation to this gathering.

Beginning to feel more composed Carmella looked back to the tree where she had left her backpack and cell phone with its camera. It baffled her that she could be so distracted, and leave it behind. If she could get one picture of the sacred circle before it completely disappeared she was sure that she would be paid extra for her article. She exhaled a heavy sigh

when she realized that leaving her camera behind meant she had lost all possibilities for taking photos, but she couldn't help smiling as Jerry supportively took her hand to guide her to climb a rock face leading up a sea cliff wall. Her heart jumped as he helped her climb vertically to a premier balcony seat high above the crashing ocean waves.

In spite of their get together not having been planned, Carmella could see that Jerry was happy to have found another moment to be with her. Soon they were sitting on the ground with their feet dangling over the cliff, enjoying each other's company. While others walking nearby were howling like she-wolves in a pack, they both sat silently spellbound in awe of the brilliant, red crimson light of the setting Sun, the misty illumination of the rising Moon, and the come-hither look in each others' eyes. Looking at the horizon where the sea and sky blended into one, Carmella asked Jerry what he thought of the title for her writing project in current progress, *The Revolving Wheel Of The Sacred Circle.*

Instead of hearing Jerry's answer, in that moment, as if some invisible force had ordained a special meeting, they were joined by one of the three priestesses who had led the circle. Wearing a long flowing blue gown that was blowing like wings in the wind, it was hard to imagine how she had hiked the uneven trail to enter their private arena. Smiling, she spoke with a British accent and giggled her way into their private meeting. "You've found the best seat in nature's theater," she commented while inviting herself to sit down next to Carmella.

Luna's wild, curly red hair was one prelude to her ability to draw attention to herself and her bold, dominating personality. There was something peculiar about her soft voice that was hypnotic, as it seemed to amplify the intensity of her words. "There is a veil of light connecting you both," she said joining their conversation. "You must be talking about something very important for there to be so much illumination between you." Within a few moments she quickly drew them into being three entwined beings searching for answers to transcendent questions that reached beyond the boundaries of time and space.

Chattering almost breathlessly, Luna confessed that while walking she was intuitively drawn to the beautiful moon-gazing couple and felt impelled to meet them. Without even a hint of humility, Luna continued, "I know my purpose is to be a channel for the matriarchal voice of the invisible masters and their wisdom. "The earth is running out of time. At a certain time, you run out of time. The right time interfaces with the wrong time. Timeless, timely, or untimely, only now is the proper time," she amplified her words in rhythm to the waves crashing below them.

Suddenly, Luna took off one of her several beaded necklaces that had a pendant of Isis, the Egyptian mother goddess, and handed it to Carmella. "Dear me, you should never join our circle without a necklace," she said with a twinkle in her eyes.

"Thank you!" Carmella replied, shyly taking the gift. She felt a blush cover her cheeks.

Sensing Carmella's unease, Luna said, "Don't worry! I made the necklace myself, and blessed it during a new moon using pyramid magic. The amulet of Isis is for your protection. Let me help you with the clasp." Luna offered, putting her hands on Carmella's back. "It's good luck if someone puts an amulet around your neck the first time you wear it."

"Okay," Carmella laughed nervously, feeling a bit anxious with Luna's seemingly familiar touch. As her hands on her shoulders seemed to send an unexpected jolt of electricity through her body, Carmella pulled away to move closer to Jerry.

Bubbling over with her love for mysticism, Luna started to spontaneously channel a moon meditation. She guided Carmella and Jerry to open their inward, intuitive eyes and see the invisible golden light of the lines of psychic energy left behind from the creation of the sacred circle. "Let's see what you can find within. If you draw on the energy of our circle, you can go back in time," she stated matter-of-factly. "When you walk psychic power lines, you can channel their light, and intensify the healing energy of the earth. Our sacred circle can be used to mend the wounds of our ailing planet." Two ravens flew overhead, sounding a cry that emphasized Luna's sense of urgency.

Persuasively adding his own explanation about the Earth's power grids Jerry said, "When you assist in this process, your mind automatically shifts to a higher level of understanding of how to work with these naturally occurring currents of invisible power. With practice, you can learn to use your intuition as an instrument to accelerate the evolution of humanity."

Even though Luna was nodding her head in agreement with Jerry, her attention seemed to be directed elsewhere. Carmella felt Luna's magnetic stare going right through her. She became filled with a strange sensation that went beyond logic, and recognized it as something akin to sensuality and seduction. Was it only in her imagination that Luna was sexually attracted to her? Why did she keep looking at her?

Without offering any clue about what lay beneath the surface of her smile, Luna continued talking to her new friends about "otherworldly" knowledge associated with vortexes, psychic realms, and invisible dimensions hidden behind the veil of Maya or illusion. Jerry agreed with

Luna, exclaiming, "Our higher purpose is to offer ourselves as vessels for pouring healing energy to the planet and those in need. The more of this work you do, the more you realize how important it is."

While they continued their talk, the fog looming over the sea began to spread its tentacles toward the shore. As its cooling mist began to fall, the light of the early evening began to fade. "Your words are very wise, but I'm getting cold." Carmella said with a quiver. "Maybe we should get back before it gets too dark to see where we've going. And I need to be heading back to town soon. My dog's been in my apartment all day, and he usually gets into trouble if I leave him alone for too long."

"Yes, it's that time of day when we all need to find warmer clothes or else freeze to death." Luna replied with a noticeable shiver. "Perhaps we'll find an excuse to talk again. Let me give you my business card with my phone number. If you're interested, call me and I will give you information about my psychic work."

Taking her number Carmella instantly thought of calling Luna to ask for an interview for her magazine article. "That's great. I'll look forward to talking with you again," she said enthusiastically.

"Luna, how long have you been a priestess?" Jerry asked.

"Some things are only for women to know," she replied without looking at him.

Carmella saw Jerry's fake smile in response to Luna's remark. But right now, instead of analyzing what might lay hidden under her friend's tight grin she decided to spend her time looking at the light of the moon's reflection playing over the waves. Her time with Jerry had passed too quickly and she didn't really want to leave. However, with every passing moment the cool wind became more savage, making it obvious that it was time to return home.

Without any words being spoken, everyone got up to leave. Carmella was happy Jerry offered his hand to help guide her along the rocky path. In the ensuing darkness, the trail seemed dangerously unfamiliar.

"Luna, would you like some help?" Jerry asked.

"No. My intuition will help me find my way," she said with sure-footed confidence.

Carmella, on the other hand, worried constantly about falling. Walking slowly, she was relieved that the light of the moon illuminated the path and it didn't take too long to travel the twisting trail down the hillside.

"Merry meet. Merry part." Luna said as they neared the meadow where earlier the ritual had taken place. In less time than it takes to say

goodbye, she disappeared down a fork in the path going toward a glowing campfire where the crowd of goddess worshippers had gathered.

"Good night," Carmella yelled through the darkness. Now feeling relieved to be back on safe ground, she let go of Jerry's hand. It was time to retrieve her backpack under the giant oak, dig out her flashlight, and find the well-worn trail to the parking lot. "Thanks for helping me find the path back here. Even though I was a bit overwhelmed walking in the dark, I had a great evening," she said to Jerry, wishing that their time together could continue.

"My pleasure," he replied with a deep sigh.

Even though she couldn't see clearly in the dim light, she had a sense he was smiling when he gave her a goodnight hug. She wasn't sure if it was Jerry's tender embrace or knowing that she would soon be safe in her warm car that gave her a feeling of being more at peace. It didn't matter. She was happy to be on her way home.

Three:
The Empress

III. THE EMPRESS

Venus Is A Tree Hugger

"Jerry, you're raiding my cookie jar again," his mother declared while walking briskly into her newly remodeled kitchen. "Do you come to visit me just because you like my chocolate chip cookies? And who are you calling on the phone?" she inquired intrusively. "It wouldn't be Lisa, would it?"

"Well, it doesn't matter, does it?" replied Jerry with an undertone of disapproval. "She's not home anyway." He hung up the phone and quickly walked to where his mother, Rowan, was standing to give her an affectionate squeeze. Jerry sensed Rowan's personal power and self-

assurance and thought that it made her seem sizable even though she only stood as tall as his shoulders.

Pushing her son's hand away she snapped, "You should give her up! A married woman isn't going to bring you happiness. I don't like my only son hanging around with some older woman who's involved with someone else. All you get from Lisa is what's left over after she satisfies her husband! What's more, you're already married to a very sweet woman who's free to give you one hundred percent of her love."

Jerry cringed as he heard his mother's remark about his wife, Stella. His mother didn't have a clue about what was going on between them, and most especially what was not. But he was too embarrassed and intimidated by his mother to explain his current situation. Instead he snapped, "Mom! Get off my back. Stop acting like I'm your little kid. I'm an adult and I make my own decisions. Besides, I'm happy when I'm with Lisa." Jerry frowned, knowing that his mother would continue to bug him about Lisa for as long as his relationship with her lasted. Why had he confided in his mom? In the past, she had always been supportive of his endeavors to find love. It irritated him that his open minded, new-age mother had surprised him with a lecture on family values when he had told her about his new love, Lisa, even though he made it clear that he treasured her for the happiness she gave. And earlier in the day, he had been excitedly anticipating telling his mom about his recent ghost haunting experience, but then he would need to tell her about his new friend, Carmella. How had she found him, or had he found her? Whatever. Now it was evident that it would be better not to mention another woman's name.

"Just because you're six foot two and a computer consultant doesn't mean that I can't tell you what I'm thinking. Don't expect me to stop yelling at you until you stop screwing around with some married woman who isn't your wife." Rowan declared while rubbing the rose quartz heart pendant that hung on a gold chain over her heart. "Those sad eyes! You look like I've mortally wounded you. Don't fret; I don't have time to talk about this right now! Moe is coming over soon, and I'm going to need you to leave so we can have our private space."

His mother's demanding tone hastened his departure. He stopped leaning against the counter and stood alert in defense of his vulnerable emotions. He could only hope for her sake that her mood would improve by the time her new lover walked in the door. "Mom, I'll leave as soon as I get a drink. Please stop freaking out about my love life. If you want to look at choosing wrong partners, think about your own ex-husband.

Remember the days when you were crying 'I can't live with your father anymore? His womanizing spirit is tormenting me to death!'"

"You shouldn't talk back to me like this! I'm your mother and I'm only worried about you because I love you. When I left your father, it was because I was frantic about what our future would hold. I did what I had to do to stop being vulnerable to your father's lies. And I didn't want you to have to live with Mark's immorality, especially since he was your daily role model for becoming a man!"

"Truce, Mom, let's not start talking about the past again. When are you going to realize that I don't want to listen to your complaints about Dad? I grew up thinking the sky was going to fall because of the crazy stuff you said he was doing behind closed doors. At this point, do me a favor and don't make matters worse by complaining about Dad or my romantic partners." Jerry turned away from his mother's glare and grabbed a handful of cookies to put in his pocket.

"Is there something you're not telling me?" Rowan asked while moving the cookie jar out of her son's reach. "I know something weird is going on, but I don't have time to pull it out of you. Being married and then getting involved with some other married woman is going to be bad for somebody, and I'm hoping that that somebody isn't you! And even though it would be good to talk about this some more, it's time for you to go."

"Okay, okay. I'm on my way. Anyway, I see your friend coming up the driveway. Do yourself a favor and don't worry about my choices so much. I'll ride my own waves, and have fun doing it. Oh, before I forget, I want to tell you about the strangest dream I had the other night. I dreamed that Dad was crawling on his knees, begging you to take him back."

"That's ridiculous. It doesn't sound like the Mark I know. Now hurry and get out of here!" Rowan howled as she pushed him lovingly toward the front door. "I don't have enough time to get ready for my friend's visit and argue with you too."

"I wasn't arguing."

"Yes, I know. We were simply chit chatting, but seriously, I need a few private moments to get ready," Rowan said walking past him to fix her hair in the hallway mirror. "And one last word: Fertility. Don't forget I'm looking forward to having grandchildren."

Jerry couldn't get out the door fast enough. Even though he would have been a bit happier if their conversation had ended sooner, he was relieved that it had ended. Because of all of his present emotional complications, he wasn't ready to talk to his mom about his love life. She was an expert at meddling in his life, and had an uncanny knack for

prying into his private affairs. He was glad she had given him an excuse to quickly leave before their conversation escalated into a real argument. Not surprisingly, he felt emotionally ambushed because she had dropped the fertility bomb yet again.

After he left and walked towards his car, he gestured a friendly nod to a broad-shouldered man who was slowly approaching the house carrying a large bouquet of red flowers. Blossoms of love or not, there was something about the guy that Jerry didn't trust. He wished his mother had better taste in boyfriends. He was sadly aware that his dear old mom, whom his dad had bitterly nicknamed the "Vagina Vampire," always required a boyfriend to distract her from recurring dark moods and their unrewarding antidote, a handful of depression meds. Jerry couldn't remember a time when Rowan's medicine cabinet wasn't filled with little orange bottles of prescription weight loss pills. She's been on too many diets and taken too many drugs for her to complain about my unwise choices, he reflected. He wasn't too far from the door to hear his mom say in her sweetest voice, "Come in, Moe. I'm so glad you're here."

Rowan, making visible her sheer undergarment that she wore under her long green kimono, smiled as she stood at the entrance of her apartment to greet her foreign friend who brought the flavor of the exotic into her life. She was happy that Jerry had left, so she could be alone with Moe.

"Yes, I'm happy too," he replied with a large grin while offering her a gift of budding roses. "Who was that young man that just left?"

"My son, Jerry. He's in his early twenties, but sometimes he acts likes he's my father, and tries to tell me what to do."

"Grown children can be like that," he said, walking into the living room.

"Yes," Rowan answered while thinking that lovers were more often that way than sons. "Thank you for my lovely roses. They're beautiful, and oh, so appreciated!" she said, smelling them before putting them in a vase.

Rowan looked over at Moe, who appeared impatient for her to finish. Giving her a big smile and moving like an awkward teddy bear, he reached for Rowan and began hugging her, but she wasn't quite ready for his advances. Feeling the intensity of his affections, she knew he was poised for love as he took her hand and walked her toward her Valentine-red sofa. Breathing heavily, he pulled her to sit down next to him and whispered with a hint of sincerity, "You are my Aphrodite, my beauty."

Rowan wasn't sure how to respond. Halfway withdrawing in hesitation, she replied, "You're very sweet, Moe. Are you sure that you're not just flattering me?"

"No, absolutely not. I think you look radiant. I want to hold you in my arms," Moe answered, kissing her reverently.

"Wait a minute, Moe. Let's talk a little before we go any farther. I need to ask you a few questions about our last phone conversation. Do you really want to marry me?"

"My sweet Rowan, I'm not in the mood to talk about this matter. Maybe after we make love, I'll be in a better state of mind for this serious conversation."

Rowan felt her body tighten and alarm bells went off in her mind. His line felt disturbingly familiar. "First make love, and then talk" had been the motto of too many men she had known both before and after her marriage to Jerry's father. She tried to shift to get more physical distance from Moe. "But, I'm in the mood to talk for a little while. I was wondering if you truly love me, or merely want to use me to get your green card?"

"Don't talk like that! Don't you respect my feelings? I've just arrived at your home, and you're already making me feel unwelcome."

"I'm not trying to be insensitive, but I need to know more about what you're feeling. I'm thrilled that you've asked me to marry you, but we've only known each other for a couple of months. Perhaps I'm a little insecure because I have a cousin who married a man who left her shortly after he got his citizenship papers. Seriously, Moe, do you really think of me as someone who you want to live your life with, or are you looking at me as an easy ticket to citizenship? Be honest!" Since her divorce from Mark, the man of her dreams that turned into a nightmare, she wasn't letting any man dictate to her who she was or what she was suppose to say or do.

"Darling, I'm here wanting to make love to you, and you're talking about things that are so complicated to discuss. Why would I bring you flowers? Why do I see you as the most beautiful woman in the world with whom I want to share my life? I solely want you - in my arms - right now!"

Rowan was happy for Moe's compliment, and his kisses were beginning to excite her. But talking about marriage felt to her like rushing things. She did hope to be married again, but she didn't want to become a victim to any man's scheming. "Well, you seem to be very loving. You don't think I need to lose weight? I have a hard time believing I'm beautiful when I look at my big belly," she said rubbing her stomach

playfully. I really need to go on a diet again, she thought to herself, being aware that for a quick second Moe looked disdainfully at her matronly girth.

"We all have our little bulges. Truthfully, you are my cougar." Moe didn't fall prey to continuing her self-defacing topic of discussion that was taboo for romance. "Rowan," he said sweetly, rubbing her thighs, "let's forget all this nonsense. I only have a little while to be with you today, and I'd really love to take advantage of our time. We can continue talking on the phone later tonight after I get home from work, but let's use this time together to hold one another."

Rowan heard him casually unzip his pants as he moved closer to her. Feeling uneasy about the speed of his passionate advance, she began giggling like a teenager. "Your kisses are so delicious," Moe said, moving his hand to quickly find a way inside her gown. But in that moment, as if by divine intervention, the phone rang, and Rowan wiggled out of his heated grip to answer her phone.

"Hello. Today? Really?" she said into the receiver amid frequent sobs of disgust. "Are they crazy? Why, yes, of course I'd love to go with you. I can get ready to go immediately," she said slipping further away from Moe, whose smile began to wilt like a tender sprout in the noonday sun. "I have a friend visiting, but he's almost ready to leave. What time can you pick me up? Okay, I'll start getting ready right now. Bye." Rowan took a deep breath and tried to hide her look of relief that would reveal she was happy to have an excuse to escape from her emotional confusion and Moe's impassioned grasp.

"Oh, dear me. I'm so sorry!" whined Rowan as she jerked farther away. "That was my friend who's an activist in the Green movement. He wants me to drive up to Sonoma County, and look at some old grove redwoods that are in danger of being logged in order for some developer to make his fortune planting a vineyard. He wants me to join the rally to fight for the rights of these trees and the spotted owls who make them their home. If I have anything to say about it, he'll have to bulldoze my screaming body before I let that happen. These ancient trees have lived a thousand years before he and his greed were even born. Sorry Moe, but my friend's coming to give me a ride to the demonstration for their preservation and he's going to be here soon."

"Someone calls, and you're ready to jump up and end our date?" Moe asked with a flash of anger in his eyes. "Now I see where I stand with you. Do you think I'm a moron?"

"Moe, this cause is so very important to me. I'd like to stay here with you, but I have a chance to help Mother Nature and safeguard a grove of

trees. There aren't many of those left. My friend only recently found out about the rally. Don't be mad at me because I want, no, I need to help. I don't want to hurt your feelings, but I can't tell you how excited I am to do something of real value. You must understand how important this is, not only to me, but also for future generations. And I'll be getting to spend time with people who are actively involved in the green movement and creating positive changes for our planet." Rowan consciously stopped herself from being too eager to talk about her friend who was picking her up in his red convertible sports car. She didn't want to tell Moe how excited she was to have a chance to be with someone who was motivating her to rise to a worthy sense of purpose and to make the most of her life.

"So your affection for trees is more important than making love with me? It's insulting that you want me to leave when I only arrived ten minutes ago."

"Moe, I'll call you when I get home, and you can come back later."

"Well, don't expect me to come back because I don't feel like visiting you any time in the near future. That's for sure."

"Moe, give me a kiss. If you really love me, you shouldn't mind that I have a chance to make some important changes to help protect our planet. Don't get stuck in negative thinking. Inflexibility drives me crazy."

"And if you're so flexible, you shouldn't mind calling me by my real name, Mohammed!" he said indignantly as he gathered his pride, zipped up his pants, and headed toward the door without saying another word.

"I love you, Moe! I mean Mohammed!" Rowan called out in a voice as sweet as candy. "Don't be angry. Mother Nature needs me right now more than you do. Please call me later."

Four: The Emperor

IV. THE EMPEROR

Party Time

Mesmerized by memories of his past, Mark lay on his couch trying to shake the fatigue of the haunting reminiscence of good times long gone. Massaging his head to awaken the present moment, he sat up, took a vial out of his shirt pocket, and carefully opened its lid. The powder glistened when he poured a thick line of it on a mirror conveniently placed on top of a nearby coffee table. Smiling, he breathed the crystals from a straw into his nostrils and waited for the euphoria that he knew would soon follow. As his mind started to soar, he watched his imagined destiny arise from shadows in the room as if they were various actors playing suitable roles in his wish fulfilling drama called Mark Wins The Lottery. How grand life is, he thought.

Forgetting that his left hand was bandaged, he reached for the nearby remote. Pain shot through his finger like a raging fire. As his throbbing agony intensified, he was jolted into remembering that he was still recovering from a recent scorpion bite in the exact spot where he had once worn his wedding ring. "I'm surprised the sting didn't kill me," he said, talking out loud. "I should never have agreed to baby sit at Rowan's house—even if it was for my own daughter. I must have been drunk to agree to her demand," he reasoned.

"Why am I still trying to prove to her that I'm a good guy?" he thought, feeling sorry for himself. Even four years after the divorce, he and his ex could still find time to argue about their two kids and her insatiable request for more child support. Rubbing his throbbing finger, he imagined the pain to be just like his angry heart that pounded fast and furiously whenever they exchanged unkind words. It offended him that Rowan always had to be acknowledged as being in the right if they were to reach any truce. Hadn't he already paid dearly enough for her trauma that his unfaithfulness caused? After all, the divorce judge had awarded her their home, their collection of art, and way too much of his paycheck.

He should have known that getting married a second time would be a big mistake. Hadn't he learned from his first wife that a woman has bargaining power in divorce court? His mind continued to spin. Two failed marriages and two prime real estate investments now belonging to his ex-wives should be reason enough to keep me happily renting my bachelor pad for the rest of my life, he told himself. But Mark knew that even after all this time, he was still having trouble forgetting the delicious smell of musk in Rowan's perfumed hair.

The knock on his front door was unexpected. Preoccupied as he was with thoughts of what went before, it echoed in rhythm with his self-proclaimed injustices. As if awakened from a hopeless dream, he got up and nonchalantly walked to the door.

He could see Mary in the porch light, smiling as he looked through the peek hole. Yes, I'm going to get some love tonight, Mark imagined as he opened the door. She may be a little plump, but she isn't shy about giving me what I like, he thought, while inviting her into his living room.

Mary came inside, moving coyly like a cat. With a heaviness showing in her eyes, she slowly asked, "Mark, sweetie, I'm in a bind. Can I borrow a little cash? I'm waiting for my paycheck to come in the mail and of course, it's a little late."

Mark noticed her conservative dress, panty hose, and Sunday-best high heels. It looked to him as if she had gone to a lot of trouble to appear

professionally trustworthy. Surely her nice appearance gave her a better chance of getting him to say "yes" than if she had simply called and asked him for money on the phone. "A loan? How much do you want?"

"If I can borrow a hundred that should help me get by while I'm waiting for my check?" Mary replied politely.

"Is that all you want?"

Mary looked surprised.

"No. I mean would you also like a glass of wine? I've got some really good Merlot," he replied, rubbing his nostrils.

"Sure. I'll have a glass," she said, forcing a smile.

The doorway to Mark's rational mind swung open with anticipation of what might come next as he poured Mary a tall glass of wine. Although the look of despair in her eyes revealed that she had serious concerns, he handed the glass to her with a big smile and invited her to sit next to him on his brand new burgundy leather sofa. Just as they both started to get comfortable, his doorbell rang again. "Well, I must be in Grand Central Station," he said with a little laugh, getting up to go to the entranceway to see who was at the door.

"And who is this?" Mark questioned as he opened the door. "Norman, my man! Come right in." His attention instantly fastened on the attractive woman standing next to his friend who was shaking with a chill. A young Mediterranean beauty with high cheekbones and rosebud lips looked back at Mark with large dark eyes. Wearing a black lace top and slinky velvet tights, she ignited Mark's libido without her needing to even say one word.

"Mark. I'd like you to meet my good friend Carmella. She's recently moved to the bay area from New York," Norman replied.

Mark, who felt an overpowering sense of attraction, could hardly take his eyes from her. "So glad you could come by. If they have women as beautiful as you in New York, maybe I should be living on the East Coast," he said, watching her closely as she walked inside.

Norman nervously put out his cigarette in a nearby ashtray and continued, "I'm wondering if we can stay here tonight. I just smashed my car. The damn fog was so thick I couldn't see two feet in front of me. As I was going around a curve, all of a sudden I hit something, and it turned out to be a street sign. We're okay, but the front end of my car is wrecked and I don't have any way to get us home tonight."

Great, thought Mark, your bad fortune might just be my good luck. Trying not to give away his delight at having more time to get to know Carmella, he looked stoically sympathetic while his mind was conjuring visions of her wearing nothing but Victoria Secret's angel wings.

Expressing concern, he replied with disconcerting hesitation, "Sure, I've got an extra room. Sorry you were grabbed by the looming hand of fog, but perhaps it was predestined to conjure your visit tonight."

"Maybe so. I also have another reason for our visit. Jerry told me that you wanted to buy some of my green supreme," Norman smugly replied while smoothing his expensive sports jacket.

"Sure. Do you have some with you?"

"Yeah!" Norman subtly pulled a pound of weed out of his large hemp backpack and handed it to Mark. "I didn't want to leave this in my car while it's being towed to a garage. If you don't have the money right now, I'll front it to you. It's not like you were expecting a delivery tonight. Besides, I trust you like my father. Your son's one of my best buddies and it makes us kind of like family. Jerry's one cool dude! Too bad he isn't here."

"Yeah. He's one of a kind," replied Mark promptly taking the shoebox-sized package and slyly smelling the contents. "I'm happy Jerry passed my message along to you. It smells great, and I'm happy to get it," he continued, while putting his new acquisition into a nearby hallway closet. Without taking his eyes off of Carmella, Mark led his friends into the living room and immediately noticed that Mary had a sour look on her face. Feeling slightly on edge, he realized that he needed to make an introduction, "Oh, and…this is my neighbor Mary. She just stopped by for a few minutes to visit."

Norman looked curiously at Mary. "I know this is crazy to ask," he whispered to Mark in confidence after instantly judging Mark's friend as being a little uptight, "is Mary cool?"

"She's a little more conservative than most of my friends, but she's pretty hot in bed," Mark replied quietly so that only Norman could hear.

Taking a seat next to her on the couch, the young man stared at Mary intently. "Nice meeting ya. Hope we're not disturbing you," Norman said beaming an artificial smile. And then as if he was a member of Sergeant Pepper's Lonely Heart Club, he pulled out a foot long bong from his backpack. "Hey Mary, do you smoke weed?"

Sipping red wine, she attempted to make a joke. "Mostly I like watching global warming from the bottom of my wine glass," she said in a tone similar to funeral chatter.

"Freaky! Obviously it's time to get this party started," Norman replied, lighting his cannabis-filled pipe. "Mary, do you want the first toke?" he asked, becoming aware that her voice and her expression seemed a little pained.

"You can let Carmella go first," Mark interjected, feeling like the alpha wolf in a pack. "Company first, and Mary's not company. She lives right around the block. Carmella, are you ready for some of Baja's best? You got it from Pedro, didn't you?"

"Hey man, don't get personal. I'm not telling where I got it, but I can tell ya, it's really good!" Norman replied while handing Carmella the lit pipe so that she could get the first taste of what he knew would be instant paradise.

Even though she felt uncomfortable being given the pipe before Mary, Carmella acted pleased to take the first turn. Trying not to look distraught from her recent encounter with a street sign that resulted in a three block, uphill hike in the cold night, she inhaled, and smiled with her eyes closed.

She looks like a statue of Artemis that I saw in a museum in Greece, Mark mused, realizing that he would like Mary to leave so that he could make himself more available to talk with his newly arrived friends. Without saying a word, Mark moved closer to Carmella and took his turn on the pipe. After a long toke, his mind seemed to spin out of control. Without success, he tried to remember how much crystal he had previously snorted. Even though he was doing his best to act normal, he no longer felt connected to his body, and became lost in thought.

Mary, trying to fit in socially, wasn't going to let everyone get high and not give it a try. Awkwardly smiling, she took her turn and inhaled from the pipe Norman handed her before she noticed Mark once again looking intensely at Carmella.

"Hey Mark. What's up? Your eyes look like they're swimming in lava," chuckled Mary anxiously, the knots tightening in her neck.

"It must be left over from making out with the volcano goddess Pele the last time I went to Hawaii!" Mark responded, sounding as though he was talking while half asleep. "Hey Norman, do you think that you could keep Mary happy while I talk with Carmella for a few minutes in private? I'm going to show her your room for the night."

"Mark! We need you to keep us entertained!" Mary whined in protest. She couldn't help but think that Mark was acting like a cad, continually looking at the young lady who had captivated all of his attention just as soon as she had sat in his favorite cubed chair.

"Don't worry, Mary! You can amuse yourself for a few minutes," Mark said, while assertively taking Carmella's hand and pulling her to stand. "You and Norman can get to know each other a little better while I'm talking with Carmella. I need to talk with her in private to check out a very personal dream that feels like déjà vu."

"I don't want to be here if you're going to go off talking to Carmella!" she stated matter-of-factly.

"Okay, okay. Get over yourself, Mary! Just hang out for a couple of minutes with Norman. He won't bite you," Mark said, lighting another match for Norman's pipe. Giving Norman a brotherly nod, Mark escorted Carmella down the hallway toward the back bedroom leaving Mary and Norman with no other choice but to try to get along in their current situation.

Once they entered the bedroom, Mark closed the door shut. Then he pulled Carmella to move with him to sit down on the bed.

She assumed that Mark understood she was Norman's date. Believing he had innocent intentions, she had passively followed him into the room, but once he closed the door she felt vulnerable.

Not wanting to be alone with a stranger, Carmella couldn't get her tarot cards out of her purse fast enough. Usually, it made her feel safe to be able to talk with her oracle, and now feeling unsure of her situation she urgently needed to get more clarity concerning the illogical string of the evening's events. Hoping to safeguard her energy, she also brought out her new acquisition, the stone she had recently found and put it on a nearby table with her cards.

"What kind of stone is that?" asked Mark. "Is that an amethyst? The color is amazing." He reached over Carmella's cards and picked up her treasure.

Carmella didn't want him to touch her special stone and reached for it, trying to stop him from touching it. "Mark, give that to me. It's my magical amulet," she protested. For unknown reasons, a current of fear shot through her body. At the same moment, the electricity completely went out and the room became dark. "Give me my stone," she repeated in a panic.

Dancing shadows filled the night air. "Wow. It's glowing, and now I can see a star illuminated in the center of it. Is it that some kind of cut crystal or is it plastic? Where did you get that thing?" Mark asked, straining his eyes to find her hand in the dark. "Here, take it."

Just as the rock slipped back into Carmella's hand away from Mark, the electricity went back on. "I found it in an abandoned house. It's my lucky stone," she replied, feeling relieved to be once again sitting in the light. With renewed composure, she smiled at Mark not knowing if she liked him or not, and started to shuffle her cards. The first card she cut from her deck was intended to represent Mark, the straight-arrow patriarchal looking man who had insisted on calling her to this mysterious meeting.

The card she chose to represent him seemed to jump from the deck. It was the Emperor reversed.

"Yes, that seems a perfect fit for me," Mark said egotistically, while he examined the image of a powerful-looking man wearing a crown. "I usually can do anything I set my mind to do. I honestly believe that the gods watch out for me and give me opportunities to promote my success. I've made my way in life promoting business investments."

Now that she heard Mark talking, Carmella could relate to his blatant sense of authority and controlling manner with a little more understanding. But she wondered if he had any social sense at all.

"Really? Aleister Crowley claims that this card is 'the male fiery energy of the universe.' The Emperor represents someone who's charismatic, successful, and often, a good leader. He symbolizes masculine vitality. Perhaps this card also represents your son, Jerry…like father, like son. By the way, do you know I'm friends with him? He's so amazing. He brings a special light into the world," Carmella said, trying to transform her uncomfortable feelings into a delightful discussion about Jerry.

Mark didn't know how to answer her. Feeling disappointed that she was talking about his son instead of him, he stared blankly and nodded his head.

Outside the bedroom, Mark's closed door seemed to create a communication gridlock. Getting more stoned and trying to be casual about the unexpected social arrangement, Norman reached over and touched Mary's leg, "Are you Mark's lover?"

Mary's eye's opened wide. Even if he was wearing an expensive sports jacket, Norman was being a bit too presumptuous for her own comfort. "Well, lately when I've made love, it's been with Mark, so I'm not too happy with Mark going into his bedroom with your friend," Mary complained loudly, brushing his hand from her knee. It wasn't the first time she'd been ditched because of another woman, and her anger was easier to express than her jealousy. "I'm really pissed right now!" And then, to make sure, Mark would be able to hear, she repeated noisily at a high, thrill pitch, "I'm really pissed at him right now!"

The bedroom door swung open. Leaving Carmella behind, Mark responded by coming out of the room with the energy of a charging ram. "What is the matter with you? What are you screaming about Mary? You're being too loud."

"Your friend was just wishing that you were out here with us." Norman remembered the cold sting of Mary's touch when she pushed his hand from her leg, and wasn't sure what he should say. Even though he was open minded to the prospect of playing musical beds, he was feeling a bit annoyed at Mark for taking private time with juicy Carmella while leaving him to sit with a cold fish. Knowing that Mark was one horny dude, he wasn't sure if he had made the right choice by asking if they could stay with him, but he didn't know anywhere else they could go without his car so late at night.

Walking gingerly toward Mary, with no regard to her obvious upset emotions, Mark's fiery nature began to show. "Come on, Mary! Stop being so uptight. Couldn't you handle having some alone time with Norman while I simply talked with Carmella for a few minutes?" He looked at Mary with a disapproving frown. Putting his hands on her shoulder, and trying to sooth the strained emotions between them, he lamented, "You're frickin' hilarious, being so uptight!"

"Mark, you're being a prick! We were making love three days ago, and now you're telling me to relax while you're taking someone else into your bedroom. And you want me to hang out getting stoned with someone I don't even know." complained Mary. "I can't handle it."

"And you're ruining my high, Mary," Mark said in a tone that made everyone aware of his underlying anger. "I thought you liked having fun."

"I do like having fun," Mary replied showing disgust in her voice, "but this is no fun for me."

"Do you want another hit of weed, or a little more wine?" Mark asked, ignoring Norman and Carmella's renewed presence. "Would that make you happy?"

"No. I want you to show a little respect and act like you did two days ago when we were together," she replied assertively.

"Well, that's not going to happen. And if you're really my friend, you'll stop acting like a possessive bitch," Mark hissed.

"Then maybe I'm not your friend, because I don't want to be your puppet on a string," Mary pouted, feeling stunned and shunned by his sharp words.

"What's up with you, Mary? Don't you want to party?"

"No Mark! You're being rude! Did you forget that you told me you loved me the other night?"

"How could I forget that?" Mark asked while reaching for his wine glass. "But right now you're acting like a wet blanket on a cold night!"

"I thought you had integrity, but no, you're an ass!" Mary replied.

"Get out of here. You're ruining our party!" Mark responded.

"Fuck your party!" Mary stated while throwing her empty wine glass at Mark who tried unsuccessfully to catch it, barely missing getting hit in the head as it flew by on its way to shattering on the floor.

"Get out before I throw you out," Mark yelled.

"I don't want to be here! It's not a party anyway. I'm leaving!"

"Not fast enough!" Mark hissed like an attacking snake while shoving Mary toward the door.

"You're a bastard, Mark!"

"Don't ever ask me for money again!"

Mary didn't have her coat. The cold wind wrapped around her like a shroud as she quickly stepped outdoors onto the dimly-lit street.

High on a rush of cocaine adrenaline Mark screamed, "You're a worthless whore!"

Just before the apartment door slammed shut, Mary saw the bonfire of scorn in Mark's eyes and Norman and Carmella squirming to find a space to peek outside from the narrow entry. "Mark, you're number one on my shit list!" she screamed as her tears started to fall in a fountain of solitary rage. Alone, her wrath slowly gave way to anxiety as she realized that she had failed in getting Mark to let her borrow a hundred dollars. Feeling the painful sting of rejection, she become aware that her recent loss of unemployment insurance benefits and her impending threat of eviction were even more depressing than her argument with Mark. What was she going to do?

Five:
The High Priest

V. CATHEDRAL

The Invincible Truth

We'll turn two hundred dollars into twenty thousand in no time, Taylor said to himself while he looked in his full-length bedroom mirror twirling the tips of his freshly dyed, midnight-black mustache. What that idiot doesn't know, and hopefully what he isn't going to find out, won't hurt him, he thought, with a sly as a fox smile. Taylor, highly regarded as leader of the gypsies, loved his family, their traditions, and their spiritualist work. Not just because he took most of their earnings, but he enjoyed watching their happiness. And making money made them all happy.

Destiny, his twenty-four year old daughter with star-bright eyes and luscious, full lips, was amazingly good at using her guiles to sweet-

talk him, at times even too good. By the time she was a twelve, she had figured out how to wrap him around her little finger and get his generosity flowing so that he'd give her more than her fair share of their family funds. She's so beautiful, it's hard to tell her no, Taylor mused, as he dressed in his dark suit appropriate for going to church.

And then there was Angel, his fifteen-year old, who had been first introduced to him by the frantic words of his wife when she called her "just an accidental pregnancy." But now, after the arguments concerning her arrival had long passed, he was so thankful that she had come into his life. Her growing breasts, like firm grapefruits, and her blossoming sensuality had made his groin twitch when he had seen her from a distance, not realizing that she was his own daughter. She certainly is getting ripe, he muttered to himself. But damn, he thought, she's the only virgin left in our family who has the inherited right to work our ancestral rites. If someone takes her to bed, her natural psychic powers will diminish. She'll lose her opportunity to be initiated into our spiritual order, and I'll fail to become presiding Grand Master. Looking in the mirror while towel-drying his hair, he saw his facial muscles tighten from thinking about it.

Her innocence will not be consummated before she has the good fortune of studying the mysteries of the triple cross and has traveled the subtle astral planes, he vowed to himself. He would make sure of that. Taylor didn't mind playing guard to keep Angel out of love's danger zone. His bullish efforts would be well rewarded once he gained the privileged majority vote in the Horned God's fraternal circle, which would be granted after she was initiated as rashani, and became their priestess who could tend the sacred fire.

He knew that she would need his help to steer her consciousness on her etherial journey to the juncture of alpha and omega, accessible only to the pure of heart. The dangers connected with reaching this summit of success would be worth whatever measures he needed to take to assure her safety and his sovereign power. If her initiation serves the invisible forces that protect and benefit his family, he was confident that her loving nature would agree to do whatever he judged necessary. So what if those less resolute than himself had lost their sanity as they crossed the subterranean sea of dreams. If needed, he had his talismans that could change adversity to benefit. In addition, he had been trained to invoke the higher powers of inner manifestation for the shield of protection they guaranteed.

Without being deceptive, he could avoid sensitive issues about her risk of diving into space beyond limited time that leads to the mystical

sphere of seven mysteries. God willing, he would do whatever he must to have an opportunity to learn the magical formulas. Most certainly these mystical treasures would be some of her recollection after her successful journey. Without discussing matters that were better left unmentioned, he was sure that Angel would approve of his plans for her. He had no idea of the true advantages the ancient formulas yielded because he had lost his first chance to gain access to them when free-spirited Destiny had managed to sneak off with her then boyfriend, Jerry, one month before her intended initiation. If it wasn't for that little bastard, she, who was smarter than most, would have been able to perform their ancestral rites. Knowing from his own past mistakes that he must be intensely vigilant, he was doing everything possible to make certain not to let a similar fate befall his little Angel. However, he would be glad when he could stop worrying about her chastity. That time would be coming as soon as she performs the Hecate ritual, he thought, as he muttered an ancient invocation. "Heavenly maiden, mother, crone, keep my youngest chaste."

Combing his long, dark but graying hair, determined to get his slight curls to lay just right, Taylor, confident of his towering patriarchal appearance, continued reflecting on his family and each person's unique value. Methodically putting down his comb into the nearby drawer and then walking toward his office desk, he turned his thoughts to another important matter, making money. Did those aristocratic fools really think his family's talent and the power of their prophecy came so cheap? Before the upcoming socialite event would be over, he'd have more money in his pocket than he could count in an hour. He was sure of that. His family had the best of training in the art of using fortune telling to weave people's problems into high finance. Knowing how proficient his wife and her sisters were at their trade, it was difficult not to start counting their money before they worked their magic.

But no one had ever learned to take advantage of people's fears like his wife, Naomi, or Know-Me, as she liked everyone to call her. Once again Naomi, who bounced around like a youth even though she was in her early fifties, had just finished buying their entire family new clothes. It was reassuring to know that his choice in a mate could wield power over CEO executives like the deep-pocketed Robert Jones. Poor guy! He really believed Naomi could bring his dead wife back from the grave. Perhaps he wouldn't have been so vulnerable if he hadn't been seeking forgiveness for his untimely act of making love to another woman at the exact same time his wife was grasping for her last breath. When he had found his wife's body, it was obvious she had not died with a smile on

her face. Poor Mr. Jones had come home late from his tryst to see in his car's headlights the love of his life on the ground staring blindly at the moon, her rigid body cold as stone. Astonishingly, she had choked on a bite of peach plucked from a tree they had planted together decades ago to honor the sweetness of their love, and her face was frozen into a sorrowful soulless glare. Hopefully the $35,000 he had just paid Naomi for communicating with his wife's dead spirit, and channeling a plea for his forgiveness would bring some relief to his torment. Taylor looked down at his new shoes. "I hope so," he thought with a smirk, knowing how the pain of guilt brought top dollar.

His thoughts were interrupted as Angel knocked on the door and let herself into his bedroom. With her long dark hair covering her eyes she announced with a loud moan, "Dad, I can't be in your ritual. I'm afraid."

Taylor's smiling face contracted into a frown. "What?"

"I've been talking to Jerry, and he's been telling me that some people lose their minds and never come back from their astral trip to the other dimension. That scares me!"

Taylor felt his blood pressure start to rise and he made a conscious effort to relax his facial expression. "Doubt is the voice of self-destruction! You must believe that you can do it. When you believe you can do something, nothing can harm you, especially when you have been anointed with the magic serum your grandfather brought back from secret caves in the Himalayas when he was a young man. It's an elixir made from an alchemical formula using salt crystals dug from a hidden quarry millions of years old. Your grandpa went where the power of magic is stronger than what any normal man can imagine. And I've told you before, Jerry can't be trusted. Look how he broke your sister's heart. It's a good idea to be suspicious of anything he tells you!"

"Well, if the elixir is so powerful, why did grandpa die so young? And why don't we know what ever happened to him?" Angel asked, sounding as if she had spent a long time rehearsing her argument.

Taylor noted how she had ignored his comment about Jerry. "When you get a bit older, I'll be glad to tell you more about what happened before your grandfather's demise. Right now, you must trust me," Taylor said while reaching over to hug his young daughter. "You have this one chance in your lifetime to visit a land where miracles are commonplace. You will see a light so bright that its radiance spreads to the farthest orbits in the universe. Don't let Jerry talk you out of becoming one with powers that are rooted in mysteries so profound that they can never be understood with logic."

"I'm almost sixteen and old enough to make my own decisions. Besides it's easy for you to tell me not to worry, Dad, but I'm the one who has to drink that weird potion. Jerry said that it can kill the faint-hearted. I don't know if that means me or not. And he said that I'll be entering a world of disembodied spirits and that one might try to take over my body." Angel replied, sounding worried and moving farther away from where her father was standing toward the door to exit his room.

"What does he know? He's just a puppy coming out of the kennel thriving on hearsay!" retorted Taylor, his anger starting to flare. "He's done an exorcism or two and he talks with weirdos who say they've astral traveled. No wonder he's scared silly and warning you of powers he'll never understand. Perhaps he should listen to his own advice and stop hanging around people who are half crazy." Then sensing her unease, he let his anger subside and said in a caring, concerned tone, "Many people wish for this experience but can't obtain it. However, since you've brought up the possibility of unknown forces, it might be useful for you to learn some practical psychic self-defense. Do you have the time for a little lesson?"

"I don't know, Dad!"

Taylor cringed when he heard her upset tone. Why do teenagers have to be so emotional, he wondered. He had a hard time accepting that Angel was in communication with Jerry. Didn't she realize how hard it was on the entire family when Jerry broke up with her older sister Destiny so many years ago?

And in response, he was having a hard time not being angry. Hearing Angel talk about Jerry and realizing how he could influence her thinking was upsetting. Why would she listen to Jerry but complain when he tried to tell her what to do?

"Let me assure you, Angel, I would never let anything or anyone harm you. You can learn to create a magic circle of protection so that wherever you go, in this world or beyond, you will be safe. If you have a little time, we can get started right now."

"Now? I don't want to do your magical stuff right now. I have homework that I need to finish. Besides, if you're really such a big important High Priest like mom says, can't you just beam me up, like they do in Star Trek?"

"Sure, of course I can," he replied with a bemused look in his eyes, "but it takes cooperation on your part to let me be 'the revealer of sacred things.'"

Ignoring her resistance to further discussion at that moment he said, "Let's do a little experiment. For just one minute close your eyes. I want

you to look through your invisible third eye that sits in the middle of your forehead. Just do this for one minute. Please!"

She sighed and rolled her eyes. "Okay, Dad, one minute."

"Thank you, Sweetie. Once you have your eyes closed, look inward and tell me, do you see a white bird or a black bird flying through the space in your mind."

"Neither one. I see a hippopotamus!" she said with her eyes closed.

"Angel, please take this seriously. Slow your mind chatter, breathe slowly, and look inside. Tell me what you see, a black bird or a white bird?"

After a few moments of silence she replied, "Well Dad, it looks kind of like a magpie and a vulture, all in one bulky bird shape. It's white and black, and it keeps flying higher and higher. Now I can't see it anymore."

Taylor looked at a Grateful Dead poster on his wall and relaxed his tense jaw. He smiled. For once his daughter was willing to listen and follow his teachings. "Great! That's a good omen. Open your eyes, Angel. You have proven with your inner vision that you will be safe. If you had seen a black bird, it would have been a symbol of black magic and potential difficulties, but you saw a black and white bird, a symbol of unification of opposites and wholeness. If your bird had been all white or totally black, you would have a hard time harmonizing the perceptions of duality that keep the mind locked in a battle between evil and good. The mixture of colors is a sign of transcending duality and going beyond the involvements of white or black magic."

"Really Dad, I'm not sure about all this mumbo jumbo. But you're obviously trying to make me feel good about taking part in your ritual."

"Angel, I want you to do this ritual because for a singular moment you will be merging with divine understanding and you will become one with the queen of the heavens. This ceremony can only be done when you're young. It only lasts a short while and I'll be by your side the whole time. You'll be richly rewarded for your efforts because you will know more about magic than adepts who are fifty years older than you. You'll have access to the akashic records and be free to read the invisible text of our ancestral linage. Things will be revealed to you that no one else knows. No one will ever be able to lie to you without you knowing."

"Dad, I understand what you want. You make this all sound easy, but I still have to think about what I want. I'm the one who has to drink the elixir. I still need to think about it." Angel said quietly, looking at the floor.

"You're the only one in our family who can do this ritual."

"Will I have more power than my sister?" she asked with what sounded to Taylor like a surge of interest.

"Yes!"

"Does that mean you'll give me more money than her?"

"You'll get more than money from participating in this ritual. You'll be united with the strength of the gods."

"For real?"

"Yes, for real."

"Okay. I'm all for having the strength of the gods. Does that mean I can have all the boyfriends I want? Hmm, maybe I should do this…. well…. I guess that, well, maybe, well…most likely I'll do it. But, don't go any farther. I'm done talking about all this mojo crap. You can explain to me later how I'm supposed to astral travel. Right now I've got a date with someone to chat online. I'm out of here. In between messages I'll be thinking about what boy I'm going to use my new powers on. See ya later, Dad. Love ya!" Angel pushed the hair away from her eyes, and looked trustingly at her father before she quickly walked out his door with a large smile on her pretty face.

"Don't worry about using your powers until after the ritual," Taylor hollered with a sigh of relief. He felt in his heart that his youngest daughter would honor his intended mission for her. Not having any desire to bring attention to details that would generate fear, he did not discuss the dark forces with her. He didn't want her to have any second thoughts. After all, her purity was her refuge, and he, the High Priest, would be her bodyguard in both the physical and ethereal sides of reality. He might not have all the answers, but he had many tricks up his sleeve passed down from generation to generation in their tradition's spiritual hierarchy that would protect her.

Whether Angel would choose to drink from Hecate's fountain of love or a Draconian spring of evil was a choice that only she could make at the exact moment when her spirit would be called to capture the nectar of the moon. Would she be able to make the distinction between the benevolent but veiled truth and malevolence disguised as virtue that mocks soul integrity, he wondered. Luckily, the power of her goodness was the best remedy for the menacing choice she would need to make.

Perhaps it was time for him to tell his wife Naomi that her Angel had agreed to be the natural successor to the priestess of his sacred order. But really, guiding her spiritual evolution wasn't his choice. It was the decree of destiny and his revered ancestors.

Six:
The Lovers

VI. THE LOVERS

Romantic Frolic

As he breathed in the crisp fragrant ocean mist, Jerry felt lucky to live in San Francisco, where he was close enough to go to Ocean Beach whenever he needed to clear his mind. Before the sun sank into the sea's horizon the sky became a kaleidoscope of mesmerizing color. It was the perfect time to climb in the dunes, carve himself a solitary seat in the sand, and let the melody of crashing waves revive his muted feel-good mood. Giving in to the temptation of possibly connecting with Lisa, Jerry took out his cell phone to call her. It's not that he was obsessing over her, but he had to try calling one more time.

"Damn, why isn't she answering?" he muttered to himself after dialing her number and hearing her voicemail greeting again.

Before the day was over, Jerry hoped to see Lisa, his clandestine girlfriend for the last couple months. Since the last time they had gotten together, four long days ago, he couldn't stop thinking about her, and his hungry body wanted to make love to her again. He reflected with amazement at how their unexpected liaison had quickly become intimate almost as if there was an electric magnetism pulling them together. But unfortunately, their fiery bond that had started in a classroom when she accidentally knocked into him while attempting to do a difficult yoga pose was stressed by an unspoken complexity. How were they to know when their eyes first locked in a silent embrace that they each already had a marriage partner?

Lisa, who was twelve years older than himself, turned him on like crazy. Despite what felt to him like judgmental knowing glances from on-lookers when they were together, he didn't mind their age difference as much as the fact that she was married to someone the same age as his father. Even so, he longed to be with her, and if it was not for Lisa, he wasn't sure if he wanted to be in a sexual relationship with any woman right now. His own wife, Stella, had sliced through his heart with words sharp as a razor's edge when she told him that she wanted to be with somebody new. The shock of being abandoned by the woman who had sworn undying love and whom he trusted to share his life had come as a brutal awakening and he was still recovering. Not surprisingly, since Stella's rejection, most women left his bruised emotions feeling cold and he was unapproachably distant. At least that's how it was until he met Lisa, his juicy lover, who proved to him that his wounded heart could still fall in love. Being aroused by her made him forget his anxiety and humiliation at his wife's rejection, and helped him feel like the man his father, Mark, the charismatic woman's man, expected him to be.

When Lisa started talking about her life, she told Jerry that her husband David, an executive who worked in the financial district, put in long hours. Getting ahead in his business was his primary obsession and Lisa struggled with being second in line for his time. Even when he took the time to be with her, it was obvious when they went out socially that he was more comfortable with his computer than conversing with her friends. And it secretly hurt Lisa's feelings that he wouldn't visit with her family, whom he hadn't seen in the last six years. His obvious avoidance of her kin created a rift, and she had given up trying to make excuses about why he wasn't available to visit. Everyone in her family believed that their father's first and only argument with David immediately after his and Lisa's expensive, debt-creating wedding put him in a sour mood from which he refused to recover. The old man should never have

accused him of using Lisa as a trophy wife, but once said, it couldn't be retracted.

Almost in tears she had told him that, as their marriage became more routine, it also became less exciting for her. Lisa complained with an unsolvable frustration that David was rarely interested in her sexually. With her Sunday School upbringing she hadn't intended to cheat on her husband, but her good-girl values couldn't withstand his frequent coldness in their bedroom. With a fiery kiss she had told Jerry that even her guilt-ridden mind couldn't persuade her to ignore the passionate connection she felt towards him.

My good fortune they're sexually mismatched, Jerry thought, while feeling a surge of heat going through his entire being as he imagined her wrapped snugly in his arms. Their special times together felt delicious even though neither one of them dared to talk about plans for their future.

In truth, for Jerry part of their relationship was pleasure and the other part was a test of patience. Something unexplainable happened to him when he was with her. When he came within four feet of her, he became like a dog in heat. Nevertheless, his biggest challenge was not giving into the aggravation of waiting for her to free her time and be with him. Usually impatient, it was easy for him to become annoyed waiting endlessly for her to call. And she'd told him not to call her at home worrying that David would overhear their private conversations.

Jerry, trying to be a pragmatist, wasn't sure how long their relationship could last, but he wouldn't deny what he felt. He knew that the chemistry between them triggered a joyful feeling that he didn't experience with any other woman, and he craved to be with Lisa whatever the obstacles. Even if she was married to someone else, their attraction was too strong to resist, and his worries about the logic of choosing the right partner didn't compete with the irresistible sorcery of her lovemaking. Intellectually he could list all the reasons why she wasn't the right partner for him, or him for her, but that didn't stop him from dialing her number one more time.

After getting her voice mail greeting again, Jerry decided to call Norman, who was next on his list of calls needing to be made. It was time for him to start thinking about someone besides Lisa, and he could count on his good friend Norman to distract him from his thoughts about her or any other woman.

Jerry dialed and heard Norman answer the phone with his typical cocky attitude. "I can hear in your voice that you're ready for some Maui Wowie. Come on over. I've got some great buds just waiting for you to smoke!"

"Okay. I'm on my way," Jerry replied, while watching the fog roll across the waves toward the shore, a sign that it would soon be too cold to stay at the beach.

"I forgot to tell you. I've got a little company." Norman chirped. "Hopefully I'll have her in bed with me by the time you get here. If I do, just wait in my living room, and help yourself to anything at the bar. Amazing good luck for you, there's another little chickie who's also at my house who can use some attention. Her name's Jodi, and she has a cross tattooed on her ass, so I call her 'Hot Cross Buns.' See ya soon buddy!"

The prospect of experiencing primo weed, getting out of his present serious mood, and meeting someone new cheered Jerry. Giving up the thought of seeing Lisa for the moment, he moved in long strides toward his car. Mentally he outlined a map to Norman's house and calculated the fastest driving route going north from San Francisco toward Stinson Beach. The finishing remnants of rush hour was a bad time to cross the often clogged Golden Gate Bridge, but he had no other choice if he wanted to visit Norman now. After saying goodbye to the setting sun, he jumped in his car, turned on its ignition, and started to drive.

In just a little more than an hour of dodging sluggish traffic Jerry was turning his wheel and going up a country dirt road pitted with potholes. The sweetness of the fresh air and the unaccustomed quiet made him think that maybe he should move from the city and its ceaseless sounds of cosmopolitan life. Doubtless though, he wouldn't enjoy driving these curving roads every morning rushing to get to his job in San Francisco. For now he was happy to get out of the city watching the tentacles of fog that swept across the hills like a legion of silent ghost ships coming home from the sea. The eerie panorama made him feel like he was driving on a moonless, alien planet. As he made a turn, an oncoming headlight blinded his vision and his mind swiftly adjusted to the one lane road and the darkness settling over the terrain that seemed to change with every new song playing on his car stereo.

As he neared Norman's home, he rolled down his window to smell the earthly sweetness as he passed a grove of giant redwood trees, and slowed his car to ensure that his wheels would securely drive the steep embankment rising high above a narrow canyon. In the distance, Jerry saw bright lights in a little house beckoning him out of the hazy darkness.

This place is ideal for the life Norman likes to lead, thought Jerry. It's tucked away from the hectic world where he can keep his life private and no one lives nearby to watch over his drug dealing affairs.

Jerry parked his car in a clearing and crossed a small wooden bridge that creaked under his hurried footsteps. Anxious to get in out of the

cold, Jerry walked hastily toward the old, two story farm house that looked like a fairy castle in the darkness. His approaching steps on the stairs announced that he was about to knock on the door.

A voluptuous young woman answered. "Hi. You must be Jerry. Come on in."

Surprised by her seemingly motionless presence, Jerry's heart jumped a beat. Although her body language was guarded, her warm smile was inviting.

"My name's Jodi. Would you like a drink?" she offered as he let himself into the dimly lighted living room.

"Sure," Jerry said, "That would be nice."

"Norman's talking privately with Carmella for a little while," Jodi said with a knowing grin. "Well actually, it may be a little more than that."

Jerry thought her expression covered an embarrassment that she was too sophisticated to willingly show. Instantly ill at ease, he needed to enlist his self control to hide his surprise at hearing that Carmella was in bed with Norman. Recently, he had noticed his two friends talking together at a mutual friend's party, but he hadn't realized that they were interested in dating one another. Carmella seemed too classy to get involved with someone stoned on drugs most of the time. In his mind, they didn't seem like a likely match.

Unexpectedly, Jerry felt a twinge of jealousy. He reached for the glass that Jodi handed to him, took a drink of what seemed to be straight Scotch, and then awkwardly tried to start a conversation. He felt the young woman's eyes looking through and beyond him and he wondered what she was thinking. As he listened to her rambling, "...the pig doesn't own me. I can go where I want...," she was saying. Jerry sensed she was in a world of her own. Feeling a world of distance, even though she stood near him, he wondered if Jodi was one of Norman's party girls who stayed with him to share in the open-handed benefit of his drug dealings. He watched her fluid movements and saw that her feet barely touched the ground as she walked back to the bar to get another drink. She must be really stoned, he thought.

As if to answer his thoughts, Jodi asked, "Do you like to get high?"

"Some," Jerry answered not being sure of how much he wanted her to know about his personal habits.

"I've got a pipe we can share," she casually announced while putting some pot into its bowl. "Norman won't mind."

"Sure," Jerry said, searching for some matches. Secretly he was hoping that getting stoned with Jodi might break her icy exterior, and that he could meet her on a deeper level.

Just as Jerry inhaled his first hit, he heard Norman's rough voice, "What's going on in here?"

Thinking that he must have done something wrong, Jerry jumped slightly, but he relaxed when he saw the grin on Norman's face. It became obvious that his question was more of a joke than a demand for an answer.

"Look at you two, getting stoned without me! If you want to get high, let's all get high together. Come on up to my room. You can join Carmella and me. We're talking on my bed." Norman started gently pulling on Jodi's arm moving toward the steps that led up the stairs.

"Come on, Jerry." Norman requested. "I want you to psychically tune into me and Carmella, and tell me what you think about our connection."

Oh, great! Not another "does she love me" question for my invisible crystal ball, Jerry thought. He felt a shadow of dread struggle to take hold of him and he immediately knew that he had made a mistake coming to Norman's house.

The red and black upstairs hallway was barely lit. It was hard to see where he was going in the dim light, but Jerry, led by the smell of sandalwood incense and the chattering of Norman's voice, followed down the corridor.

Norman's bedroom was candlelit and mirrors covered the walls and ceiling. "You know Carmella," he said to Jerry, "Come on, sit down on the water bed with us. Take your shoes off and get comfortable."

Jerry agreed but then backed away from the bed as soon as he saw Carmella's bare breasts. How weird to see her naked twice within the last couple of weeks, he silently mused. Trying not to be obvious, he couldn't help but stare and noticed that she was wearing zebra-striped underpants. How beautiful her nearly-naked body looks in the candle light, he thought, feeling uncomfortable and wishing he was anywhere else.

"Don't be so uptight," Norman said, mocking his friend's hesitant stance. "Come and join us."

Nonverbally searching for clues as to what Carmella was thinking, Jerry held himself in check and kept his eyes from watching her. He had thought her to be more reserved, but he was quickly changing his opinion. Jodi reached for his hand and pulled him to join everyone sitting on the bed. As if watching a movie, he became aware of Jodi playfully bouncing like an energetic child, making the waterbed move the group up and down as if they were riding waves on the surf.

"Stop moving around so much, Jodi," Norman demanded, "we'll all be sea sick."

In defiance, Jodi jumped a couple of feet closer to Norman on the bed, causing Carmella to spring up and down as if she were a frog hopping on a lily pad. Jerry, finding it a little difficult to enjoy his present circumstances, began inching his way toward the edge of the bed. He couldn't ever remember feeling possessive with his female acquaintances until this moment, and he didn't like it. Confused, he wasn't sure what to do with his unexpected emotions, torn between jealousy and the unanticipated stirrings of desire for Carmella.

"Open this bag." Norman requested, handing Jerry a small brown grocery bag.

Jerry opened it, reached in, and to everyone's surprise, pulled out a white plastic dildo. As if it was radioactive, he quickly dropped it back in the bag.

"Damn! Wrong bag!" said Norman with a chuckle.

"Here's the bag I want you to open," he said reaching under his nightstand and grabbing another small brown bag that he handed to Jerry.

After seeing the contents of the previous bag, Jerry wasn't sure that he wanted to know what was inside this one, but with a naive curiosity, he peeked inside. His eyes widened as he saw a large, clear cellophane envelope filled with white powder. He looked back at Norman.

"Let's get high!" Norman pulled a tray shaped mirror from under the nightstand and took the bag from Jerry. Smiling, he poured the white powder onto the mirror and deftly divided the crystals into eight thin lines. When he was done, he handed it to Jerry with a small silver spoon, and said, "Have the first toot, buddy."

Jerry had expected weed. Sometimes you just take whatever life offers, he thought, trying not to look surprised. He considered possible withdrawals and what could happen when going to work the next day. No worries, he told himself. He'd be able to handle his computer duties if he only inhaled a little.

The others waited patiently for Jerry to snort his lines, and then each took their own turn. Before Jodi, who was the last in line, had finished, Norman's hands were rubbing Carmella's thighs and he began whispering mischievously in her ear. Giggling, she tried to embrace him by wrapping her legs around his middle while turning her back toward Jerry.

Even if the bed hadn't been making him bounce around, it was hard for Jerry to sit still and watch the love birds embracing. His mind was racing back to when he and Carmella were checking out the haunted house, and to when he had seen her naked at the full moon ceremony.

At those times he hadn't thought about her in a sexual way, and after spending time with her, he hadn't even called to continue their friendship, but now he felt an unpredicted attraction towards her. And worse yet, with her gold bangled arms wrapped around Norman, his battered spirit wilted in an icy shroud of an unfamiliar aloneness.

Jerry, who was not known as a wild child in his circle of friends, began to realize that he was too stoned for his own comfort. Through his mental haze, he knew he needed to be moving, or doing something, but he wasn't sure of where he should go, or what he should be doing. His felt like an underwater video camera filming "Lost at Sea" while his body floated in space within touching distance of three aliens blurred from recognition.

"Hey buddy! Why don't you give Jodi a massage? I know she'd like it." Jerry heard Norman through a jumbled echo chamber in his mind. "And can you dim the lights?"

"Who says I'll like a massage?" Jodi snarled, her body obviously tensing.

"Come on, baby. Relax! Jerry's one of my best friends and I know he can give you a great rub." Norman replied, pulling up one of Jodi's feet and lifting her toes toward his mouth. He stuck his tongue between her two largest toes and started licking them making Jodi squeal and move about like a tiger on a chain. Everyone on the bed, including Jerry who was feeling out of his element, began to rock with the frantic tsunami waves that were rolling up from inside the water mattress.

Carmella looked angrily at Norman's advances toward Jodi. She quickly started to move away, but Norman grabbed her with his other hand and put his arm around her shoulder holding her tight and caressing her breast as if it was his bounty.

"Jerry, what do you think of these two babes? They come around here and I get them high and look how they treat me. Jerry, come on, my man! It will be nice if you help me keep my lady friends happy."

Feeling that he may have snorted too much of the white powder, Jerry intellectually rejected his confused feelings for Carmella, and Jodi had already faded into complete insignificance in his mind. Truthfully, he didn't want to play an active role on the impromptu stage of Norman's bedroom playground. He liked intimate moments, but he couldn't be happy being part of this foursome, no matter how high he might be.

Admittedly, seeing Carmella nearly naked was getting him physically aroused, and that was something he hadn't anticipated, especially since his heart had been beating in unswerving rhythm to his thoughts about Lisa. Neither had he expected Norman's sexual openness with his lady

friends to transmit a tantalizing heat across the bed. Jerry couldn't deny feeling turned on, but he could still say no to becoming involved in someone else's sexual entanglement. He didn't want to spoil the party by telling the group that he believed sex was a sacred act, and he didn't want anyone to know that he was sweating profusely as if he were sitting in Hades. He just wanted to hide under the covers and get away from it all. Should he stay nearby or could he make a discreet exit, he wondered, feeling slightly sick.

"Jerry, buddy, why are you sitting so far away? You look lonely. Come over here next to Jodi!" Norman coaxed.

Jerry felt robotically numb. He thought for an instant about moving toward her, but then Jodi suddenly jumped up and moved quickly off the bed. Without a word, she scampered out the bedroom door and disappeared.

"No Jerry. Don't get up," Norman commanded in a rough voice, pointing to Carmella.

Jerry felt anxiety rolling inside his belly. He wasn't sure about this *menage a trois*. Previously, he didn't get turned on by Carmella even a little bit, but now he was feeling territorial towards her, and wanting her to leave Norman's bed. "Norman, this isn't the kind of meeting I had planned. I'm feeling a little gun-shy." Jerry managed to sputter as he started moving off the bed.

Before his feet were planted solidly on the floor, he was knocked off balance by Carmella who giggled, then lunged at him, and pulled him toward her. Jerry felt his mind and body go limp while trying to surrender to her grasp. She held him close, so close that he could smell her sweet perfume and feel the softness of her firm breasts. He wished that Norman would go away, but instead he moved his body to physically intertwine with them and together all three rolled about as if they were stones having their rough edges smoothed in a tumbler. Norman, growling like an animal in heat, created a wild spectacle from which Jerry wanted to escape.

Suddenly Carmella screamed, "Stop it!" and in a tantrum hit Norman with her fist.

Awakening from his daze, Jerry jumped from the bed, and tried to pull the frantically thrashing Carmella far away from Norman. She managed to scratch Norman's shoulder and even in the dim light, Jerry could see their faces frozen in anger. With a gentle firmness, Jerry held Carmella at enough distance from Norman that she could no longer hit her squirming target.

"Namaste! Namaste! Relax!" Jerry said soothingly as he looked Carmella in the eyes and tried to calm her down.

Not wasting a moment, Norman sprung up from the bed and ran to the bathroom. "What's biting you?"

Jerry, left alone with Carmella, couldn't believe how quickly this crazy situation had materialized. Hopefully she wasn't mad at him too. "Carmella, please stop crying and pull yourself together. Come on, what's wrong? We can just leave if you want. Norman's out of here. Stop crying." He whispered tenderly trying to calm her shaking body.

"That bastard bit me. I just want to punch him!" she replied, her arms crossed over her chest

"Norman's high. He's not thinking right. Drugs can make people act crazy. You'll be all right." Jerry said, stroking her hair, and relaxing his hold on her tense arms.

She started to cry as she grabbed a corner of the sheet to stop the bleeding from the bite. "Oh shit!" Jerry looked at her breast and was horrified to see blood oozing from her nipple.

As if Jerry was in the middle of an X-rated video, in that moment Norman came running back into the room wearing nothing but chaps and a Zorro mask. While cracking a long black whip, he wailed, "I didn't want to hurt ya, baby. I was playing with ya. I love you, my precious!"

"I need to get out of this room," Jerry muttered in a tone of frantic urgency. He wasn't sure if it was the right choice to leave, but he couldn't think of anything else to do to change his unpleasant emotions. He was getting angry, and was unaccustomed to the confused emotions he was feeling. Why wasn't Carmella making any efforts to leave? Frustrated by a feeling of helplessness, he moved away from Carmella, hoping she was smart enough to take care of herself.

Looking at Norman and seeing him butt naked in black leather chaps turned the moment into a comedy of errors. Was Norman crazy? Jerry couldn't get to the door fast enough. He refrained from making insults about Norman's wrinkled bare ass, even though he considered it to be the perfect thing to do. Instead he quoted Aleister Crowley as he walked out the door, "Love is the law—love under will." It was obviously going to be a long night.

Seven: The Chariot

VII. THE CHARIOT

Duality Isn't For Sissies

"I'm getting out of here. I need to clear my head," Jerry told Jodi, who was sitting in Norman's living room with her head buried in her hands. "Want to come along? Some fresh air will make you feel better, too. We can go get coffee or something. And please stop saying that you feel like dying? It gives me the creeps."

Moving her head slowly as she turned toward Jerry, Jodi stared blankly at him. Jerry felt uncomfortable seeing her small, semi-naked body, and handed her some clothes from the couch, hoping that they might belong to her.

She pulled a sweatshirt over her head, smoothed her hair, and then said weakly, "I took too much of that shit. I thought it was going to be

coke, but now my body is telling me it was meth. I hate that stuff. After the high, it makes me feel like I'm about to die."

"I think it was coke, except it feels like it was cut with something cause I feel wired for outer space. Next time he offers me something, I think I'll pass, but right now it might help if you stop playing with your hair, stand up and move. Even taking a few steps will help you feel better." He took her trembling hands and pulled her up to her feet. "Let's go outside. The night air will breathe some life into you."

"I'm an Indigo Child, and no one tells me what to do," she said, sounding irritated and pulling away her hand. "I'll do what I want to do, when I want."

"I'm not telling you what to do, I just know that if you choose to go outside, you'll feel better." In that moment his intuition told him to leave without her, but he resisted this impulse. *Why did he feel the need to rescue people from themselves,* he wondered. Considering his present condition he didn't have the mental strength to take care of anyone beside himself.

As soon as Jodi had finished getting more clothes on, Jerry grabbed what he hoped were her shoes and led her toward the exit. "I don't like to wear shoes," she complained as she saw them in his hand. "Besides, those aren't mine."

"Okay, Jodi," he said leading her out the door, while trying not to feel annoyed. "Hopefully your indigo aura keeps your bare feet from stepping on any sharp rocks or thorny trip vines."

He thought he detected a slight smile, and was relieved to see that she wasn't too stoned to follow his lead down the steps.

Walking close together, he wondered if they looked like disgruntled lovers trying not to touch. Jerry had keen night vision and guessed he was better at seeing in the dark than his new acquaintance. He moved slowly to make sure she could find sure footing on the narrow path leading to the parking area where his faithful, four wheel chariot awaited them.

As soon as they were starting to go across the old wooden plank bridge, Jerry stopped walking. He sensed a presence watching them and looked carefully in all directions. In a voice of muted distress he said, "Do you see that?"

Jodi froze. "See what?"

"That pulsing light across the bridge!"

"What light?"

"That blue-green cloud of haze! I haven't seen anything like that since I was fifteen. It's a Seega!" he whispered.

"What?" Are you dreaming?" she asked sarcastically. "Maybe you're hallucinating."

"Not dreaming! It's an ancestral spirit tethered to the earth by ancient rites for wrongs they committed when they were alive. Their souls are damned, and their ghostly forms are doomed to walk in solitude as punishment for their crimes." He felt himself trying to hide his shivers that were a mixture of growing anxiety and the cold of the night at the same time as he conveyed his urgent news. "The neighboring water elementals of the creek, the Waktcexi, their supernatural caretakers, stand guard over them as their perpetual wardens."

"You're bullshitting. I don't see anything!" Jodi said in a skeptical tone, "I'm having enough trouble just taking one step after another. I don't need another problem."

"I thought Indigo children are supposed to be psychic. You don't have to believe me," Jerry replied. "But I see it. Luckily, they have a difficult time crossing water. So if it tries to bother us, we can go back across the bridge and the creek spirits will block it from crossing our path. But right now, it's far enough away that we should be okay. Hurry up! Let's get to my car," he said pulling her to quicken the pace.

Before they could reach his car, Jodi screamed. "I just felt something cold and sweaty shaking my neck! I'm scared!"

Simultaneously, they broke into a run to his nearby car. "Let's get out of here," he said breathlessly while he nervously unlocked the passenger door, opened it, and Jodi jumped inside. Jerry then rushed around his car to get to the driver's front door. He too could feel icy hands shaking him as he fumbled with the keys, and it took all of his strength not to run away. "*Avante, avante!*" he shrilled. "Stay back, spirit of the dark!" His adrenalin shot like wild fire through his mind and he accidentally dropped his keys.

"Jodi, open the damn door," he commanded while picking up his keys from the cold ground. He couldn't believe that Jodi was so dumb that she didn't know to unlock his door from the inside the car. Looking over his shoulder in the dark, he felt an unfamiliar chill, and in frenzy his trembling hand tried in vain to fit the wrong key into the locked door.

He could see Jodi crying and sinking down into her seat with a moaning fright as if she were trying to become invisible. Jerry realized that she was too stoned to help and even if she tried, she would only get in his way. Summoning all his energy, he found the right key, and managed to unlock his door. His mother had always said that he could be depended upon in an emergency, and most of the time she was right.

Relief spread through him when his car door finally opened. He hastily dashed inside, and sunk into the safety of his familiar seat. Sweat

dripping from his forehead, he was ready to be finished with this current venture and go home.

After a few moments that seemed like an eternity, he turned on his headlights, started the ignition, and gunned the engine.

"What was that?" Jodi sobbed.

"It's an entity associated with turbulent powers and evil forces. Only the water spirits can withstand its murky temper. They work as etherial guards to keep it from doing harm," Jerry said while driving his car like a chariot racing to escape danger.

"Well, I felt its cold hands on me and the water spirits didn't protect me." Jodi pouted.

"That's because the water spirits didn't move fast enough to use their power against it when it tried to grab you. Maybe they couldn't stop it in time."

"Why didn't it attack you, like it did me?" she asked, sounding a bit more relaxed as they zoomed farther away from the uninvited excitement.

"It did, but I called on my totem to protect me and stop the Seega from harming me." Jerry answered while trying to calm his breath and restore his mental equilibrium.

"What's a totem?"

"How old are you? You haven't even heard of a totem?" Jerry noticed that his voice sounded incredulous, but he was surprised she was so naive.

"And you're such a smart-assed big shot because you know what a totem is. It sounds like you think a little too highly of your stupid self." Jodi promptly gave Jerry the middle finger. "I don't need you to put me down. You don't even know me."

Jerry felt her attitude hit like a left cross to his jaw, and backed off. "We don't have to fight about what I know or you don't. A totem is a spirit animal you call on for protection. For example, I just called my raven friends to come to my rescue. Black as coal, they're invisible in the dark, and they can peck out someone's eyes if needed. The Seega couldn't even see them coming." Jerry answered, wondering what he was going to do with Jodi, whom he was finding more and more unpleasant.

Restraining his combative impulse, he continued, "Native Americans say that if you want a totem, you have to find what animal is attracted to your energy and which one you feel a kinship with, or at least, discover one you can communicate with on some inner level. I've spent a long time calling raven energy into my life. I've searched for their habitats, collected lots of their feathers, and have taken hundreds of photos of

them. I've even created a sacred space to represent their nest in my room. I can make sounds that are identical to their calls."

"Well, I guess that means you're a bird brain, right? Is there an animal that can make my head feel better? That's the totem I want right now! I'm freaked." Jodi replied.

Jerry struggled to keep his composure. "Dolphins play a significant role in healing physical problems. Maybe you can call on a dolphin to help you and ask if it wants to become your totem. And yes, healing is important to both of us right now. I'm feeling on the jagged edge. That was some pretty nasty stuff we inhaled. Hopefully, a cup of warm tea will help."

Jerry's cell phone rang, but before he could answer his phone, it went dead. "Damn! My signal's gone. Good thing we're almost to town." he said to Jodi who was turned away from him and looking out the window.

They continued to remain in cold silence as Jerry sped down the highway in what he jokingly called his chariot of the gods, and he began to wonder what he was going to do with Jodi. She couldn't even hold an intelligent conversation, and her combative attitude annoyed him. Although she was cute, his interest in rescuing her from Norman's crazy drug scene was waning.

Happily, he soon saw the lighted signs for an all night café, and drove into its nearly empty parking lot. Wrapping himself in his warm Peruvian poncho, he got out of the car, breathed the cool ocean air, and forcing himself to be the gentleman his mother taught him to be, walked around the car and moved to open Jodi's door. Without looking at him, she got out of her seat, and moved quickly toward the café door.

As he shut her car door, Jerry gritted his teeth thinking about his current predicament. Catching up to her, they walked into the fisherman's café, where he could see her clearly in the bright lights. In the dimly lit rooms at Norman's house he hadn't realized how young she was, but as she stood in the light Jerry could get a good look at her. Jesus! She's jailbait, he thought to himself.

"Hey Jodi, how old are you anyway?" Jerry tried to sound nonchalant as he looked around for the right table.

Jodi looked at him with widened eyes, and smiled. "How old do you think I am?"

"Seventeen." He guessed while walking to the back of the café and taking a seat in a well-worn booth.

"Nope. Guess again." She answered coyly as she moved to sit across the table from him.

"Oh, great. We're going to play a guessing game. Are you nineteen?"

"No. I'm sixteen." Jodi replied as if she couldn't care less about her age.

"You're sixteen!" He bit his lip to hold himself back from swearing. "What are you doing hanging around with Norman anyway? He's almost twice your age." Jerry tried to hide his surprise by looking at the menu.

"I met him one night in San Francisco when I was panhandling on Broadway, and we went out and got high together. When he found out that I didn't have a home, he told me that I could stay with him."

"And so you went home with him?"

"Of course! I'm not stupid and, besides, Norman's one cool dude," Jodi replied.

Her girlish smile reminded Jerry of a mischievous child waiting to steal candy from a bowl. Realizing it was not a good conversation to have in front of the matronly waitress who was standing at their table he quickly changed his topic of conversation and said, "I'll have a cup of black tea, please."

With her eyes hardly leaving Jerry, Jodi said, "I'll have some fries and a double latte."

Before continuing his chat, he waited for the waitress to walk away from their table. "Were you living on the streets?" he inquired, feeling a knot tightening in his stomach. He had walked by too many sleeping, homeless women on the cold sidewalks in the city, and it wasn't a pretty sight.

"Yeah. For about three weird months. Right after I got to the city I met this guy, Simon, who took me home with him to get high and make love. At first we were just fooling around and having a good time, but then he started pushing me out the door to make money for us by selling my body. He'd beat me till I'd bleed if I refused. After a couple of beatings, I knew that the only way I could survive was to stay high and work the streets to make him money. I wanted to get away, and plotted what I could do. When he realized I was trying to leave him, he followed me everywhere, and told me that I didn't have a choice. He'd hold a blade to my face and threatened to slice me from my vagina to my nose if I didn't come home."

"One night after I had worked about twelve tricks, and Simon was stoned asleep, I took my money and got on a bus to visit a friend who lived in Daly City. I knew that Simon wouldn't know to look for me there. I'd met this nice guy through my work who wanted to help me get out of my business even though he was one of my repeat customers. He was young, tall, and good looking, and he told me he could get me a job

working as a waitress at the Fairmont Hotel where I could make lots of money legally." Jodi paused for breath then continued.

"I didn't get why a handsome guy had to buy love. Maybe because he was raised to be a strict Catholic, he didn't feel like he fit into the San Francisco scene. Even though he complained about it, he was living at home with his mother who couldn't speak of anything but the fear of God. He was an adult, yet she kept telling him not to have girlfriends because if he would have sex with them he would lose his special god given gifts. To keep her happy, he never told her about his private life. He joined a single's club where he paid hundreds of dollars just to meet lots of nice women, but he hated the match-making parties. He said it made him feel like a piece of meat on display at the butcher shop."

"We got along really well. He didn't mind paying me for my services, and trusted me enough to give me his phone number. Good ol' Jordan said that I could call if I needed him. That night when I was running from Simon, I took him up on his offer, and called him for help. Since he couldn't take me home to meet his mother, he rented a room for us to share from one of his friends who had a spare," she said grabbing a napkin to rub her dripping nose.

Lost in her story, both she and Jerry didn't even notice the waitress hovered over them now with their order of fries, tea, and latte.

"So you went from living with one man to living with another," Jerry said trying not to show that he was troubled by her story. He had heard about teenage runaways surviving on the streets, but couldn't believe that he was drinking his newly arrived cup of tea with one.

"Well, what was I suppose to do? I started living with two men, my new guy, Jordan, and his friend. Being free of Simon, I stopped taking drugs which is something I knew I needed to do. I slept for most of seven days. But when Jordan wasn't with me, which was most of the time, I started getting bored. I thought about going back to my old neighborhood in the Tenderloin where I could easily score dope to get high again, but I was afraid of running into Simon. Jordan was kind to me though. He bought me some fancy clothes and took me to meet one of his friends who is a manager of a restaurant in the Fairmont. He told him that I was eighteen and had experience as a waitress. His friend offered me a graveyard shift and I started working it. I didn't like following in the footsteps of my mother who worked as a waitress, but I was willing to work to change my life."

"So what happened next?" asked Jerry, showing an obvious interest in her story.

"If we didn't have customers at three or four am, my boss, who had been asking me to go home with him so that he could make me breakfast after work, told me that I could rest or sleep in his office. Well, one slow night at work when I was really tired, I took him up on his offer and fell asleep on a cushion on the floor in his office. I woke up to find his hands going up my pants, and I busted him in the eye. He fired me that night, after only ten days on my new job. But that was okay with me. I didn't like the stiff collared uniform I had to wear. It was yellow and gold and it made me look like a wilted daisy. But without any money I started living in so much fear that I almost wanted to return to my parent's home in Indiana."

"Why didn't you? Wouldn't that have been easier?" Jerry inquired, not knowing whether to feel sorry for his new acquaintance or admire her.

"My mother's third husband was a scum bag. She married him when I was twelve. Over time, he and I went from hating each other to becoming friendly. He let me know that he liked me to wrestle with him and I liked having a chance to punch him. But, after a while my mom started getting angry at our bouncing around. She told me to stop bothering him and if I didn't stop, she'd yell at me to go to my room. Then, one night while she was away from home working a late dinner shift, my step dad and I were clowning around, and getting really rough with each other. Before I could stop him, he pulled my blouse over my head and grabbed my boobs, but I kicked him as hard as I could in his balls to end our brawl. I ran to my bedroom and locked my door. He was really pissed. He swore at me from outside my bedroom door and told me that he'd torch my mom if I told her what he tried to do, and I was sure that he'd do it. He had such a bad temper, especially when he was drinking - which was most all the time." Jodi explained while looking almost robotic.

Jodi was so matter-of-fact that Jerry thought he could be talking with a mannequin if he didn't know better.

"After a couple weeks, I couldn't take him being so lovey-dovey with my mom and glaring at me like he wanted me to die, so I ran away as fast as I could go."

"Wouldn't it have been safer for you to tell your mother?" Jerry said feeling a knot tightening in his stomach.

"No! She was too busy making money to pay the bills to talk with me, and besides, we didn't have that great a relationship. She let me know that she couldn't wait for me to start making it in the world on my own. I felt like some kind of a burden on her back. She was tired of working so

hard, carrying such a heavy load just to survive, and not being able to pay our bills, and her body was hurting." Jodi's voice became barely audible and Jerry guessed she was trying to hold back painful emotion that was obviously rising to the surface. "But, the last time I called home I found out that my mom had died. She died and I didn't get to say goodbye to her! Since no one knew where I was living, I wasn't told about her death, and I didn't get to go to her funeral. I have a feeling she's mad at me even on the other side." By the time she had finished her sentence, Jodi's tears burst through the dam of her pent up emotions.

Jerry didn't know how to react. Uncomfortable hearing her list of misfortunes and realizing that she had problems larger than he could solve, he noticed a heaviness sitting upon his shoulders. Coming down from his earlier high, his mind was feeling like burning toast. After listening to Jodi's narrative, he now felt even more of a sense of responsibility to take her somewhere safe, in spite of his headache. Fighting his fatigue, Jerry decided that it was time to finish his tea and leave the restaurant. Perhaps he could figure out how he might help her once he got some sleep. With a little more time and a clear mind, he was sure he could think of some way to help fix her predicament. "Do you want to go to San Francisco with me?" he asked, getting ready to pay the bill. He was feeling strangely transparent to everyone who looked at him even though he was wearing two layers of clothes.

"I guess so…I do love the city." Jodi continued while getting up from the table. She offered Jerry her hand, which he refused to take, making it obvious that he didn't think it was a good thing to do. Jodi didn't mind that Jerry ignored her hand. She was accustomed to relying on her own self to get through hard times. Before leaving the cafe, she swaggered by two different dining tables before she was offered the cigarette she brazenly asked to borrow.

Jerry felt annoyed waiting for her. The entire night was not going at all like he anticipated. Damn, he thought, her life had so many problems, but he didn't want to inherit a new set because of Jodi. Even so, he knew there must be a better solution than returning Jodi to the crazy scene at Norman's.

"Okay, let's get out of here, but don't light that cigarette in my car." Jerry exclaimed as she approached him looking for matches in her bag. His mind was balancing between compassion and frustration as he opened the café door and felt the cold wind outside.

"You're not going to take me back to Norman's?" Jodi asked while they walked to the car and she lit her cigarette.

"No, I need to go back to San Francisco and go home so I can get a few hours of sleep before going to work tomorrow, and besides, I don't want to cross paths with that spook again." He said taking the cigarette out of her hand and throwing it on the ground before helping her into his car.

"Don't go out of control on me," Jodi started to protest. "It's cold and the middle of the night, or I'd walk back to Norman's. It's a good thing that I don't really need to smoke that cigarette, or you'd be listening to my bitching!"

There was dead silence in the car as Jerry pulled out of the drive. The night shadows hugged the back roads as they drove into the southern Marin hills, and the fog rhythmically appeared and disappeared as if a dancing phantom in the darkness. Without warning, a deer ran in front of the car and Jerry slammed on the brakes only to have his car skid sideways across the misted highway. Within seconds he'd hit a deer with enough force to create a loud smashing thud.

"Lucky there aren't any cars coming from the other direction," Jodi spat. "I hate hurting innocent creatures. Did you kill it? This is just like when my dog got hit by a car. I had to keep it on my lap while my mother drove us to the emergency vet. Just as we got to the clinic it died in my arms, and I'll never forget it."

Jerry sighed with obvious stress. He was annoyed about the potential damage to his car and Jodi's obvious lack of approval was alienating him. "Let me pull my car off the road, and I'll go outside and pull the deer off the road."

The cold slapped him in the face when he opened the door and jumped out. He walked to the deer lying in a pool of blood on the road. He shined a light from his flashlight into its eyes and the deer starred back without blinking. Oh no, this is a sign from the gods that something is very wrong, he thought to himself. But Jerry was someone who would always try to find something positive in any situation. To relax his mind, he looked up into the night sky to search for the constellations. Breathing deeply, he closed his eyes, whispered a short prayer for the deer's peaceful passing and then with focused attention, took out his knife and cut off its tail. He had wanted a deer tail to put in his ju-ju pouch to attract protective power, and the universe had just provided. He looked at the canopy of stars and offered a note of thanks to the Great Mystery for the tail and the fact that his car was still intact.

"What is that!" screamed Jodi when Jerry entered the car and started looking for some paper to wrap the tail that was in his hand.

"It means the deer's life was not lost in vain," Jerry said to Jodi who was crying again. "A deer's tail has power to invoke the spirits of nature."

"What do you mean?" Jodi asked between sobs.

"I mean you should stop crying and just be happy we didn't get hit by another car when we swerved across the road." Jerry grunted, not feeling like sharing his hard earned shamanic wisdom with a kid whom he knew wouldn't understand.

"I feel terrible!" Jodi wailed.

"Get your head together! Life has bigger problems than a dead deer. Listen, do you have any place you want to go in San Francisco?" asked Jerry, wanting to change the subject.

"No, but you don't have to worry about it. You can just hold your deer's tail or your dick or whatever you want to do!" she howled.

"Listen, smarty pants, if you keep mouthing off to me you can walk in the cold back to Norman's house." Jerry replied, feeling annoyed at her again.

"Aren't you one super cool dude! You just want to leave me stranded on a highway in the middle of nowhere?"

His foot automatically started to press the accelerator with more force than was practical for the foggy road, but he desperately needed to get home and return to his familiar life. He was on his way to getting a few hours of necessary sleep in his warm, welcoming bed, and he wasn't going to let her stop him. Surely he could drop Jodi at his ex-girlfriend's apartment in San Francisco.

"If you can't think of any place, I know somewhere you can stay tonight." Jerry told Jodi, hoping he could count on Destiny's kindhearted nature to offer her a place to sleep.

The Golden Gate Bridge looked to him like a welcoming friend as they approached it. Feeling a sense of relief, Jerry was sure he was doing the right thing for both himself and Jodi. Everything would work out just right he silently told himself.

For Jodi, the lofty illuminated towers looked like the entrance to a fairy castle partially hidden in the mist. It was the butterflies soaring in her stomach that let her know this golden doorway to the city was a beacon of hope, a totem of despair, and a harbinger of known and unknown dangers from which she could not run.

Eight: Strength

VIII. GRYPHON

The Rape of Innocence

"Jerry! What are you doing waking me up at 3 o'clock in the morning?" Destiny moaned as she answered the door of her apartment. Destiny would much rather not have been awakened by her ex-boyfriend and his barefoot friend whose red swollen eyes looked as if she had been partying far too late into the night. In spite of giving them both a half-awake look of disgust, she invited them inside. After they came in, she realized that she wasn't awake enough to entertain guests, and turned quickly to run down the hallway to her room, jump back in bed, and pull the sheet over her head. Perhaps Jerry and his disheveled friend would

leave, she thought, hoping that the knock on her door had only been a dream.

Following Destiny to her room, Jerry boldly pulled away her covers so that she couldn't ignore him. With wide eyes and raised eyebrows he spoke in a whisper, "Will you be a sweetie and help? Jodi needs some place to stay and I can't take her home with me. Can she sleep in your living room?"

"You must be out of your mind!" She pointed to the door. "Get out. Leave me alone!" Destiny wailed, trying once more to pull her covers over her head. Why did Jerry only knock on her door when he had a problem, anyway, she wondered while preparing to flex her veto power.

Jerry's voice took on a pleading tone. "Please, I can't take her home with me and she needs a place to stay. Besides, I won't let you go back to sleep until you say yes," he implored while gently stroking her hair that was sticking out from under the covers.

Former teenage sweethearts, Destiny and Jerry had remained good friends even after they had broken off their once stormy relationship, and in spite of their differences they still had an endearing connection. After all, they had lost their virginity to one another during a wild escalation of passion, and that special gift of love could never be repeated with anyone else.

"Who is she and what kind of problem is she running from?" Destiny asked, opening her eyes to scan the darkness in the room before she reached for her pillow and put it over her head. She knew enough about her longtime friend to understand that he wouldn't bring a stranger into her home in the middle of the night unless there was a problem.

"She doesn't have any place to go. Can you let her stay with you tonight? She's only sixteen." Jerry said, pulling back a corner of her sheet, and giving her a gentle kiss on her forehead.

"Take her home yourself, you've got a bedroom!" Destiny turned away from Jerry to show her annoyance, but her heart had a weak spot for him, and that always gave him an advantage.

"My apartment is so small. I'd be walking on her if I tried to go to the bathroom. You've got a lot more space, and besides you're a woman, and you can talk woman to woman with her. I've got to go to work in early morning, and I need to clear my mind without worrying about her. Give me until tomorrow to come up with some other ideas as to where Jodi might go. I'm sure I can find someone else who will be willing to help her."

"Do you think I'm so asleep that I don't know the real reason you don't want to take her home with you? Stella isn't going to be too happy

knowing you're hanging out with some other women, let alone a teenager, is she? But I also know that you're serious about not letting me get back to sleep tonight if I say 'no'. Go get a sleeping bag out of my closet for her. She can sleep on the futon in my living room. And then get out of here!"

"You're the greatest! Honestly, I mean it. '…And the kisses of the stars rain upon thy body.' I owe you a big one," Jerry answered not wanting to confront Destiny with the fact that she knew nothing about the character of his frustrating relations with his wife, Stella.

"Let's see…You're quoting from Crowley's *Book of Thoth*, aren't you? Hm, that's impressive, but the big question is: what do I want you to do for me?" she replied, already thinking of what she wanted in return for her favor. "You'll have to crawl in the dirt like the worm you are to repay my helping hand."

Jodi, who had been listening to her friend's conversation while she stood in the nearby hall, walked into the dimly lit room, "Thanks!" she said meekly. "I won't be any bother."

"Jodi, this is one of my dearest friends." Jerry said smiling. "She had a tough time growing up with her Dad, too. We used to call him 'Taylor De' Toro' because he was so domineering, but we made our own decisions in spite of his heavy-handedness. I'm sure she can understand your struggles and I promise that she'll take good care of you. Tomorrow after I get some sleep, I can help you figure out where it's best for you to go." Jerry opened the closet door, quickly found the sleeping bag, and then threw it to Jodi.

"Your bedding, madam." Jerry said before he turned toward Destiny and without making eye contact gave her a kiss on the forehead. "Thanks for being a sweetie and letting Jodi stay the night. I'll get out of here now so you can go back to sleep."

"Come on, Jodi, let me show you the way to the futon," he said walking out the bedroom door. "I'll check in with you tomorrow, Destiny. Adios!"

"You're such a nice guy," Destiny yelled sarcastically as she heard her door shut behind him. She guessed that as usual, he was oblivious to her feelings. She was really pissed at him for waking her in the middle of the night. Now her mind was awake, awake enough that she started thinking of her recent absurd argument with her present boyfriend, and with those kind of thoughts, she was sure she wouldn't be able to get back asleep for a long time. She'd tried to distract herself from thinking about her handsome, curly haired Nick and their impasse by spending the late evening studying Deepak Chopra's *Seven Spiritual Laws of Success*. She'd fallen asleep with her book as her pillow. Unfortunately, shortly thereafter, she was awakened by dogs running and barking in the

hall outside her apartment and people shouting loudly for them to shut up. Her night was starting to look more and more like she was watching a soap opera called "Untamed Emotions."

It was especially upsetting that others took her kindness for granted. It seemed as if she was always expected to do things for others, even if she didn't want to do them. Early in life she had been assigned the role of being a good girl, since she was the oldest sibling, and was called the "responsible one." Too many times she had done things for others, not because she wanted to, but because other people demanded it and she had been conditioned not to say "no."

She shouldn't live solely to please other's expectations, she told herself. She needed to learn to do things differently, and the sooner the better. Maybe she would just starting telling everyone who wanted something from her "No! Absolutely no way! No, I'm not going to take in your stray friend for the night, no, not me!"

Thinking more logically now, she realized that's what she should have said to Jerry.

One sheep, two, three sheep, four, oh damn! Would she ever get to sleep again?

A daring, bright teen, Jodi knew more about love and hate than most people her age. By the middle of the next day, she was tired of listening to Destiny advising her about what she should be doing with her life. Destiny sounded too much like her mother who always told her what to do. By the time she had put the sleeping bag away and their late lunch was finished, she was rudely told to wash the dishes. It didn't take long before she could feel the cold truth behind Destiny's fake smile and sensed she was an unwelcome guest. Disappointed that Jerry hadn't called, she didn't want to waste any more time hanging around grumpy Destiny. She was ready to do something more exciting than sit in an apartment waiting for someone to maybe arrive.

She had plenty of experience being on her own. Because she hated the cold windy city of her childhood, she had longed to travel, and San Francisco, the fun loving hot spot, had beckoned to her. To follow her dreams of freedom, she had stuffed her backpack with her favorite hand-me-down clothes, her first childhood teddy bear, a couple of cans of tuna, potato chips and cookies, and used her school bus pass to go downtown. She had saved just enough of her babysitting money to buy a one-way ticket to California. Without even saying goodbye to

her mother, she jumped on a westbound Greyhound bus and rode solo across the country.

Mature for her age and naturally endowed with the assets that many women pay highly to obtain surgically, she attracted men's attention and knew it. Hanging out and listening to music in Golden Gate Park created a world where romance was easy to find. When she first arrived in the "Cool, Gray City of Love," she experimented with making out with different guys and sampled an endless, easily available supply of euphoric drugs. Her favorite pastime was dancing exotically without a partner to the beating of the Congo drums that rocked her core. But once she hooked up with Simon he wouldn't let her do that anymore. Although heterosexual by nature, once he made her start walking the streets to get fast, easy cash for their drug money, she had been forced to explore what it means to swing both ways. Thankfully, her life had been better lately, she had found a new strength, and she didn't like to think about that part of her past.

Happy to be away from Destiny and outside in the fresh air, she walked down Haight Street in the twilight to catch a bus to downtown. Even though the sidewalk was alive with colorful characters moving about, she didn't feel like trying to connect with anyone and kept to herself. A young man with a guitar stopped to talk to her, but she wasn't interested in having a conversation with someone who wanted her spare change—as if she had any to share. She was lost in her thoughts thinking about her new friend Jerry, and couldn't stop giggling about the weird, ridiculous evening they had bouncing together on Norman's water bed. Knowing how crazy men were, including Norman, she wondered if anyone could ever make her believe in the prospect of finding true love.

As if hit by lightening, the blow on her shoulder came from behind her, and a rough hand covered her mouth so that she couldn't scream. When she finally got a glimpse of the man's fierce eyes, horror overcame her as his strong arms dragged her toward his car in a back alley. Caught in his vise like grip, she could move only in the direction where his forceful arms shoved her, and no one was close enough to even notice. Jodi bit his hand and started to cry out, but he quickly muffled her scream.

"Shut up, bitch!" her assailant hissed as he pushed her through the door into his car. He held her painfully immobile with the dominance of his massive weight as he got into the car. Climbing over her, he deftly moved into the driver's seat. "Don't try to move, or I'll kill you! You're coming with me," he said while using one hand to hold her tightly and

the other hand to start his ignition. Slowly with precision, he backed out of the alley and started down the road.

"Please," she pleaded, grasping to find courage in her voice, "Please stop holding me. You're hurting me!" She looked at the door. With all of her strength she struggled to free herself from his grip and then jumped toward the door, began to open it, and was willing to risk her life and leap from his moving car.

Acting as if he had captured a rare prize, he swiftly regained his hold. Pulling her to closely to his side, he held her by the arm so tightly that Jodi thought he was going to break her wrist. His silence made Jodi aware of the muscles frozen like ice in her body that were locked in fear, struggling yet unable to move. Her mind raced to find a way to escape, but she couldn't release his threatening grasp. While the car moved through back city streets, currents of adrenaline pounded her entire body, making her feel like her heart was about to explode. There was no one to hear her scream and she couldn't run. Where was he taking her? Would she live through this night?

The car slowed and went toward a freeway underpass without streetlights. The ominous threat of darkness came into the sedan like a parade of angry gremlins as he stopped his car, and turned off the ignition and the car lights. Parked where dim shadows frolicked menacingly in reflections from distant lights, the waning moon appeared to frown in sympathetic understanding.

"I'm afraid" were the words Jodi repeated silently in an unending refrain as her mind raced to find a reality other than the one she was facing. Please God, let me wake-up, please let this be a bad dream, she thought. Her stepfather, who was angered by her disobedience and her teenage rebellion, had told her that she'd probably get killed if she didn't listen and left home as she had threatened she would do. Was he about to be proven right?

Her driver, grinning in a grimly macabre way, pushed her to where he could slap her repeatedly, shattering her ebbing will to escape before he tore off her shirt. "Please don't hurt me," she repeated while grasping for breath under his massive weight.

"I'm not going to hurt you," he said grabbing her crotch. "Just take off your panties. Now!"

Even though her body was rigid with fear her resolve was still intact. "No!" she cried.

"Well then, I guess I'll do it myself." His fist slammed her shoulder as if it was a sledgehammer hitting a nail. Yanking her hair, he pulled her to lie beneath him on the seat, engulfing her with his bulky, sweating

torso. The smell of alcohol on his breath as he forced his grotesque kisses on her made her stomach turn. Jodi tried moving away, but the pain from another blow rendered her immobile. With all the anger she could muster, she spit in his face. But he seemed to take it in stride and showed his crooked teeth in a lopsided smile as if enjoying her plight.

She could feel his hands moving toward his fly. She started trembling as she realized that she, who would freely give herself to just about any sincere appeal of love, was about to be raped. Feeling his fingers rubbing her soft private parts seemed like a bullet piercing her soul. "No, please, no!" she pleaded. His answer came with his tongue reaching deep into her mouth.

The lingering pain from his forceful blows invoked a terror she never before imagined. Her body quaked with a throbbing dread. Was death near? She wanted to vomit, but she was frozen motionless from her fear.

Crushed by his brutal nature and hoping her life wouldn't also be taken, she couldn't summon the courage or the strength to refuse his words, "Do it or I'm going to kill you!" he yelled.

"I'll do anything you want," she blurted, "just please don't kill me!"

Time lost its meaning as the present seemed an eternity of living in the hell of enduring his loveless passion. Never before had Jodi felt such misery and her fear entwined with anger as if a fire going wildly out of control. Where was the pleasure she had previously experienced when making love? She tried to detach from the horrific sensations that she felt as he penetrated her.

The thrust that signaled his climax came after what seemed like an eternity of living in hell. He removed his body's offensive embrace with a jerk, and watched her body go from rigid to limp. "That was so good," he remarked, zipping-up his pants. "Where do you want to go now?"

Jodi could hardly believe his words. Weakly, she fumbled to get back into her torn clothes. "Can you take me home?" Jodi barely spoke, feeling a faint flash of relief that her nightmare may soon be coming to an end.

"Sure! Where do you live?" he grunted as if he truly cared for his prey.

In shock, but happy to hear his words, Jodi blurted out the names of the cross streets where she had once shared an apartment with her previous boyfriend, Jordon. Feeling as if she had been nearly released from the grip of approaching death, the prospect of being taken to a safe haven felt like a titanic miracle.

Silently he drove through the city. Jodi's hope returned as she saw her old familiar neighborhood, and she realized that he wasn't going to kill her. He was really going to let her go.

Time seemed to stand still, but eventually he stopped his car at her designated street corners. Without looking at her driver, Jodi opened the door, and swiftly jumped out. She tried to read the license plate number as her predator drove away, but in the dim light the rapidly receding numbers blurred, making them impossible to read.

In the cool fresh air, the flame of her spirit re-ignited. She ran to the entrance of her old apartment building, rang the bell, and waited for someone to unlock the lobby door. A loud buzz signaled the door could be opened. After running up two flights of stairs she was standing in front of the former sanctuary that Jordan had once provided.

Even though the door to the apartment couldn't open fast enough, the familiarity of safe surroundings slowed the tremulous beating of her heart. After being invited inside the cozy living room, her previous roommate, Mike, and Jordon her one time knight in shining armor, turned down the stereo to listen to her tearful outrage.

"What happened to you?" Jordan asked.

Jordan's eyes became large as saucers and his brow tightened with stress while he listened to Jodi. "I'm out-of-here!" Jordan responded, acting like a cowardly lion. He turned away and got his jacket before he made his way to the door.

Jodi struggled to hold back her tears. Her heart sank as she watched him walk out the room without as much as one glance in her direction. Under her present circumstances, how could he not even consider giving her a few seconds of emotional support? Stunned, his response stabbed her like a knife as she sadly watched him disappear from view.

Mike could not believe his friend's callous behavior. "The pig!" he exclaimed, shaking his head in disappointment and offering Jodi a supportive hug. "Let's call the police to report your situation," Mike insisted. "Hopefully they can catch the bastard who hurt you, and that should help you feel better."

Jodi's body crumbled into a heap on the floor and her body began to shake. "Why me? I hate my life," she cried.

Mike tried to console her by holding her in his arms, but Jodi pushed him away.

"Don't touch me," she screamed.

Shortly, two young rookie cops were knocking on the door. They entered the room looking as if they were entering a crime scene where everything is suspect. "Are you the woman who is reporting the rape?" one asked, in a voice cold as ice.

Embarrassment and tears accompanied her reply. How do you talk with strangers about something this painful, she wondered, feeling a red

blush covering her cheeks. "Yes," she said through her tears. She couldn't think clearly about what she might say.

"Are those the clothes you were wearing during the rape? Please take off your underwear. We need to see it," one of the cops requested matter-of-factly, as though talking about the weather.

Shame became waves of oceanic torrents of anger as they held the crotch of her underwear up to the light. Oh my god! she thought, this is just as horrible as being raped.

"We're keeping these as evidence," one police officer said, putting her torn panties in a plastic bag. "You need to come to the station with us to fill out a report. Our doctor will examine you for STDs and gather evidence with samples of DNA."

Can death be any worse? Jodi wondered while trying hard to remain stoic. An eruption of anger gave her the courage to walk out Mike's door with the officers who were politely ignoring her while escorting her to their car.

"Get in the back seat," one said, opening the car door. "It won't take long for us to get to the police station."

Mutely she did what she was told. "I just want to die!" she murmured to herself as she got into the police car and felt her heart sink toward the floor.

Nine: The Hermit

IX. BLUE BUDDHA

Lighting The Lamp Of Wisdom

Jerry, thinking about his recent experience at Norman's and trying unsuccessfully to focus on the work piled on his office desk, was obsessing about his insecurities and yearnings. He criticized himself for bringing Jodi to San Francisco the previous night and making himself feel responsible for her welfare. He remembered telling her and Destiny that he'd call today, but he was preoccupied with feeling annoyed at Lisa, who hadn't returned his phone calls and now he didn't feel like calling any one. Why was she playing cat and mouse games with his emotions? He had shared his soul secrets and confessed his love to Lisa. How could

she not return his calls when she knew how much he cared for her? His uncertainty was being triggered more and more with every passing minute his phone didn't ring.

Using work as a fitting excuse, he delayed calling Destiny, whom he believed could be depended upon to take care of Jodi for a just little while longer. Besides, he needed some space to clear his mind, and soon enough he would return to check on his new friend, jailbait Jodi, as he'd come to call her.

In addition to his worries about Lisa, and his headache from partying a bit too much the previous night, Jerry was also preoccupied with the uncommon sighting of the Seega and its goblin-like glow in the darkness. Being fascinated with the supernatural, he wanted to scrutinize the ghostly presence by Norman's parking area without the drawback of Jodi's whimpering. And he needed to make sure Carmella was doing okay in relation to Norman's strange antics.

As soon as it was quitting time at his job, Jerry wasted no time leaving his desktop computer, and soon found himself behind the wheel of his car. Pretending that he was a race car driver, he weaved in and out of the frustrating rush hour traffic trying to relax his mind while watching day turn to dusk. Once across the Golden Gate Bridge, he smiled knowing he was on his way back to Stinson Beach once again.

Confused by his trial-and-error relations with women—lately it seemed mostly error—he realized how tired he was becoming of worrying about his love life. For a moment he considered changing his plans and going home to bed. He had been sadly over analyzing his relationships, and he knew that thinking about Lisa or worse yet, his wife, would be more draining on his emotions than a distracting road trip to investigate the supernatural. He became increasingly excited as he thought about the scary creature in the parking lot and wondered what it was doing at Norman's. His mood brightened as he realized that this trip complemented his new resolution to more deeply awaken his inner sage and improve his magical skills.

Exiting the main highway, he followed the same route toward the coast that he had taken yesterday. Lucky for me that I don't need to talk with my wife, Stella, he thought to himself while rolling down his window for a breath of fresh air. "No, I didn't just think that!" he said out loud, surprising himself as he heard his own bitterness in his cynical voice.

In his last phone message from Stella, she had been wondering why he hadn't called her, and moaned that he didn't love her anymore. He felt henpecked by her new form of nagging. Previously, against his will, he

had to respond to her demands to create an open relationship in relation to her new age vision of love after she had become interested in dating someone new. And now, after spending so much time mending his upset emotions, he didn't feel like lending insensitive Stella his ear so that she could complain about their relationship. Her changing viewpoint about the meaning of their marriage vows had broken Jerry's heart and changed his life forever.

By the side of the road, small eyes reflected his car lights like mirrors in the Sun, reminding him that he needed to pay more attention to the wildlife in his surroundings. Watching the shadows play in the oncoming darkness, he was happy to return his thoughts to the countryside and take another break from traversing the tortured endless tunnels of his emotions. The narrow, winding Highway One was beginning to feel familiar as he drove along looking for the turn he needed to take to Norman's. In spite of the approaching darkness, it didn't take long to find it. He rolled down his window and smelled the fresh sea air. Energized, he zoomed up the bumpy, gravel road to his destination.

While parking his car, he didn't notice any sign of the Seega who presently seemed less of a concern than the knots twisting in his stomach. They were giving him the signal that he wasn't as confident returning to Norman's home as his mind told him he ought to be. Getting out of his car, he realized that he didn't know what to expect after the strange drama he had experienced the previous night. Remembering that he had taken Jodi from Norman's home without saying a word to his friend about it gave him a slight sense of apprehension. Nevertheless, Jerry was pleased to see the little house in the woods shining with a light indicating that Norman was home. Walking slowly, he approached the front porch.

"Anybody home?" Jerry called into the crisp air as he knocked. "Hello! You told me that I'm always welcome back, and I'm here. Can I come in? Come-on, open the freakin' door. It's cold as a witch's broomstick out here." Jerry stared behind into the dark to see if the Seega had followed him, but nothing was there.

After waiting a couple minutes he heard footsteps approaching the door. Norman, with his hair in disarray, peeked his head outside. "Are you alone?"

"Yeah, alone! Can I come in?" Jerry asked offering a large smile in response to the strong aroma of pot that drifted out through the door.

"Sure Jerry, hurry up, it's cold out there. Where's the brat?" Norman asked while scanning the empty darkness for motion.

"Do you really think she's a brat? I took her to the city and she's staying with my ex-girlfriend. You two certainly went at each other in a

weird way last night," Jerry said, trying to make his conversation light-hearted as he walked into the living room.

"Maybe. But I really like her, even if she is a bit crazy and stubbornly pig-headed. With her around I always have a buddy who wants to get high with me." Norman answered without looking at Jerry.

"Sure... Like you only want to get high with her." Jerry teased.

"You can leave right now if you think you know more about me than I do," countered Norman. His eyes grew large and showed obvious signs of being reddened by a lack of sleep. Jerry suspected that he would easily become irritated if there were any more innuendos concerning Jodi.

"Oh come on, it's no big deal," Jerry playfully exaggerated while taking a seat on the edge of a chair. "Like I came all the way from the city just to offend you? You know I think your tripping out with her is really cool."

Norman looked at Jerry with his kingpin manner, and then stared coldly away as if something important in another room needed his attention. Speaking with his lips drawn tightly together he muttered, "What's up? It's a little unusual for you to be here two nights in a row, isn't it?"

Jerry knew that it was time to tell Norman what was on his mind. "Something I saw here last night made me want to return."

"Oh, really? It wouldn't be that you want to take Carmella to stay with your ex-girlfriend in the city, would it?" Norman smiled, but his voice sounded guarded as if he was talking to a rival. He moved close to the fireplace and threw in a log. "Damn place is so damp. Living among the redwoods it always feels cool and I never seem to see enough sun." He turned and ignored Jerry. His attention focused on a novice punk rocker who was dancing provocatively on the "Pants Off Dance Off" show on MTV.

Not wanting to take Norman's attention away from the dancer's nearly bare butt, Jerry cautiously waited ten minutes for the program to finish before he spoke again. "Ya know, the California Indians seemed to be a lot cleverer about living with the redwoods. They said not to reside under these green giants because bad spirits live among them. And to be honest, this is main the reason I had to return tonight. Do you know that you have a Seega near your parking space?"

"A what?" Norman replied sounding curious.

"A Seega. It's an evil spirit who's condemned to live on the earth. It's not free to go to the other side," Jerry explained. "I saw him last night right in the middle of your parking lot."

"What?" Norman asked, suddenly sounding more alert.

"Really," Jerry replied, becoming more enthusiastic. "I learned about them the hard way when I was sixteen. I got stuck living with one in a house my dad rented that was built on an old Indian burial ground. The damn thing drove us out!"

"Here we go again," said Carmella, who had silently walked into the living room. "Jerry, are you seeing more ghosts? You must be hard wired to see ominous things that go bump in the night."

"I believe him," replied Norman. "Not too long ago a friend of mine was sleeping in his camper in the parking lot. In the middle of the night, he felt something pounding on his chest. It woke him with a terrible fright. Feeling something invisible attacking him, he jumped out of bed. He came screaming up here at four o'clock in the morning wanting to sleep in the house yelling that there were spooks in the parking lot. The next day he moved his van as fast as he could right after it became daylight."

"I want to go see this spook," Carmella said. "Seeing is believing!"

"Okay! We can all go, but you better take a flashlight," Jerry suggested, realizing that her eyes told him she was high enough to see anything.

"Oh, you mean we need the hermit's lamp to shine light on our path?" questioned Carmella.

"Carmella, this isn't about the tarot."

"I can't help it, Jerry. You remind me of the hermit. Even though you hide under the disguise of being a computer geek, you light the path so that others can follow. Here you are, once again, taking me on a mysterious tour to see the underworld of material reality. You'd be a perfect match to the hermit if you just wore a hooded cloak and carried a serpent staff."

"Well, I don't know if I'm flattered or insulted, but what's important here is that we each find a flashlight so we can clearly see our path in the dark," Jerry answered sounding aloof. He made a conscious effort to avoid sounding interested in her comments or forming a connection with her.

Norman cynically joined in the conversation, "Jerry can't be a hermit cause he's married. And what about me? How come you never say any of that cool tarot stuff to me?"

"Don't be jealous. It's because you're not into metaphysics," she replied as she turned away from both men.

Norman grabbed Carmella. "You don't know what I'm into."

"Okay. Are you into metaphysics?"

"Not really," Norman replied with a grin while pinching her thigh.

Carmella glared at Norman and walked away to find her jacket.

Soon they each had a flashlight and they walked outside to follow the meandering footpath. In the dark, the tall Sequoias looked like Titans boldly defying the wind. Coyotes howled in the distance affirming the untamed restlessness in the air. Moving sure-footedly, Jerry remained quiet except for his exhilarated breathing that broadcast his excitement.

"Where across the bridge did you see this thing?" asked Norman when they neared the ravine leading toward the parking lot. "I don't see anything."

Jerry's eyes scanned the distance. "Look to the left. There's a circle of light hovering close to the earth that spirals upward toward a faint glow about two inches higher then my head."

"I don't see anything. Where exactly is it?"

"Maybe what you really saw is a space alien and it's already transported itself home," chided Carmella.

"Perhaps plain reality's too boring and you need to communicate with imaginary friends," Norman said sarcastically walking in the direction where Jerry had pointed. He boldly pushed past Jerry to get a better look across the bridge

"It's not a fantasy. I see it; I can't believe that neither of you do," Jerry declared. "Can't you see it?"

"Maybe if we had more to smoke, we'd see it too," Norman announced, giggling like a child.

"Oh, sweet!" replied Jerry in a serious tone. "Aren't you funny? If I were either of you, I wouldn't go over there. You don't want to provoke it. It looks like it's getting ready to..."

"Norman, Let's not walk any farther," Carmella said looking into the darkness. "Come on; let's go back to the house. I don't need to see any blinking lights to believe Jerry. I'm willing to take his word that there's something over here."

With his extraordinary night vision, Jerry could see the Seega arching its ghostly back like a tiger getting ready to attack. Within a matter of seconds, Carmella flew up in the air looking like a puppet being pulled on a string. Faster than Jerry could blink his eyes, he watched her land on her back flat on the ground. Norman moved quickly to help her stand on her feet, but she screamed when he tried to pull her upright. Had she broken her leg? In an instant the night became more ominous by her wailing cries of pain. Jerry felt an unwelcome steam of adrenalin shoot through his spine.

The gurgled sounds came next. "Give stone back!" reverberated in an echoing hum of vengeance.

Jerry strained to decipher the nearly inaudible words the ghost muttered. What is it trying to say, he questioned within his mind.

"Come back over here! Hurry up! You both need to get back across the bridge where he can't easily follow," Jerry blurted out between breaths. Seeing Norman's inability to help Carmella, he chanted a mantra for psychic protection, and ran to help Carmella who was lying on the ground sobbing.

"I can't put any weight on my leg," she hollered. Her body began to shake and she started crying.

"You'll be okay. Just try to stand up and walk. We're holding you."

Jerry tried to lift Carmella with the help of Norman, but it soon became obvious that Norman was too stoned to be helpful. Looking to Jerry like a scarecrow blowing in the wind, he busily swung his arms in the air trying to fight off the invisible presence. Jerry tried to lift Carmella on his own, but he could hardly support her weight. Jerry watched the Seega grow in height and the light emanating from his brow change color from violet to blood red. Kneeling on the ground next to Carmella, he witnessed the Seega pull something ominous from behind his back. Jerry focused his eyes and realized that it was light beams woven together in the shape of an ax. Just as it was about to use this ethereal weapon to strike against them, Jerry felt the rush of adrenaline give him a surge of unexpected strength. In an instant, he picked her up and carried her back across the bridge where he knew they would be safe. Norman fearfully tagged close behind swearing defensively into the air. Once across the bridge, Jerry watched his friend promptly flee in the direction of his home.

Although Jerry was left behind with Carmella, he didn't mind. He knew his friend was too stoned to cope with this emergency. Besides, he was enjoying holding Carmella, even if she was moaning in pain. With his support she relaxed enough to stand on one leg and she attempted to walk, or at least stumble on her own. With his help she could walk a little, even if they had to stop every other step to make sure she could continue to move on the path with him.

"Thanks Jerry, let me try to get up the stairs myself," she said when they arrived back at Norman's. "Well, maybe I can use some help," she said sitting on the bottom step.

"Okay, how can we best do this?" Jerry asked. "Can you put any weight on your hurt leg?"

Norman looked down at them from above. "Shouldn't you try to hurry? That thing can't bother us here, can it?" he asked in near panic.

"I can't move. I hate pain. I want to just sit and let someone beam me up the stairs." Carmella said sounding a note of anger.

"Teleportation isn't going to happen and getting chilled by the cold isn't going to help either. Come on, let's get you into the house," Jerry said summoning up his strength and then carrying her up the stairs as if she were a Barbie doll and he was her Ken.

Norman, who had turned on all the lights in the house began racing around as if in a panic. "Okay. Let's see what you've done to yourself," he said as Jerry laid her on the living room couch. Norman squinted his eyes to look at her leg. "Oh shit! Your ankle's twisted."

"Is it that bad?" Carmella asked. "I was just standing there when I felt something push me down. You were there. Did you see what happened, Jerry? Did you see it push me down? Whatever happened out there happened so fast. It was so weird, and the smell was as if someone had opened a coffin."

"I tried to warn you both, but you didn't believe me. I think I heard it say something about wanting a stone." Jerry replied in a matter of fact way. He turned to Norman. "Does it look like she needs to see a doctor?"

Norman shook his head. "Yes, but not at this time of night! She'll have to wait until morning because I'm not leaving the house tonight."

"What do you mean?" Carmella asked.

"Just a minute," replied Norman as he went to a different room.

Carmella rubbed her ankle. "It's swollen. I need to go to the emergency room. It's open all night. I can't wait till morning. I'm in too much pain." Carmella wailed, "Call 911!"

Norman quickly returned to Carmella's side. He had a gallon glass pickle jar filled with a variety of different color pills. "This is my very own pharmacy in a bottle," he boasted.

"Come on baby, let's get you stoned. You won't feel so bad after you take a couple of these." Norman said, handing her several brightly colored pills.

"You're crazy. I'm in pain. I need a doctor, not pills. I can't even walk." Carmella started sobbing while Jerry gently touched her badly twisted ankle.

"Take these pills and you'll feel no pain," Norman told her. "I promise to take you to the doctor in the morning. I'm too wired to drive you to town now. Hurry and take these." Norman commanded. "You need to get comfortable with the idea of staying home cause we're not going anywhere tonight!"

"Norman, you're not in touch with my feelings at all! Jerry, you can take me to the hospital, can't you?" Carmella pleaded.

Norman looked with distain at Jerry. Just then the phone rang. "Don't answer it," he asserted. In unison, they stopped talking long enough to listen to the call on the answering machine when it turned itself on.

Jerry's eyes widened as he heard Jodi's feeble voice on the message machine. "I'm at the police station in downtown San Francisco. Can someone come and get me?" she asked before hanging up.

"Oh crap! Sounds like more bad news. It's time to put Carmella to bed," Norman said sounding to Jerry as if he was captain in charge of a sinking ship.

Jerry hesitantly agreed. He felt overwhelmed. Disagreeing with Norman could ruin their friendship, especially after feeling that he'd blundered by taking Jodi away the previous night. Perhaps he could persuade Norman to take Carmella to a hospital. In reality Jerry was in agony about both his own and Norman's enormous role in Carmella's condition. And what about Jodi's phone message? Rescuing one friend was enough for him in one night, but with the ring of the phone and Jodi's cheerless message, it sounded as though he needed to go back to the city to help another. "Carmella, you're one of my favorite friends, but Norman's planning on taking care of you. Jodi sounds like she's in a mess and I need to help her, too." Jerry said trying to be stoical. Turning away from Carmella, he followed Norman out the door to have a private moment to discuss their situation.

"You know man, I don't want to go anywhere past my front door for a while." Norman confided. "Even the parking lot is way too much of an ordeal for me. I'll reward you with some really primo weed if you go pick up Jodi and give her a ride back here."

"Sure. I'm all for that, or at least I'll try to find her," Jerry said his voice echoing the tenor of dismay. "I'm curious as to why Jodi's at the station and I'll do everything I can to get her out of there. I'm on my way," he said searching his pocket for his car keys as the two walked back into the living room where Carmella was still moaning.

"I'm too stoned to drive you anywhere," Norman repeated to her in a petulant voice that proclaimed to Jerry that he was feeling sorry for himself.

"You self-centered jerk." Carmella screamed from the couch. "I've called 911."

"I told you those pills will take away your pain soon. You're acting stupid!"

"I don't want your damn pills. I can't walk. While you were playing Mr. Cool with Jerry I called 911 for someone to come and get me."

"Carmella, you're an idiot. Jerry! Don't leave. You've got to help me get my pot plants out of sight. And I need to hide my stash. Do you see anything that I could get busted for?" Norman shrieked as he started running around the room.

"Not if you get your pot out of sight," said Jerry, not believing that he was witnessing another crisis happening for the second time within an hour. Feeling like he was becoming a rescue service for Norman and his lady friends, Jerry anxiously questioned, "How about if I leave now and go get Jodi? It's not the police who are coming; it will be the paramedics in an ambulance. They don't bust people. But it will be better if you open the windows so it doesn't smell so much like pot smoke in here."

"Sure, man. Can you help?" Norman asked hysterically as he sat down the potted plant in his hand and ran to open a window.

"Just for a minute. I've got to hurry cause I don't want to get stuck on your one lane driveway facing an ambulance in the dark without any place to turn around." Jerry quickly began to open windows and doors without saying another word. A grimacing cold quickly filled the rooms.

"It's time for me to go," he said, moving to walk out the door. "I'm sorry, Carmella." He felt his heart wrestle with a burden of sadness leaving Carmella when she needed him. He couldn't even look at her as he walked out the door. To make him feel worse, since hearing the plea in Jodi's disturbing phone message he couldn't shake the feeling that he had done something else terribly wrong. It felt like a storm cloud burst upon him and now the thought of running into the spook seemed to be the least of his problems.

As Jerry was leaving he heard Carmella scream to Norman in a tone as cold as a winter wind, "There wouldn't be this problem if you had listened to me, you crazy ass."

"Stop bitching! It's not too late for me to carry you back down to the driveway to wait for your ambulance. Maybe then you'll get a broken jaw to go along with your broken ankle," Norman mumbled with hostility.

From outside on the front porch Jerry watched Norman rush about carrying his marijuana stash and pill bottle out of the room.

"I was willing to take you to the hospital, but I wanted to wait until morning when I'll be sober enough to drive," Norman yelled.

"Sorry, but I need someone to help me now. If you were in pain and your ankle was twisted like an animal balloon, you'd find a way to go to the hospital, too." Carmella said bursting into tears.

"Enough crying! You win. Thanks to your phone call, I don't have a choice in the matter. You're going to the hospital. Jerry's going to get

Jodi, and I'm going to be alone. I don't like being alone when there's a spook outside."

Jerry moved quickly. He took a deep breath in the cool air and was happy to be getting farther away from Norman who was sounding more and more like a spoiled child. Before he got to the parking area he turned around and took one last look into the house and raised an open hand to send Carmella some Reiki healing energy. Almost cartoon like, Norman was rushing around the room precariously holding several pot plants in his arms. Jerry would have liked to laugh, but it was a serious matter.

Ten: The Wheel of Fortune

X. TRISKELION

The Mandala of Karma

Too bad Julie had to get pregnant, Mark thought shaking his head in dismay. Feeling his curly hair rubbing against his cheeks, he brushed it back into place with his hands. His fingers couldn't ignore the expanding empty space created by his receding hairline and his somber mood intensified. It was obvious that he would have to do more than his fair share of grandparenting after Julie would have her child. Seventeen years old, unmarried, and showing all the signs of having a tough time adapting to motherhood, his daughter's pregnancy was not a happy thought. Who would have imagined that it would be his youngest child who would first make him a grandpa?

Perhaps he could more easily forgive her situation if she hadn't annoyed him by trumping his authority when she slammed shut the doors of communication, refusing to name her bastard's father. Foolishly, Julie, whose flat chest was noticeably expanding in relation to her growing belly, had followed in her mother's footsteps by getting pregnant too early for her own good. Why couldn't Rowan have saved their daughter from this dire fate, Mark wondered, feeling a smoldering resentment toward his ex.

He detested the burden this unexpected situation placed on him. Although he had been happy to be a dutiful father and share custody of his daughter with Rowan, he would never willingly volunteer to have an infant move into the room next to his, but now he didn't have a choice. He gradually became aware of the knot in his stomach and wondered if Julie's announcement that she planned to live with him instead of Rowan was going to trigger his ulcers. His frequent visits to the doctors had taught him that it didn't do any good to hold on to anxieties and let them eat a hole in his stomach. He tried to relax. "Be here now," he told himself while resolving to put his daughter and her pregnancy out of his mind.

Taking his mental focus away from Julie, Mark began to think about his own priorities. At the present time, besides freeing himself from his worries about Julie, his most important mission was attending his lodge meeting, a long overdue gathering to support men's liberation. Quite different from most of his lodge assemblies that were inside locked doors, this one was being held outdoors at a campsite near Devil's Slide and it had sport competitions—not that he was fit enough to join in those activities. But he possessed other qualities. Without contest he claimed the prestigious role of Master of the Initiation Ceremony. And tonight he looked forward to hearing two young men recite their secret oaths, a prerequisite for joining his fraternal order that seemed to have more than its fair share of older guys talking about what's wrong with the younger generation.

Mark hurried to pack his bag with his ceremonial clothing. Before long, he finished everything he needed to do, picked up his baggage, and left his home to walk to his car in a nearby garage. Shivering in the brisk wind, he hoped that the chilly weather wouldn't deter the other men from venturing out in their traditional robes. Once in his driver's seat, he kicked over the engine and smiled with self-satisfaction as he heard it growl like a tiger. Accelerating his way through the hills of Twin Peaks he made rapid progress toward his destination, and by the time he had reached the coast, all previous concerns had left his mind. Enjoying his drive on the serpentine highway going south, it didn't seem to take long

to find the secret place where he could join his lodge brothers and play his part to jolt the party into fifth gear.

He felt so alive in the countryside away from the confines of his apartment walls. Even though his home was comfortable enough, he yearned to be in nature, but seldom took the time to get there. He used the excuse that it was much easier to watch environmental programs on his large screen TV than to hike in the country.

Lost in his imaginings, Mark drove past the "No Trespassing" sign without seeing it and turned into the campground parking lot. What a rich world I live in, he thought as he looked for a parking spot amongst the many new or nearly new cars and trucks that had arrived earlier.

Getting out of his car, the moist air greeted him with an unwelcome chill and he grabbed his heavy coat. Looking through the darkness beyond a grove of tall trees he could see a glimmer of light from a bonfire. Hurrying along, he followed a long shadowy dirt trail to meet his companions. As he approached the welcoming crowd of about twenty-five men he shouted to everyone the call of the brotherhood, "Greeting, Serpents and Warriors!"

"One circle, joined destiny," many answered amid tribal shouts.

"You're late, Marcus," said an older man who momentarily stopped smoking his Cuban cigar. "We've been waiting for you to start our ceremony. So get yourself a beer and let's get this show on the road. The natives are restless!"

"When you're lucky enough to become an Adept in this organization, late is being on time," he replied with a tone of superiority. Even though Mark knew that he was in a group of extraordinary men, he wished they wouldn't be so anal. "While you get our initiates into the Westward quarters, I'll take a few minutes to get into my robes."

"You're the boss, Marcus," one man replied. "Don't worry. We'll be having a good time while we wait."

Mark went by himself into the concealing darkness of a ring of trees where he could change his clothes in private. He took his ceremonial headdress out of his bag, held it out in front of him, and admired it. He loved having the opportunity to show off his hard earned authority by wearing this towering crown of achievement. Moreover, in his dark robes he would be nearly invisible in the flickering shadows of firelight, but his headdress would make him the center of attention. Besides, it wasn't something he could wear very often so it would be regrettable to miss an opportunity to parade the cosmic symbol of his office and display its magnificence.

When Mark emerged from the dark fully dressed in his regalia, the other men made way for him to pass in a titanic wave of movement. He walked to the front of the group and stood on a bench in order to tower above everyone. "Put down your drinks brothers, it's time to listen to the voices of those who wish to join us," he began. "Each of us needs to hear the oaths that will join them with our brotherhood. Once they swear their allegiance to embody the values that we uphold, no one can destroy our unity. Listen closely to their voices to hear whether they are worthy of wearing our crest."

Mark looked stern as he waited for everyone to become quiet. His voice was benevolent yet commanding as he spoke to the two hopeful initiates. "Your fortunes may be bueno-good, or mala-bad. As you join our journey, your goal is to go beyond this world of duality, the good and the bad, the wealthy and the bankrupt, and to learn how to turn the wheel of fortune toward the destiny you wish to achieve. Initiates, what is the wheel of fortune?"

The first initiate, a tall, well-built young man named Richard Wiseman, answered in a way that made it apparent that he'd had too much to drink, "A game show on television with a hot lady who turns the wheel for prizes."

Oh no, thought Mark, I don't think this Mr. Wiseman, good-looking or not, belongs here, but we'll soon find out. Hopefully our next man can do better. "Okay, Jason Green. It's your turn to answer this question. Will you please explain the wheel of fortune?"

"Head Master, with all due respect to my fellow initiate, the wheel holds the essence of the principles of the brotherhood. It is the Sri Chakra of ancient times, the all-seeing eye of God, the karmic wheel, the evolving mandala of the zodiac, the sacred hexagram that bears truth beyond thought."

"Yes, very good," replied Mark feeling a sense of relief. "Also, the wheel is related to the goddess of fate, Dame Fortune, some call her. As it spins, it is Lady Luck who turns destiny in your favor, or against you, if she disagrees with your ways. In days of old, gamblers prayed to her to win wealth and greater prosperity. Let us all call to her by her name!"

The men shouted loudly in unison, "Fortuna, Mistress of our night!"

"Sustainer of our fortunes, for our silver, gold, and material bounty we give thanks." Mark bellowed. "All right initiates, what do you need to start this journey?"

"Only faith," they answered in unison.

"What expectations do you have of our secret works?"

The first initiate, Richard, uneasily blurted in a broken slur, "I know that you will guide me to a better life."

Next Jason, the second young man, replied without hesitation, "Understanding and power over the universal vexations of success: anger, greed, bewilderment, delusion, envy, slander, and scorn."

Mark suspected that he had spent many hours studying the brotherhood's teachings. "Good answer. You'll do well in our brotherhood." Mark spoke his approval directly to the Jason without even looking at Richard. He stepped down from his podium, and walked up to both initiates. Mark reached for a Grecian urn that was filled with Cabernet, and then poured a half glass measure of wine for each man to drink. "Is your glass half empty or half full," he queried.

"Half full," they replied in a unified military shout.

Mark continued, "Always remember the message of this drink to empower your body, mind, and spirit to wins over antagonistic forces." Changing his emotional tone he spoke candidly, "Initiates, hear what I am saying! If you are inwardly drawn to take this path, you are requested to show your trust for your new family. To prove that you deserve to enter our inner sanctums, you must do one thing we request. Tonight, both of you must allow one of our worthy archers to shoot a beer can off your head with a bow and arrow."

"Oh, shit! I can't believe this!" Richard said to Jason, grimacing with apprehension.

"Yes, it's true. You said you had faith in us, and the foundation of our group connection is built on trust in one another. By submitting to this trial you will prove your trust. And most importantly, once you have passed this test, you must each sign an oath with your own blood that you will consciously rise above mundane mediocrity and strive to elevate your standing in our brotherhood. Also, in your first year you must agree to do fundraising for the noble purpose chosen by our group."

"That sounds less difficult than having someone shoot a beer can off my head," Jason moaned looking at several of the men who stood around him. "How are we going to raise funds if the arrows end up going through the middle of our foreheads?"

"Yeah! Do we really need to prove that we want to join your group? Cause if I must let some drunken lodge brother shoot a can off my head in the dark, I'm leaving now," Richard added assertively.

"Okay, that's your choice. But the person who's shooting the arrow is an excellent marksman and stone-cold sober." Mark maintained.

"I don't care. I'm not doing it. I'm out of here. You guys are a bit too weird for me anyway. And that hat you're wearing should be put in a

coffin and buried," Richard sneered as he took a few long steps away from Mark.

Even though Mark wanted to tell him off, he held himself in check since he knew everyone was watching. In his position of leadership he always had to prove he was worthy of being followed, and he suppressed any strong reactions. Trying to sound totally detached, he declared, "We don't need your disrespect. You don't have a clue what's going on here. Luckily for us, you're the lesser of the two initiates, and the stronger man is smart enough to know the value of our group. He's not a coward."

"Well, fuck off, Markass! I'm leaving this dumb ceremony! Jason's just more stupid, not more courageous…that's obvious!"

"Enough nonsense. We bid you farewell, Mr. Not-So-Wise." Mark replied and turned his back toward Richard. "Come, Jason. It's time to show your valor," Mark directed, dragging him by the arm.

Driving from the police station, the city streets seemed endless. Jerry, feeling like a navigator through the outer boundaries of time and space, drove enveloped in a mental fog. Colors that his logical mind knew didn't exist darted in front of his car lights. Spirits from another world, he thought to himself. Every few minutes Jerry heard a muffled sob from Jodi, who sat in the seat next to him curled in a fetal position. He reached over, put his arm around her shoulder and gently stroked her hair. Jodi didn't respond.

"So much for the tough girl living in the city," Jerry tried to joke. In his heart he knew that her silence and barely audible moans were natural to the misery she must be feeling. If she only had more common sense, he thought, maybe she wouldn't be in this mess, and neither would he. Even though his own stress was making his nerves feel jagged and he wanted to fall asleep to escape from his impending sense of disaster, he felt mindful enough to pilot them through their middle of the night odyssey. Driving through the maze of the foggy avenues, he turned the car out of the flat grid of streets and rapidly began to ascend the hills of Twin Peaks.

"This doesn't look like the road that will take us to Norman's." Jodi said.

"Don't worry. It'll be okay. I'll take you back across the bridge to Norman's after I get some sleep, which I desperately need in order to be able to go to work tomorrow morning. I'm taking you to my father's house in the city for the night."

Jerry did not want to believe that he heard these words coming from his own mouth. He knew that he was getting sucked into feeling responsible for her, and he wasn't happy with the thought. Any optimism he had had about Jodi not interfering with his life had waned an hour ago at the police station when she announced that she had been raped. Seeing her misery triggered his willingness to do anything to help her, even though being with her ran counter to his common sense. He tried to detach from thinking about the consequences of his involvement in taking her from Norman's and bringing her to the city. What role had he played in the unfolding evolution of Jodi's karma? Was he responsible for what had just happened to her?

Fighting his building sense of guilt, he knew it was definitely time to find his own bed and end the current craziness of driving all over the Bay Area. He was starting to feel like a taxi cab driver, but without getting paid for his time or his gas.

"I'm not going to make that sixty mile round trip again until after I've had a good night's sleep," he told Jodi with the hope that she could understand his quandary. His energy was waning and he started looking forward to his dreamtime that would refresh his mind and perhaps bring answers to questions concerning Jodi's uncertain future.

"Toxins in my mind, toxins in my brain," the man on the radio was singing. Listening to the rhythm of the beat, Jerry could easily relate to the punk lyrics. He dreaded getting up early and going to work later in the morning. He felt a sense of relief that his work was almost over, but he became more aware of his frustration when he remembered that during the past week he hadn't seen or heard from Lisa. Fortunately pushing her and their last erotic encounter out of his thoughts was a lot easier with Jodi sitting right next to him whimpering like a child.

"I want to go back to Norman's," Jodi persisted. "I have a place to go."

"I'm delighted that you have somewhere to go. I would be glad to take you to Norman's, but I've already had one exhausting trip to his place earlier in the evening. When I left Norman's to come here to pick you up, Carmella was on the way to the hospital. It's not a good time to go there. And can you please understand that I've got to get up at six in the morning and get ready for work? I need to think clearly when I get to my job. So I'm going to go home to get some sleep before it's time for me to go to work in the morning. I will take you to Norman's tomorrow as soon after work as I can pick you up. And besides, we're just arrived at my Dad's, and you'll be able to get some sleep soon too. He's a really good guy. You can trust that he won't let anything happen to you. And most likely my sister Julie is staying there too."

Jerry knew it would be better if he arrived at his father's home with a gift of pot, but he had forgotten this protocol, as he had been preoccupied with the teenage runaway sitting in his car.

Things were far from perfect. He could hardly get Jodi to walk down the sidewalk. His dad hadn't been notified they were coming or that he was going to ask him to let Jodi spend the night. But surely, he wouldn't mind giving a young woman a place to stay since he had an empty bedroom in his place. If he or Julie weren't there, he'd use the key his dad had given him to open the door, a privilege that he hadn't previously needed to use.

Jerry knocked several times and was relieved when Mark opened the door. "Hi Dad, I was worried that you weren't home."

"I wasn't, but I just got here."

"I have a favor to ask of you. Can my friend stay here tonight until I can pick her up and take her to Norman's tomorrow after I get off of work?"

Mark looked at Jodi.

Lucky Norman! He thought. He always has young pretty women hanging around. "Sure, come on in. She's welcome here. A friend of yours is a friend of mine." Once Mark looked at her frozen in the light he wondered what kind of mess she'd gotten herself into. It was obvious that she'd been crying. He hoped Jerry hadn't been giving her a bad time. "Show her my spare bedroom in the back. I was just getting out of my clothes to go to bed myself." Mark replied.

"Where have you been?" Jerry inquired.

"You won't believe it, but I've been at a campout gone wrong."

"What do you mean?" Jerry asked, noticing an unusual furrow in his father's brow.

"First, show your lady friend to her room, and then we'll have a chat before you go home to your Stella."

Relieved, Jerry showed Jodi to a room that had papers and boxes spread all over the bed. "You can shower in there," he said pointing to the bathroom. Without further conversation he spent ten minutes clearing the large amount of clutter from the covers while Jodi sat on the floor with a look of doom on her face.

When he had finished he said, "Everything will be all right. I promise to return as quickly as possible and give you a ride to Norman's. Tomorrow will be a better day." Jerry bent down and hugged the unresponsive Jodi goodnight. Then he gave her a little kiss on the top of her head, turned, and left the room. He tried not to notice the middle finger she pointed his way.

One minute later, Jerry was in his dad's kitchen. "So what's up with the campout that went wrong?" he asked Mark who was pouring himself a large vodka-and-soda.

"I was master of ceremonies for our club's meeting, and we had chosen a new initiate. As part of the orientation, a man was going to shoot a beer can off his head with a bow and arrow. The archer, who wasn't suppose to drink, but I found out later, had one drink too many, missed his target and hit the poor guy in one eye." Shaking his head in dismay, he continued, "I can still hear him screaming. We called an ambulance and rushed him to the hospital. The doctors said that he's permanently lost sight in his eye and that the accident almost cost him his life. To make matters worse, his buddy who had witnessed this fiasco from afar got into his truck to run for help, but because he was so stressed, he accidentally put his gear in reverse and drove backwards into someone's new Mercedes. The Mercedes rolled forward and crashed into a tree so that it was smashed in both the front and the back end," Mark gulped for air sounding totally exhausted. "I wish I would have had your friend Carmella's magic stone with me. Maybe this all wouldn't have happened."

"What magic stone?" Jerry asked.

"She was here the other night with Norman after he crashed his car a few blocks down the road. She showed me an extraordinary stone that glows in the dark, and said that she found it in a some abandoned house," Mark told him.

"Oh really?" Jerry said feeling a bit surprised. Instantly his intuition told him that Carmella had found it in the haunted house they had recently visited together. Oh no, he thought remembering the words he thought he'd heard the Seega speak.

"Yes," Mark added. "But now I just want to get on a plane and fly to Timbuktu because I don't want to be here tomorrow to answer the damn phone. I know it's going to be ringing off the hook. I'm usually happy to lead our pack, but not now. I can't even imagine how much the legal fees are going to be to sort out this fiasco. It might even mean the end of our Lodge." Mark lamented. "I need another drink and then I'm going to bed."

"Dad, it's not your doing. It's destiny playing itself out, and you can't control it. Best thing is that you relax, try not to worry, and get some sleep. I'm going home, but I'll come over after work tomorrow, find out how things are going for you, and pick up Jodi. Please tell her to stay put until I can get here and take her back to Norman's. Keep her busy by

letting her watch TV." Jerry requested before giving his dad a sympathetic pat on his back, and hurrying out the door.

What a crazy night, he thought. He had wanted to tell his father about Jodi's situation, but after hearing his father's problems and seeing him so shaken, he decided not to add further stressful complications to his evening.

And now on top of everything else, he couldn't help but wonder about Carmella's stone. How had she gotten it? And worse yet, he especially didn't like the unexpected feelings he was having toward her. Feeling a migraine starting to emerge he turned his thoughts toward finding his car and making his way home. All he wanted was to put everyone's problems out of his mind, fall into bed, and go to sleep.

Eleven: Justice

XI. JUSTICE

A Free Spirited Fling

"It's very complicated, and hard to talk about," Stella confided to Naomi. "I just want to cry when I think about it, and usually I do. My pain is so deep; I haven't talked with anyone about it. Even though I've been keeping my situation a secret, I feel like if I don't tell someone soon, I'm going to explode. That's why I'm here. It's taken me a while to get up the courage, but I want to tell you what's going on, and then maybe you can help me. Jerry and I have been married for five years. He always talks about you and your family, and says that you're an amazing card reader. I feel like I can trust you."

"Thanks for your vote of confidence, Stella. I hope I'm worthy of Jerry's good review. Please tell him thank you for me." The older woman sat back in her chair, and looked deeply into Stella's eyes. She felt Stella's

sorrow, and decided that it would be better to stay quiet and give the young woman an opportunity to unburden her soul. *Young people seem so plagued with tortured emotions and a lack of trust*, she thought. *These days they can talk to their computers, but are afraid to talk with one another.* She was glad that her storefront office was inviting so people felt safe coming inside to talk and share their concerns with her.

Stella wrung her hands as if she were cleaning laundry, and continued, "I was very attracted to Thomas when I first met him at a work convention. I couldn't stop thinking about him. I felt that we were soul mates. I wanted to pursue our connection, but Jerry, my adoring husband, would never allow such a thing. When I first started telling Jerry that I wanted our marriage to turn into an open relationship he got angry and didn't want to hear about it. He was opposed to letting me see someone else. He seemed so insecure and immature and we fought about it a lot. I told him that having an open relationship would be an exciting opportunity to grow. We each would become emotionally wiser by opening ourselves to new people than if we stayed in our same old fashion way of being together."

Naomi nodded with understanding. She was glad that the sun had started coming through the crystals hanging in her window and that rainbows were beginning to dance throughout the room. The dancing prisms of light helped her distance herself from feeling sad for Jerry, whom she liked and respected as a gentle soul. She had watched him grow up starting as a young man in junior high school when he began dating her daughter. She thought that he and Destiny had made a perfect couple, even if he was a bit mercurial. Secretly, she had wished that they would have stayed together forever, but what vote did she have in teenage affairs? Not many young men were as in touch with the supernatural as Jerry, and that made him a perfect match for her family.

Naomi watched Stella sit nervously in her chair. She wished she could say something to help her relax. She looked at the statue of Kuan Yin, the Asian goddess of compassion, standing in the corner, and then looked around the room searching for a sign from the gods that they would help her give an impartial reading to the young woman sitting in front of her.

Without changing the expression on her sad face Stella declared, "After arguing for several weeks about transforming our traditional marriage vows, and watching Jerry sulk around our apartment, I told him that he didn't have a choice. I didn't want him controlling me with his conventional idea of our relationship. We didn't sign a contract to have an exclusive connection. I was so sure about what I was doing; I persisted in creating a major change in our lives."

"It's as if every detail is engraved in my mind. I kept telling him to be happy about new possibilities instead of being stuck in his narrow-minded viewpoint. Since I believe in being honest, I wanted him to know that I was going to start seeing Thomas whether he liked it or not. I longed to be free without needing to hide my actions or feel guilty. Jerry, my sensitive, supposedly New Age husband, complained that he 'didn't see it coming.'"

"I told him that it would be great if he were to also start seeing someone new. I knew that if Jerry were with someone else, he wouldn't be so angry with me, and I wouldn't have to deal with his insecurities." Stella's tears ran relentlessly down her cheeks.

Naomi interrupted her trying to be supportive. "Before you go any farther, please take a tissue and dry your eyes."

"Yes, thank you. I haven't been feeling very balanced lately. It's like I'm obsessed with Thomas…he's been absorbing so many of my waking thoughts. I was even willing to risk my relationship with Jerry for him. When I first met him, I couldn't wait to spend more time with him. I felt like a piece of ripe fruit, and he was going to be the man to harvest me."

"We talked on the phone for hours. Thomas bought me a cell phone so that Jerry wouldn't have to know how often we were talking. He made me so hot, even on the phone."

Naomi didn't reply. She smiled, waiting for Stella to go on.

"My relationship with Jerry became more difficult as he tried to adjust to having this new kind of relationship," Stella continued. "We stopped talking about open relationships so we could actually keep talking to each other. Our communications became more and more stressful. We would argue, and our quarreling became heartless. We soon stopped being intimate. I watched him mope about in a slump, and then he stopped coming home after work. Between his work schedule and mine, we hardly had time to see one another. And when he was home, he wouldn't tell me what was on his mind, or what he had been doing. Then after a month of barely talking to one another he let me in on his little secret. He told me that my plan to change the terms of our relationship had succeeded. He now also had a new lover. I acted delighted for him, but inwardly I felt terrible."

"I couldn't sleep that night. My mind was spinning as I questioned my choices. What I had with Thomas was playful, affectionate and I could talk about anything and everything with him. But after I slept with him he totally changed. Everything that created a passionate connection for us stopped. Whenever I saw him, he continued to stimulate me like a lone wolf nearing a she-den, but he was no longer available. I tried

being nonchalant when I spoke with him, but I embarrassed myself by shamelessly offering him an opportunity to make love. Lightheartedly, he told me that he had other things he needed to do."

Naomi thought about the sword-wielding hand of justice and took a deep breath. Trying not to judge Stella's personal choices she said, "Eros sometimes plays tricks on our hearts when we get too attached to the physical side of love."

"That's for sure." Stella sank down further into her chair, "A week later, the last time we talked, I joked with him about the craziness of our relationship and offered to make mad passionate love with him. After all, he was responsible for provoking our initial sexual relationship. That's when he told me that he couldn't become involved with me because his extended family didn't want him having relations with a married woman. I was livid. Extended family! How crazy is that? I hadn't been sleeping with Jerry because of my feelings for Thomas. I had put my life on hold to be with him, and he 'wasn't ready!' I tried to hide the disappointment that clawed at the deepest core of my being. After all, I was a patient woman. I had waited a long time for Jerry to finally propose to me, and I now I would need to be patient again and wait for my new man to want to continue our relationship."

Stella stopped to wipe away her steady stream of tears.

"I became agitated and anxious," she went on. "As Thomas felt me needing him more, he started withdrawing. He made it clear that we weren't going to be having an intimate relationship after all. Why did it take him so long to let me know? I'll never understand him or any other man. I feel like such a vulnerable fool. What was he thinking when he bought me my own cell phone so that we could talk privately?"

It was half a minute before Naomi spoke. She adjusted her position in her chair, watched the moving rainbows the crystals cast upon the wall, and looked back at Stella.

"So, you exchanged your harmonious relationship with Jerry for the dream of a more fulfilling, but unborn love. How strange the twists and turns of romance." Naomi shook her head sadly.

Stella nodded.

"After many hours spent crying on my pillow I began thinking that perhaps it was my wedding ring that had made Thomas feel safe with me. When I took it off, my freedom to be with him prompted him to show me his phobia of commitment. The closer I tried to move toward him, the farther away he moved. When I became fully available to him, he froze like ice on a winter pond."

Naomi could see Stella holding back her anger as she reached for another tissue.

"Now, although the opportunities are scarce, whenever I find the chance, I'm trying to improve emotional communications with Jerry. I feel so vulnerable and I don't know where our relationship is going. Maybe I've killed any chance of getting back together with him. I know he's involved with someone else right now and he's gone most all of the time. He says he still loves me, and I know I have only myself to blame for setting him free to become involved with someone new. He keeps telling me to stop resisting the changes that I've set into motion."

"Jerry's a good looking young man. I wouldn't expect him to stay home waiting for you to finish your affair," Naomi said with a bit of sharpness in her tone.

Stella winced.

Naomi examined her eyes to gauge her reaction to her words. She had been consciously trying not to negatively judge Stella's confession but knew her last comment implied disapproval.

Stella tried to lighten the conversation. "He wants me to get into metaphysics more. Jerry says that magical energy can be used for healing the body and mind, opening our heart, and transforming consciousness. He says that's ultimately what life is all about."

"That may work for Jerry, but who are you? Do you want to study metaphysics? Actually, it might be more worth your while to study Tantra. What's really important is to focus more on your own personal needs and those might not have anything to do with metaphysics. Think about what you can do to mend the broken link in your connection."

"The truth is that right now, I'm clueless about what to do," Stella said. "Tantra sounds beyond me. I know it has something to do with yoga, but that's about it."

"Don't worry, dear," Naomi replied. She picked up a wooden box sitting on a nearby table and took out a deck of cards. "Let's use my tarot cards to get some clarity. Why don't you shuffle them, and while you do, think about your relationship with Jerry."

Naomi handed Stella her cards.

Stella closed her eyes and slowly mixed the cards. After a few moments, she looked at Naomi and asked, "Is this enough shuffling?"

"Yes, dear, now cut the cards wherever your intuition tells you to cut."

Stella closed her eyes again, took another deep breath, and then cut the cards.

"Now choose a card. The one you select will give insight into your relationship," said Naomi. "Specifically, this card will tell you something about the best direction for you to go on your journey with your husband."

Stella hesitated, fingered one card, and then pulled out another that was hiding just beneath it.

"What card is this?"

Naomi smiled. "This card is a good sign. You have cut the cards on the eleventh major arcana card, Justice. It corresponds to the sign of Libra, which is the sign of balance, harmony, and commitment in love. It represents the importance of staying centered and keeping your inner balance in order to find your path to happiness. It's telling you to carefully weigh the pros and cons of your present choices and decision-making in relation to your husband. Check resources on sex, such as Tantric texts. Or, if you can't find any of those, read the latest issues of *Cosmo* to research how you might gather your strength to seduce him into making love with you. The planet Venus linked with love, is associated with this card, so you should be able to find a pleasurable solution."

Looking into Stella's eyes, Naomi searched for visible signs to her immediate reaction, and then asked, "You're still living together, right?"

"Yes. Sort of, but he's not home much except to sleep."

"Trust me. Sooner or later you'll find the right time to talk with Jerry and rekindle his passion for you. Don't obsess on your fear that your marriage is destroyed. You have time to fix it. Find your balancing point where you feel centered in your power as a beautiful woman."

"But what should I do?"

"Focus on healing your communications with your husband," Naomi commanded. "And start being sexually playful again, even in little ways, like running your fingers through his hair. Remember the best times you had together, and start acting toward him now like you used to act toward him then."

Naomi saw that Stella's tears had stopped and she felt her change of mood. "Negatives don't have to play out in life," she said. "Request a healing from your guardian angel, who is always with you. In your mind, visualize Jerry coming home and embracing you. Dark forces can more easily play themselves out in love when there is fear. To help you clarify and improve your situation, literally change the lighting in your home. As a reminder to connect with the healing power of light, get some light bulbs that emanate a natural yellow glow. Yellow rays link you with your solar plexus where you can feel your personal power and confidence. Stop worrying about your recent transgression, and open up and reveal

your sense of loss without him. And don't forget to forgive yourself. You can't always be right about everything."

"Thank you for being so encouraging. I'm so worried about making more wrong choices that I have knots in my stomach, but it makes sense for me to try to be more confident," Stella answered. "Honestly, things feel so wrong. As I spend time alone now, the more I am fantasizing about having children with Jerry. I feel so sad that I can't tell him that I want to become the mother of his children since he will hardly ever talk to me."

"You sound so passive and weak as you say that," replied Naomi sounding slightly annoyed. "I'm going to give you an affirmation that I want you to remember. Whenever you start to worry, mentally utter the command 'stop!' Then repeat to yourself: 'I am balancing my inner scales of justice with love, peace, harmony, and trust.' When you're trying to fix things with Jerry, think loving thoughts and send affectionate feelings toward him."

Stella looked doubtful but hopeful at the same time. Naomi watched her sitting anxiously in her chair and realized that she needed something more. She took Stella's hand in her own. "I could even," she said softly, "give you a love spell that my grandma taught me for fixing broken hearts. But for the power of this spell to work, you have to be willing to pay dearly. Stains of sin and ignorance can only be removed if you're willing to act beyond what appears normal."

"How? What would I need to do?"

"First, I must ask my guides for their consent to give you this spell. If they give me their permission, I can offer you their instructions about how to magically heal the discord in your marriage. Also, I will pray to Mother Mary for Jerry's seeds to be planted in your body. If God is in accord with the sincerity of your spoken words, you'll have a baby growing in your belly in a short time." Naomi eyes looked upward as she sat silently for a few minutes.

Stella continued, "I'm so tired of trying to change my emotions without seeing any change."

Acting as if she didn't hear Stella, Naomi said, "Okay, I have finished talking with my guides. They told me that you won't need to wait long for what you most want. They also said that you presently despise Thomas, and to jump-start your healing, you need to tell him the consequences of his flirting with you. They have also prescribed the payment for the spell I will give you, if you wish to use my remedy. Because you are Jerry's wife you are considered to be part of our extended family, and you need only pay half of what a stranger would normally pay. Finally, if you want me

to help you with this spell, you will need to do some work on your own, and it may take a couple of weeks or a month to see any results. For my time and effort in working with you, you will need to pay me a thousand dollars."

Stella caught her breath. "A thousand dollars? Can I take time to sleep on this decision?"

Naomi let go of Stella's hand.

"No, you need to act like an adult and make your decision right now. You and I both know that you're whimsical by nature, and your fears will cloud your mind if you take too much time to deliberate. My time is too valuable to waste on holding your hand while you tip-toe around your thoughts about it. Just say yes or no to working with me before you leave." Naomi's voice had become like that of a captain calling commands to an ocean liner that was in trouble.

Stella exhaled. "Yes, I want you to help me." Her voice sounded pleading, yet resigned. "I'll do anything to get Jerry to love me again."

"All right. First, complete your obligation to pay me, and then I'll ask you a couple of important questions. Besides that, you need to have complete faith in me. I need to warn you, that once I start working invocations for you, if you do anything to counteract the energy I send, you will be in danger of psychic attack by my ancestral guides."

Stella visibly trembled, and then said earnestly, "Jerry has told me that you're a powerful healer. I won't do anything to block your energy. I promise. I need you to help me." She got out her purse and found her checkbook. "I can give you seven hundred now and the balance day after tomorrow when I get my paycheck. Does that work?

"Okay. We have an agreement," declared Naomi as she took Stella's check. "Can you bake an apple pie?"

"Yes."

"Great. I'll go to the kitchen for some items that you'll need to get started," said Naomi. She got up and went through the door into the adjoining room.

Shortly, she returned to her parlor with nine red apples in a wicker basket. "These apples will be the essential part of your love potion. Their red color inspires passion and their sweetness will help you attract sexual love back into your life. Nine is the number that signifies transition and moving through life's hurdles. To create a positive environment ripe for love, you will weave together a spell using the Biblical serpent's choice for Eve's seduction of Adam: the apple, said to be the source for the birth of the human race."

"Now takes these and go. Don't let anyone else touch them." She handed the younger woman the basket. "I will call you and give you detailed instructions for their use once I know you and these apples are safely home."

Stella looked bewildered. "I'm excited, but a little afraid. I've never done a spell before."

"Don't worry. Everything will work out." Naomi said as she gave Stella a supportive hug and then walked her to the front door.

Twelve:
The Hanged Man

XII. ECLIPSE

The Sacrificial Altar

Unfortunately for Jerry, the next day when he was supposed to pick up Jodi at his father's and take her back to Norman's place near Stinson Beach, he couldn't get off work at his normal quitting time. On his desk was a time-sensitive proposal that had to be completed right away. Because of unforeseen last minute changes, he was in a panic to have it turned in before the eight PM deadline. He had only two hours before it needed to be delivered, and if he didn't have it done, he could count on his boss giving him a truckload of grief that he didn't want. Worrying about Jodi, he called his dad once again to check on her, and to tell him that he'd arrive just a little later than expected.

Julie answered the phone.

"Hi brother, what's up?" Julie said.

"I need to check in with my friend Jodi," Jerry replied. "Can I talk with her?"

"You could if she was here, but she went out with Dad." Julie said, her voice revealing little concern.

"What? Where did they go?" Jerry asked with a feeling of alarm.

"How do I know? Dad said something about taking her to see dolphins. He didn't bother inviting me."

"That's crazy! Where are they going to see dolphins?" Jerry said in a tone of voice that showed an unusual degree of concern.

"How am I supposed to know?"

"You could have asked where they were going. Do you know when they're coming back?" Jerry, who was normally calm, covered his feelings of anxiety with a veneer of irritability. "You're joking, right?"

"No, not really." Julie replied in a cavalier manner.

Jerry became more agitated as he sensed the unhelpful attitude in her tone of voice and changed the subject. "What are you doing at dad's if he's not at home?"

"Mom's got this rich, new boyfriend who's taking her on some tree saving eco-vacation in Brazil, and she doesn't want me to stay home alone. So I'm moving in with Dad. I was just unpacking when you called. I can't believe it; it's disgusting! Mom goes from this guy to that guy, and yet tells me that I can't have boyfriends at home past eleven at night. And I can't handle her constant complaining that I don't do anything around the house and her yelling, 'Pick this up and pick that up,' and 'Hurry up and clean the living room because my friend will be here any minute,'" Julie complained.

"I just visited Mom a few days ago and when I was leaving, I saw a dark-haired man coming to your door. Is that the guy who's flying her to Brazil?" Jerry asked.

"That must have been Moe. No, that one's out of the picture now that she's met her latest Mr. Wonderful with his hot little sports car. He's about fourteen years younger than she is. I think he's a dork, but Mom is all excited about him and can't talk about anything else."

Jerry didn't think he could handle more drama.

"Thanks. I'll phone Mom and check to make sure she's not doing anything stupid. But, hey, do me a favor. Tell Dad to give me a call when he and Jodi get home. Better yet, tell him not to go anywhere with Jodi because I'll be picking her up right after I get out of work to take her to Norman's."

"Why are you so worried about Jodi? She's almost my age, ya know. She told me so. Isn't Stella giving you enough love to keep you from hanging around with jail bait?" Julie said with considerable sarcasm.

"Cut me some slack here, Julie! I told her I'd help her. She wants to go to Norman's and I'm not interested in her except to keep my word that I'd give her a ride to his house. Stella couldn't care less what I do, anyway!" Jerry tried to sound upbeat even though Julie's question about Stella caused a heavy feeling in his chest.

"Really? Your wife doesn't care that you're hanging around with big-boobed young girls?" Julie teased. "Perhaps I should talk with her and get some lessons in not worrying about the man I love."

Jerry's fingernails dug into his palms. "Don't horse around with me, and please, don't call Stella. I'm at work and I've got a deadline to meet. Julie, I don't have time to talk with you right now."

"Well, I won't call Stella, not just yet. But I'm not an idiot, and if you don't tell me what's really going on with you and Jodi, I might."

"I did tell you." Jerry replied, a note of panic in his voice. "Now please, be the sweetie you are, and don't hassle Stella. Maybe I'll see you later when I come to pick up Jodi. Bye."

Jerry hung up the phone, exhaled deeply, and then looked at his computer screen. He could feel knots of tension expanding in the back of his neck. Where had his dad taken Jodi, he wondered? Jodi was so young. Certainly, Mark wouldn't make the mistake of being interested in someone Jerry left in his care who was almost the same age as his teenage daughter. *No*, Jerry thought, *that would be crazy*. There had to be a good explanation. Jerry needed to focus on his work, and he didn't have more time to waste thinking about his father and Jodi if he was going to meet his deadline. He looked at the clock, and told himself that he'd be driving Jodi north across the Golden Gate to Norman's soon enough. Besides, he didn't want to play the role of her daddy who needed to worry about her. Or so he told himself as he tried to keep what happened to her the previous night out of his mind.

As he worked furiously to meet the pending proposal deadline, he accidentally hit the wrong key on his computer keyboard and erased his last half hour of work. He'd been working so fast that he hadn't hit the save key as often as he normally did. He went through a momentary downward spiral of panic, and then pulled himself together with the realization that even feeling crazy would have to wait until later. Maybe when he had some spare moments, he'd have some time for self-examination or even make an appointment to see a shrink. "I am opening my heart to greater wisdom," he told himself. But despite the repetition

of his positive affirmation, there were way too many things weighing on his mind, especially the whereabouts of Jodi. Looking around the empty room, he felt relieved that most everyone had left the office and no one could witness his aggravation.

His mind raced back to earlier in the day after his stress levels nearly peaked. The normally good-natured Carmella had sent him several distressed text messages to convey her hurt and anger. She had told him she was thankful that after last night's grueling episode at Norman's the doctors only needed to put her ankle in a temporary brace, but never the less, she was walking slowly with pain, and she was blaming both him and Norman. Later a phone conversation had gone from bad to worse when he asked her if she had found a stone the day they were exploring the haunted house. "It was only a stone," she had replied with what Jerry thought was an undertone of embarrassment. "What else did your father tell you?" She then continued with a list of complaints about Jerry's lack of communication in their car ride home after that frighteningly bizarre incident in the haunted house. How was she to know that he wanted her to report every detail of her experience? Until that day she had never entered a haunted house, and she didn't like it even a little. Understandably, today hadn't been the best time to talk to her about it.

Between her tearful calls, Norman had phoned and angrily accused him of being at fault for Carmella's trip to the hospital. His string of swear words also let Jerry know how furious he was when Jerry hadn't delivered Jodi to his door as expected.

"Name calling isn't going to help," retorted Jerry after Norman had called him a flaming asshole. He had bitten his tongue to keep his cool at work and refused to tell Norman what was really on his mind. He felt guilty that he hadn't acted more assertively to stop Norman and Carmella from walking toward the ghoul. After all, he was the only one who could see it. But at this time, he needed to push aside his panic and focus on completing his work.

At that moment, as if fate was having fun at his expense, Jerry's work phone rang again. Thinking it to be his dad, he anxiously picked up the receiver. He was surprised to hear Lisa's voice on the other end of the line. He immediately perked up. "Lisa, what's going on? I've been worried because I haven't heard from you."

"Oh, sweetie, don't be mad. I've been missing you so much! It's just that I've been so busy at work and at home. I haven't had a spare minute to call you."

"Yeah, I know life can get really busy. I've been busy too, but not too busy to miss you. You know I'm happy to hear from you. What's up?"

Jerry inquired feeling his heart beat fast as Lisa sounded excited to be talking with him.

"I was wondering if we can get together tonight. My seriously frail mother-in-law who lives in Florida fell down some stairs, hit her head on a metal railing and landed with her legs in the same position as a young athlete doing the splits. My father-in-law thought she was dead and called 911. Luckily, she survived the fall, but is in the critical care unit in the hospital. So my dutiful husband bought a plane ticket to Miami and is presently on his way to visit his mom in the hospital. For now, I'm a free woman. Is there any chance we can get together tonight?"

Jerry groaned inwardly. He had been desperately hoping to spend time with Lisa, and now when the opportunity presented itself, everything else was demanding his attention. He searched his conscience.

"I've promised someone I'd give them a ride to Marin County later." He fumbled for words, trying not to lose Lisa's offer or to complicate the conversation by telling her that he was responsible for driving another woman out of town.

"Oh darn. I need you to give me a ride too," Lisa giggled.

Jerry was pulled in two directions at once. He felt his craving for Lisa in his body, but he remembered Jodi's anguish and the commitment he had given to take her to Norman's. If he were going to have any peace within himself, his need for Lisa would have to wait.

"Lisa, I want to be with you, but I can't just rush over right now. I'm working against a deadline to finish a proposal that has to be turned in tonight, and my time's already committed after work," Jerry said. He could hardly believe that his sense of responsibility was being a roadblock to his desire for Lisa. "But, after that I'm available, and I'd really love to see you. Once I have a better idea about things, I can call and let you know what time we can get together later tonight."

"Okay. Since my husband is out of town, you can come over any time, really. This is such a great chance for us to be together. As long as I know you're coming, I'll stay up and wait for you."

"Okay, my love. I'll be there as soon as I can." Feeling breathless, Jerry hung up the phone, and then immediately tried phoning his dad, but Mark still didn't answer He sighed deeply, rubbed the kinks out of his neck, and looked back at his work on the computer screen.

Mark had been wasting no time trying to get to know Jodi, but she seemed suspicious of his interest in her. Still he knew how to sweet-talk

his way into becoming her friend. Any pretty lady friend of Norman's would be welcome on his own list of friends, and his dignity wasn't going to let their age difference interfere with having a good time, even though she seemed to barely notice what he said to her. He made it his challenge to get her to talk with him for longer than her usual five-second replies and to turn her frown into a smile. She was an ambiguity that he wanted to clarify, and a welcome distraction from the numerous calls he received about the problems concerning his recent lodge meeting.

After he had made Julie and Jodi dinner, and then watched Jodi wait impatiently for Jerry, Mark used his finesse to get her to agree to go to the beach with him to watch the sunset and look for dolphins. He knew he wasn't misleading her by tempting her with the possibility that she might see dolphins jumping in the waves. In San Francisco, anything was possible. Even if he had spent his entire life going to the beach without seeing a dolphin there, they might see them today.

Sitting in his parked car at the beach, they could easily hear the incessant crashing of the waves against the shore. The mixture of the misty fog and the last rays of the sun turned the sky into a turquoise, pink, and orange symphony of color.

"I'm so sorry that we haven't seen any dolphins," lamented Mark as he tried to console Jodi. "But even so, the sunset is lovely."

"I have a headache. All I see at this beach are signs saying 'stay out of the water, shark attack.' Can we go back to your place and find out if Jerry's there yet?" She sounded annoyed.

Mark had spent the day trying to make her feel comfortable in his home and wished she could show a little gratitude. "Yes, of course. But I need to make a stop at my friend Taylor's house to pick up something. He has a daughter who's about your age. Maybe you two could chat for a few minutes, while I talk with my buddy."

"Okay," replied Jodi who groaned a heavy sigh. Disappointed that she hadn't seen any dolphins, she passively went along with Mark's request. If she hadn't felt so miserable, instead of waiting for Jerry she would have gladly left his place to hitch hike a ride to Norman's. But, after what had happened last night, she didn't have the strength to venture down the road into the unknown. It felt safer to wait for Jerry, even if that meant taking a round the town drive with his father.

Darkness overtook them as they arrived at Taylor's front door and said their hellos. Jodi preferred not to look at Taylor when they walked into his house, and was annoyed that she was forced to listen to Mark complain about some accident that had happened the night before, and how this could mean a potential lawsuit. She knew that if anyone had the

right to object to the unfair, troubling events of the preceding evening, it was herself. Yet, she had no desire to tell these strangers about her much larger problems.

The air in the large room seemed to vanish when Taylor reached out and put his long fingered hand gently on Jodi's shoulder.

"Would you like to join my friends and I tonight? We were just getting ready to do a ritual before you arrived. Do you know that young women have magical powers equal to a dragon breathing fire?" Taylor asked her.

"I don't believe in dragons," she replied moving out from under his touch. She knew the instant she heard his strangely melodious voice that it was time to leave.

"Maybe you should," he responded, smiling at her while putting his hand under her chin and lifting it so that she would have to look up at him.

Jodi froze, looked in Taylor's eyes, and said nothing. *If this guy believes in dragons, he must be crazy,* she thought. Taking a deep breath she summoned the courage to shuffle several steps away from him. Even though he seemed nice enough, there was something odd about him.

"I think fate brought Mark here to help us tonight," Taylor continued. "My friends are waiting downstairs for me to lead them in doing a very important ritual. I'm going to summon the departed so we can speak to the spirits on the other side. Perhaps among other things, they can give us some needed answers to Mark's predicament. You can join us in this rare opportunity to talk with the deceased. Do you know anyone on the other side who you would like to speak with?"

Jodi couldn't believe this bizarre situation. All she wanted was to get back to the relative comfort of Norman's house in the woods. She looked at both men and wondered if there was any truth to Taylor's mumbo jumbo. Could this man with eyes like an eagle really talk with the dead? If so, it seemed like a chance she shouldn't pass up. "Well, my mom's on the other side, and I'd really like to talk with her," she said slowly.

"And I'm sure that she'd really like to talk with you, too." Taylor responded, his voice sounding a note of triumph that made Jodi cringe. "Mothers always miss their children and long to be reconnected. I'm sure with your help, we can invoke her spirit to appear."

Although Jodi's first instinct was to run, she missed her mom and longed for the chance to tell her she was sorry for running away and not being home to help her when she lay sick and dying. Maybe her mom would forgive her and help relieve her unrelenting sense of guilt and grief.

"What do I have to do?" she asked

"I'm sure Taylor will let you know," replied Mark who was intrigued by this shadowy yet interesting synchronistic occasion.

Without speaking, Taylor gestured for Mark and Jodi to follow him down a long narrow hall toward a doorway. After Taylor opened the door, they quietly trailed behind him as he walked down a dozen, short narrow steps into a noisy room that looked like an old two-car garage converted into a meeting hall decorated with Turkish rugs on the walls. Several ornate ceiling candelabras lit the space that was crowded with about thirty people, dressed in black, mingling about, talking, laughing, and drinking. Some were dancing wildly to an African drumbeat being broadcast from overhead speakers. Others were eating while standing next to a banquet table covered with chocolate and sugar glazed desserts.

"Help yourself to anything you want," Taylor offered, before leaving Mark and Jodi at the refreshment table and disappearing into the crowd.

Jodi was looking at the decadent feast, but her stomach was too knotted up to eat. But she couldn't resist staring at the people in the spirited crowd. Soon, the dim lights became even fainter and the music stopped. Jodi could hear her heart beating as the crowd fell silent and everyone turned and faced one corner of the room. There sat Taylor in a throne-like chair with large palm ferns behind him. He wore a kingly helmet made of what looked to Jodi to be bones, a black robe decorated with strange gold symbols, and a large jewel pendant cross over a triangle around his neck. Attended by two semi-naked women kneeling before him, he looked like the king of the Apocalypse. Taken aback, Jodi felt a shiver race down her spine. Using their fingers as paint brushes and the flow of their emerging menstrual blood as an artistic pallet, both women methodically drew a magical circle on the floor around Taylor and themselves. When the circle was completely drawn, they each sat on the floor on opposite sides of Taylor, looking toward him as if they were loyal guard dogs protecting their master.

"Tonight we are going to use the hermetically sealed *Doctrine of the Ritual of High Magic* to create the impossible," Taylor announced. He stood up and raised high his crystal skull staff. "I welcome you all. This ceremony will summon those whose spirits are free to roam the invisible realm of the Netherworld. Also, it is my special honor to ordain Angel, my daughter, as virgin priestess of the Lords of Truth. Holding the oracle of wisdom above her third eye, she will sojourn to the conjunction point of Alpha and Omega, where only the pure at heart can enter. She has agreed to ask the guides, gods, and goddesses of the four corners of the earth for our redemption and privileged rebirth. Following the traditions of our ancestral path, she has been instructed in how to travel

to the astral planes where she will follow Hecate's invisible path to the sphere of seven mysteries. With the goddesses' blessing she can bring light out of Chaos, and access the forbidden scrolls that map the route to hidden treasures guarded by the disembodied spirits of those who live in invisible subterranean planes."

Is this for real? Jodi silently questioned.

As if a green light had turned to "go," the crowd started to murmur and someone in the back of the room shouted, "What if she succeeds in getting there, but can't find her way back?"

"Don't corrupt our vision of success with your lack of foresight, and cast the doom of doubt by asking such a question! Her very DNA knows how to travel inside these planes of nether reality, and her purity functions as her talisman. This work is meaningful for us all, and Angel is first in line to achieve the reward of such an honor. If she doesn't feel right about accepting this prestigious invitation, she can withdraw at any time." Taylor responded firmly.

Suddenly, the lights flicked on and off and on again, and a brass bell was rung loudly three times. The silent crowd parted to open a path down the middle of the room, and Angel, dressed in a long white wedding gown with a lace veil covering her face, advanced rhythmically toward her father's throne. She pulled a large black pit bull on a chain behind her and together they walked to the magical circle.

One of the two women inside the circle spoke sharply. "Before you can enter, you must say the magic words to open the invisible gate."

"I knock three times on your door. One knock is for each of the Teutonic masters, The Three Witnesses, by which the invisible is made visible, and light becomes tangible matter," Angel whispered.

"If you are not afraid to embrace the darkness, you may enter," the other woman inside the circle said, sounding a genuine echo of concern.

"I am not afraid," Angel replied.

I would be if I were her, Jodi thought feeling anxious for Angel.

Then Taylor's assistant took a dagger from her belt and cut an invisible door for the young woman to enter their private magic circle.

Angel walked to the foot of the ceremonial chair, and her dog followed. Just as Taylor was getting up to give Angel his chair, the dog lifted its leg and pee ran down his black boot. "Damn dog!" he complained while shaking his foot.

"Angel, by your own free will, you agree to be part of this ritual, is that right?" Taylor asked.

"Yes. I want to do it," Angel replied.

"And you have been instructed on how to vacate your conscious awareness, and dive into astral space to explore the hidden inner planes?"

"Yes."

"And you have been instructed in maintaining your mastery over any chaotic spirits or grosser elements that you may encounter as adversaries along your way?"

"Well…I hope so."

"You must answer yes or no."

"Okay. Yes. I've been instructed," she said.

"Remember, at all times you must hold your cross that you are wearing around your neck with your right hand. Your left hand is free. If you encounter any difficulties, lift your left hand, and we'll bring your conscious spirit back to the room as fast as the speed of light. The elixir of your magic is in your faith in being triumphant. Visualize your confidence and success at all times. Now sit in my chair," Taylor commanded.

Angel moved immediately to the seat. She looked to Jodi like a small child on a too-big papa bear chair. Taylor's two women attendants drew near, lifted her veil, and kissed her on the forehead.

Taylor called out, "Mistress Nostradame, please recite your sacred code and induct our Angel so that she may enter the inner planes."

Following Taylor's directions, the woman who had opened the invisible door in the magic circle chanted a song in a foreign tongue while she walked around Angel and her dog three times in a clockwise circle. She stopped chanting when she reached Angel's left side, and pulled out from her pocket a golden locket on a chain.

"Angel, watch the golden ball. Watch it swing back and forth, back and forth. Relax your mind. You are falling asleep. You are falling deeper and deeper into sleep. You are relaxing. You are falling fast asleep. You are now asleep. Feel your spirit as it frees itself from your body. Let your unconscious spirit awaken, and let yourself fly through space." The woman smiled an all-knowing smile, and then she said, "Tell me where you are at this moment."

"I'm surrounded by dark clouds and I can't see anything." Angel answered sounding as if she were talking while in a state of deep sleep.

"Angel, to help you go where you are needed, we won't talk with you for awhile so you can embark on your journey," Taylor spoke softly. He then turned to the crowd, and as if he needed to supply a reason for everyone to assemble, and then he spoke loudly, "Let us all remember those on the other side. Use your soul's longing to invite the departed into our room." Taylor was silent for several minutes before continuing.

"Ascend-Descend-Awaken to rest in our shadows. Make your spirits easy to discern. We welcome you to walk among us and anchor in our bodies so you can live through us this night. Eat through our mouths, dance with our bodies, experience and enjoy this soul feast of wine and food. Are any spirits here with us tonight?"

Taylor continued without skipping a breath. "I am calling the spirit of the mother of Jodi. Jodi, raise your hand so everyone will know who you are. Jodi, call your Mother. We are humbly asking you to be one with us. Your daughter wants to hear from you, and I will deliver any message you have for her."

Embarrassed, Jodi raised her hand and looked at everyone staring at her. *If only I could hide,* she thought while Mark pushed her closer to the front of the circle.

Taylor was silent for a couple more minutes.

"Yes, she's here Jodi. She wants you to know that she loves you very much. And she's trying to help you from the other side. She knows that you miss her and she misses you too."

I'm sure he's not channeling my mom, Jodi thought. *Anyone could come up with those lame comments.*

Taylor continued channeling, "You need to be reminded of your pure heart. Since you were a child, you have been vulnerable to those who want to use you. Your soul is pure, but you have forgotten this truth, and your heart is being contaminated by the lust of world. You have sacrificed your innocence and your honor. By playing into the temptations of dark forces you are losing your sensitivity to hear the murmur of your own soul, and forgetting your true purpose. Your mother says to tell you that she looks forward to the time when you will be together again. And just so that you know that it's really her, she wants me to tell you that she forgives you for stealing her pearl necklace that you're wearing tonight. She's happy that you have something to remember her by."

Jodi felt her body go into shock. No one knew that she'd taken her Mother's pearl necklace when she ran away from home! Jodi felt her cheeks turn blazing red and tears stream down her cheek . "Mommy, I miss you. What I should do with my…..?"

Just at that moment, Jodi was interrupted. Everyone's attention in the room shifted to Angel as she roared a deafening screech that sounded like a raven had been shot in mid-air. Taylor turned toward his daughter, who ripped off her cross pendant, threw it in his face, and jumped to stand on the seat of his royal chair. Angel looked at the crowd and laughing uproariously she screamed, "You're all going to die hideous and vile deaths. You think that Father Time will allow you to be late to arrive

at Death's doorway, but you'll be there sooner than you think." Then she pointed to one woman and said with loud certainty. "Your husband is screwing his mistress right now while you're at this stupid party. Maybe if you didn't stink, he'd be fucking you instead." To another woman she shrieked, "Do you think that by wearing that ugly black dress you can hide how fat you are?"

Angel's pit bull started barking viciously at the crowd. Jodi turned and started running for the door in competition with the crowd, which was moving toward the stairway leading to the exit like a disturbed hive of hornets. Pushing and shoving, everyone hurried to get to the upstairs door and Jodi was being knocked out of the way. She was relieved when someone illuminated the room by turning up the lights, but now it became easy to see that the room had turned into chaos. Jodi looked back to the altar and saw Taylor reaching for his daughter's hand. In response Angel kicked him in the groin. Things were going badly.

One of Taylor's female attendants who had been holding the dog's chain now urgently put in it in his hand. Slowly, both attendants walked away from the magic circle, but once out of reach of the angry pup, they pushed their way through the crowd, ran up the stairs, and flew out the door leaving Jodi and the less aggressive far behind.

Before Jodi reached the top of the stairs, she looked back at Angel and her distressed father who was acting like a juggler balancing his ebbing sense of authority with a hard to veil nervousness as he held the growling dog's chain to restrain its gnashing teeth. Angel, her eyes staring wildly, spit furiously at her father, but then sat back down on the chair and became silent as stone. Jodi felt someone grab her hand and pull her out the door and down the hall toward the front entrance.

Meanwhile, the room had emptied of everyone except for Mark, Taylor, and his daughter. An eerie quiet filled the once vibrant room.

"I thought you gave her instructions on how to protect herself," said Mark incredulously.

"I did," responded Taylor who looked as if he was going to cave in from the pain of seeing his daughter being in such a destructive state of possession.

"Angel, my sweet daughter, do you remember the chants for protection that I gave you?" he asked. "We can chant them together. They go: Om Parve…"

"Stop jackass, those chants might work for virgins, but ….guess what you stupid old man….I've been sleeping with my boyfriend for the past two months after you go to bed. I'm hardwired for sex, drugs, and whatever comes my way." Angel cackled like an old witch. "And right

now, I'm planning on doing a lap dance on horny old Mark and you and I both know that you're too decrepit to stop me!"

In complete shock, Mark jumped back.

"Angel! Come to your senses! You're the child of my dearest friend! Taylor, I'm going to leave and phone for help. I know you can communicate with Angel and bring her back to her normal self. Just keep encouraging her to reclaim her body."

Keeping his eyes on the make shift stage Mark walked backwards toward the exit. As he turned to go up the stair, he kept looking back toward Taylor and his writhing daughter. Once he made it up the stairs he ran outside where he found Jodi, tearful and stunned, waiting for him on the front steps. "Let's go!" he commanded.

Hurriedly, they both walked to Mark's car. Jodi gratefully climbed in, and locked her door. In her mind they couldn't drive away fast enough to calm her shaking sense of reality.

Thirteen: Death

Dancing the Karmic Tango

When Jerry finally got out of work and arrived at his dad's, he was surprised that no one was home yet. He used his key to enter the empty apartment and then waited impatiently for Mark and Jodi to return. *Some days don't work out the way you plan,* Jerry thought to himself. Hadn't he told his dad not to let Jodi go anywhere? He didn't expect his father to be out with Jodi, as he had told him that he intended to take her to Norman's as soon as he got out of work. With neither Jodi nor his father present, it was obvious that he was going to have to wait for their return.

Trying to focus on something other than his impatience, he called his father's cell phone, but Mark didn't answer. Carmella, who had annoyed

him on the phone earlier in the day, also didn't answer when he tried calling her. And even though he wanted to talk with Lisa, his intuition told him that it was better to wait to talk with her until later when he could see her. Again he began to think of Jodi and a strange chill went up his spine. Certainly he didn't have to worry about his father's intentions, or did he?

Trying to put any uncomfortable thoughts about Jodi and his father out of his mind, he picked up the remote, and settled on watching a television show about the ghosts of Alcatraz. After looking at his watch and sitting anxiously for another twenty minutes, his stress could no longer be ignored. The tension in his shoulders began throbbing. Trying to rub the tension out of his neck, he began to question what he was doing wasting his time waiting for people when he could be with Lisa. What a strange twist of fate that Lisa was finally free to be with him, and he wasn't available to be with her. He was getting more and more annoyed as he wondered about where his father had taken Jodi. Why couldn't he have left a note telling him when they'd return? He'd give them fifteen more minutes, and if they weren't home by then, he was leaving to go to Lisa's.

The moment Jerry decided that he wasn't going to wait any longer, he heard keys unlocking the front door. The mismatched couple, a tired looking older man and a teenage girl with downcast eyes, was silent as they walked into the living room "Where have you two been?" Jerry asked impatiently as if he was the parent and they were his disobedient children. "Didn't we have an agreement that I'd come here to get Jodi after I got off of work today?"

His father gazed at him with a strange look that appeared to Jerry to be a mixture of confusion and fear. "Sorry, Jerry. We got caught up in some unplanned events. Jodi's been in a rush to come home and meet you, but I had some errands that got in the way of getting back any earlier."

"You could have at least called me! Couldn't you be a little more considerate?"

"You sound just like your mother. Don't ask me anything about what I need, just start the judging."

"Dad, you're way out of line tonight, and I don't want to get into an argument with you. I've worked hard all day, and I didn't expect you to be out so late and keep me waiting. I don't have a lot of free time, you know."

"I thought you said you didn't want to get into nagging tonight."

"No! I said that I don't want to get into an argument with you. I didn't say 'nagging.'" He turned to Jodi. "Come on, it's time to take you to your friend's house. Norman's been waiting for you. Earlier today I told him I'd get you back to his place by sunset and that was a couple of hours ago."

"Jodi, maybe you can fill Jerry in on what happened tonight so that he gets off his high horse," Mark said.

"Thanks a lot, Dad," Jerry replied sarcastically, wishing that his father would have communicated differently. If he had only opened up and said a meaningful word or two, perhaps he would have gotten some sense of what was going on inside Jodi's mind, but it had never been easy for Jerry to talk with his dad.

After ill at ease goodbyes, Jerry and Jodi left Mark's apartment. Even though they didn't talk to one another, the cool breezes coming off the ocean persuaded them to agree to walk quickly. When they reached Jerry's car, Jodi blew a smoke ring in Jerry's face before putting out her cigarette. In spite of her obnoxious behavior, he opened her door, trying to trust that he was wasn't living a bogus reality, but was living with integrity. "Are you doing okay?" he asked.

"I've been better," she mumbled with her head down while getting into the car.

He went around to the driver's side of the car and got in. "Where did you go with my dad?"

"We went to some weird séance," she said robotically.

Instantly Jerry felt a knot in his stomach and sensed that something terrible had happened, but he wanted to know for sure. "Who had a séance? Where was it? What happened?"

"It was some weird guy dressed all in black and his weird daughter who was dressed in a white wedding gown. I think it might have been your old girlfriend's sister. Anyway, if you want the details, talk with your weird father who knows where it was. And don't ask me any more weird questions."

Ignoring Jodi's wall of defensiveness, Jerry responded, "I'm sorry that I couldn't take you back to Norman's any sooner. Last night, I was so stressed. I had to get some sleep so I could go to work today and not be a zombie, but I'm here now taking you to Norman's, just like I said I would, so please don't be angry at me."

Jodi looked at Jerry for one quick minute before looking away, and then said, "I'm not angry. I just think you're a jerk, and I'd rather not talk to you. So I won't."

Jerry imagined that she was still upset from the events of the previous night. Even though she didn't want to talk, he felt relieved to know that

his father had simply taken her to a séance. In spite of the uncomfortable silence, a heavy weight lifted from his shoulders from knowing that at this moment he was taking her to Norman's to fulfill his agreement. As soon as his task was complete, he'd get back to the city and hopefully connect with Lisa before it became too late.

After leaving the Golden Gate Bridge and its dimly illuminated towers far behind, he soon began navigating the twists and turns on Highway One. Even though he wasn't sure that taking Jodi to Norman's was in her best interest, he couldn't think of anywhere else to take her.

Throughout their drive Jodi remained coldly silent until they reached Norman's driveway and she let out a sorrowful moan. Jerry reached across the seat and put his hand on her head. "Everything will be okay," he said sympathetically.

"Don't pet my head like I'm some kind of a dog," Jodi growled.

Jerry couldn't believe her response, and pulled his hand away, and thanked God that they had finally arrived. He scanned the driveway for any signs of a ghostly presence before he parked in front of the wooden plank bridge leading to Norman's house. He looked at Jodi but she kept staring out the car window. He got out of the car. With his flashlight helping him make his way in the dark, he walked to Jodi's door, and opened it. Jodi appeared to be sleeping. "Come on, we're here," he said softly.

"What about that Seega thing?" Jodi asked.

Jerry shined the light on the ground next to her. "I've already looked near by and I haven't seen it. Just in case it's somewhere close, we should hurry up so we can get going before we see it or it takes notice of us." He took Jodi's hand to help her out of the car, but she pulled her hand away.

"I'm scared."

"Don't worry. It's only a short distance to Norman's, and I'm here with you," Jerry replied offering her his hand.

Acting as if she didn't hear him, Jodi got out of the car, and started moving toward the bridge.

Jerry closed her door and rushed to follow behind her as she sprinted fearlessly up the footpath. Luckily, there was a scattering of moonlight to make it easier to dodge the uneven ruts on the trail and to help them find their way to the little house in the clearing in the redwoods.

After a few breathless minutes Jodi was starting up the first step on the stairway leading to Norman's brightly lit doorway. She turned to look back at Jerry. "Aren't you coming?" she asked.

Jerry who had been right behind her was already turning to go the other way in the direction of his car. After Norman's insulting remarks

on the phone earlier in the day, he didn't feel like doing anything but delivering Jodi to his door. When he had explained what had happened to Jodi in the city, Norman had heartlessly blamed him for her incident. Why couldn't Norman realize that he wasn't empowered to stop the unrelenting hand of destiny? "No. Norman's angry at me and besides, I need to get back to the city."

Even though she felt angry with Jerry for his role in placing her in the situations that had led to her recent terrible ordeals, he was at least someone familiar, someone who showed her kindness in the harsh and frightening world of heartless people. She hated to admit it, but she even enjoyed his corny enthusiastic outbursts about life and magic. "But I want you to come with me." The sound of her voice evaporated in the lonely darkness. Her eyes pleaded with Jerry to come in, to stay with her for at least a little while. Beneath her veneer of apparent indifference Jodi was desperate for someone to care about her. She had realized that Jerry's commitment to drive her back to Norman's showed a trace of the simple human caring that she so needed.

But Jerry had already taken several steps in the other direction, and didn't see the look in her eyes or hear her weakly spoken request. He had fulfilled his responsibility to her, and only wanted to leave. He didn't even care if the Seega would be in the parking area or not. He only had one concern and that was whether or not Lisa would be willing to see him this late in the evening.

Lost in his thoughts about his uncertain love life, he returned to his car, kicked over the engine, and turned his wheels in the direction of San Francisco. He was mindful of not speeding in order to avoid getting a ticket. He had gotten too many of those in the last year, and didn't want to add the fear of losing his driver's license to his list of worries. As soon as his cell phone regained reception after being in a dead broadcast zone, he dialed Lisa's number, and waited for her to answer.

"Lisa. Hi!"

"Jerry, where are you? It feels like I've been waiting all night." She sounded sleepy.

"Do you still want to see me?" Jerry asked, his mind whirling with the fear of rejection.

"Yes darling," she answered. "Get here as quick as you can, before I fall asleep."

"I'm almost there, so wait up for me," he said, blowing her a telephone kiss before hanging up his phone. He could feel his body tingling with desire, as he turned southward on Highway 101.

Jerry was happy to cross the Golden Gate Bridge, and didn't even mind paying its steep toll to enter the city. Finally he arrived on her street, but then had to endure a frustrating twenty minutes of lost time while he looked for a parking spot. Good thing his car could fit in a tight space, he thought as he finally squeezed his car into a narrow space between two driveways.

Breathing heavily from excitement, he rushed to find her home. He'd never been there before, and he felt a bit taken aback when he saw the size of two tall stone pillars marking the entrance to her building. He stopped, took a minute to slowly inhale the salty air, and told himself to relax as he walked through a sculptured archway and up a stone stairway. Finally, he was knocking on Lisa's door, and every thing else in his life could wait. In spite of the previous obstacles, he would soon be in her arms.

"Hello, Jerry. Come on in," Lisa said as she opened the large carved wooden door.

Jerry hurried inside and immediately started to hug Lisa. "I've been in a rush to get here all night. I'm sorry it's so late."

Lisa reached to embrace him. "I've been missing you so much," she said as her lips reached for his. "I'm so happy you're here."

Jerry felt his body become alive with the warmth of her kiss, as if a river of fire was flowing through him. Lisa's touch was electric. Without hesitating, she took his hand and led him down the hall into a room that looked like a Moroccan caravan filled with the glow of soft candlelight. In an adjoining room, not far from the pillow-adorned king size bed, a heart-shaped Jacuzzi was bubbling a warm invitation. Lisa stopped holding his hand, moved two steps in front of him, and turned to look at him. "I want you to see something that I bought just for you," Lisa said, taking off her robe and letting it slide to the ground.

She was wearing a black lace strapless bodice that showed the delicious curves of her slight breasts. Below it, he could see her pierced belly button adorned with a sparkling diamond chain. Her black sheer hose smoothly entwined with a purple and black lace garter belt to highlight the outline of her thighs. A tiny g-string decorated in the shape of a heart glittered in the dim light when she moved.

Jerry's body began throbbing with excitement. He stepped forward, pulled Lisa toward him, and melted into her arms. He could smell a sweet fragrance on her skin and smiled at his good fortune to be holding her. As they kissed, their lips were like magnets that couldn't separate. His hands slid to her nearly bare buttocks.

At that moment, the phone in his pocket sent a ring of harsh reality to disturb their special occasion. "I'm not going to answer that," Jerry murmured without stopping his heated kisses.

"Okay with me," said Lisa, as she tightened her arms around him, making their bond inseparable. After a kiss that seemed to last infinitely, she giggled, put her hands on his shoulders, and then jumped up and wrapped both of her legs around his waist. His hands caught her firm bottom to support her weight. He felt like a scorched desert coming alive with the first drops of a drenching rain.

Swift as a fire stoked by the wind their kisses became more excited, and he carried her toward the bed. As if fate was playing a bad trick on his good fortune, Jerry's phone rang again. Lisa playfully reached into his pocket and took out his phone. Her eyes squinted to see the caller ID name and number of the person who was calling. In a cold unfriendly tone Lisa said, "It's someone named Carmella." Unexpectedly, Lisa then hit the answer button on the phone and placed it next to Jerry's ear. Jerry looked at Lisa with exasperation, freed one hand and took the phone that she had stuck in his ear. Falling from his grasp, Lisa pulled away, jumped from Jerry's partial embrace, and stood glaring at him as if he was an intruder.

The loudness of Carmella's cries enabled her voice to be heard clearly in the room as she said, "Jerry, answer the phone. It's an emergency. I need your help. Please answer the phone. I'm freaking out. Help, please!"

Jerry looked sadly toward Lisa and took a deep breath. Their interaction had changed seamlessly like a tango dance moving rhythmically without missing a beat. An alarming sense of disappointment rippled through his body.

"Jerry, are you there?"

"I'm here," he said reluctantly.

"Guess what Jodi did tonight?" Carmella asked.

"What?" Jerry replied without emotion while looking at Lisa and faking a smile.

"She drank a fifth of vodka and took Norman's gun and shot a hole in her head."

Jerry froze in shock and then slid to the floor. "No!" Jerry cried. "Oh God! Is she dead?"

"She's in the ICU at Marin General Hospital. She's alive, but she's in a coma and no one's sure if she'll pull through. After the ambulance left with her, the police came and took Norman to the police station to ask him questions about what happened. He's there now. And you, Jerry, are

on my biggest shit list. Why did you have to bring a psycho like Jodi to Norman's?"

Avoiding Lisa's stare, Jerry replied defensively, "I brought her to Norman's because he asked me to bring her back, and she wanted to go there. She didn't want to stay in the city, and Norman liked having her around. He made me feel like I was betraying him because I had encouraged Jodi to leave his place."

"Well, now his house has yellow tape around it and no one can go in. I feel so terrible." Carmella replied.

Lisa was vanishing into the mists of Jerry's consciousness. "Do you know where the bullet went into her head?"

"I don't know for sure. All I know is that Norman's really freaked out. When he called me from the police station, he wanted me to find him a lawyer and get him out. He didn't say much about Jodi except that after she shot herself, and the emergency people came to help, he didn't want to go with her in their ambulance. He went nuts. Just like he refused to go to the hospital with me when I got hurt, Norman wouldn't go with her. After she was taken to the hospital, he ran to clean his drugs from around the house, and flushed as much as he could find down the toilet. When the police got to his house, he was very drunk and extremely high. He locked himself in his room, but realized that he had to open the door for the police or they were going to break it down. They asked him a few questions, then handcuffed him and took him to their station."

"Did he say if she was on drugs?" he questioned. "Do you know if he had sex with her?"

"How do I know? Norman wasn't willing or able to talk much from jail. Besides, he knows that I don't like talking about his other girlfriends," Carmella admitted. "But I do know it's not going to look good if they find his juices inside her body."

Jerry felt his grief expand as if it were a vice tightening around his mind. "If Jodi managed to commit suicide, it doesn't have anything to do with Norman or having sex with him. Jodi's a little crazy to begin with. She probably would have decided to blow her brains out sooner or later. I know Norman well enough to think that he wouldn't give her enough drugs to make her lose her mind and he'd never give her a loaded gun to play with."

"True, but she's a minor," Carmella said.

"Yes, that's definitely going to be a problem."

"Can't you get off the phone already?" Lisa asked with a note of irritation.

Jerry stopped talking and looked at Lisa. He felt his face flush with a silent implosion of anger.

"Whatever happened in her mind that made her want to end her life, we don't really know," Carmella continued in his ear. "Once, I overheard her say that the devil was controlling her thoughts."

"Get off the phone already," Lisa commanded while shaking her hips like a sultry dancer.

Jerry ignored her. "Were you at the house when this happened?" he asked Carmella.

"No," Carmella said. "The truth is, I was a bit jealous of her connection with Norman and I didn't want to be there when she was there and have to watch her hang out with him. I made a point of leaving right after she walked in the house earlier in the night. And, I thought she was a bitch because as soon as she saw me, she gave me the finger. But right now, I'm just angry with her for creating such a mess. She's the reason Norman's in jail. She certainly wasn't concerned about any of us when she decided to pull the trigger!"

"If someone's crazy they're not going to be concerned about anybody else. But, it's not a time for judgment," Jerry said feeling sweat dripping from his brow. "What I really need is to help Norman. I owe him for all the good energy he's given me over the years. I wonder if I can get into his house."

"Maybe we can blame Jodi's father," Carmella suggested. "She told me that he committed suicide after leaving her mother and her when she was a young child. Maybe that's why she got the idea."

Lisa handed Jerry a glass of wine that she had newly poured, and then hissed, "Jerry get off the phone. We don't have a lot of time together, and we have something that we need to talk about!"

Jerry ignored Lisa, tasted his wine, and went on talking to Carmella. "I don't want Norman to take the blame for what Jodi did. And we'll never know what really happened in Jodi's mind unless she survives the gunshot."

Lisa jumped to grab the phone from Jerry, and yelled loud enough that Carmella could hear, "I'm not going to stand here and be quiet any longer! You need to get off the phone. Tell whoever's on the phone to go cry in her beer and let you enjoy your evening!"

Jerry grabbed his phone in time to hear Carmella say, "Oh Jerry, I'm sorry for disturbing you. I didn't realize you were in the middle of something. We can talk tomorrow. I'll try to find out what's happening to Norman and see if he can be released from the police station. Don't

worry about anything. I'm sure everything will be okay." And then Jerry heard Carmella's phone line disconnect.

Jerry looked at Lisa, who was making goofy faces at him. "Lisa, this isn't a time to be funny!" he said, turning off his phone.

"Yes, my dear sweet, Jerry. I'm sure that you're feeling sad after listening to someone cry on your shoulder about her foolish friends. But don't let your woeful phone call stop our party. Right now, I have something to offer you that will help you forget that nasty call, whatever it was about. I promise to make you feel so much better." Lisa extended her hand to Jerry, and pulled him toward her bed, giggling like a wanton child.

Fourteen: Temperance

XIV. POLARITY

Two Cups of Love— One Silver, One Golden

"I love you, honey pie," Lisa said to Jerry as they sat on her bed covered in dark blue satin sheets. Lisa had thought about asking Jerry to explain his recent phone call, but it sounded so serious that she was afraid their time together could turn into a murky discussion of someone else's crisis. *Live for the moment,* she thought, *and don't worry about problems until they come home.* Lisa knew as she looked at Jerry that right now there wasn't a problem. She'd been hoping for a time when Jerry and she could explore their relationship without their customary short time limit

and interference from other commitments. This evening had been the perfect time.

Jerry shifted nervously in his seat, and looked blankly at the floor. Lisa could see the look of sadness on his face.

Turning to look at Lisa Jerry replied, "I've been wanting to be with you for so long. I was beginning to think that we wouldn't see each other again. If it wasn't for your smile, I'd be going crazy thinking about my friend's problems right now. I just need a few minutes to get my head out of their troubles and shift my attention to you."

"I want you to be happy. Remember when you told me that I stir your soul?" Lisa said, determined not to let anyone steal the moment. She would do anything to distract Jerry from his worries, she thought. Smiling she began to unbutton his shirt and then started lightly biting his tight muscles that rippled down the front of his chest.

Her long hair tickled Jerry's bare skin. He loved the sensation of her tresses sweeping across his midriff, and his mind gradually began to move away from the call he had just received from Carmella.

Lisa unbuckled Jerry's belt, untucked his shirt, and began to cover his belly with her kisses. "I love that our evening has opened to finally have time together. We fit so perfectly together," she said, putting her arms around him, gently pushing his upper body down onto the bed, and moving her body on top of his.

Jerry moaned as she buried her head between his shoulder and neck and started to playfully nibble his ear. At last, he could relax and let his body melt without reflecting on the unfamiliar coldness of Lisa's behavior while he was on the phone with Carmella. The moment was becoming more agreeable with every kiss, and its electric charge produced high voltage. "Yes, we're a great fit. What a wonderful surprise it was to get your phone call asking me to come here," Jerry said, pulling her bodice down to unveil her naked breasts.

"What a minute. You haven't said that you love me," Lisa replied, removing her bodice and strategically rolling her hips back and forth in an exciting rhythm over his body. She noticed Jerry beginning to smile.

"If I'm a little slow saying I love you, it's because I'm waiting to see how much you love me before I commit to telling you how much I love you. But, I want you, and find you so deliciously attractive," Jerry said before he grew silent and began to cover Lisa's soft fragrant skin with an abundance of warm, moist kisses.

Jerry's stroking of her body became more intense and her body tingled with excitement. Lisa's king size bed was just the right size to accommodate their raging desires. Each movement turned the flame of

the heat between them up higher until Jerry couldn't wait any longer to taste the sweet silkiness between her legs. He slid his body toward Lisa so that his hands could gently open and caress her inner thighs.

But Lisa sat up abruptly and pulled away. "Wait a minute. I need to hear you say that you love me."

Jerry moved his hands to further caress her. "Let my actions speak for themselves," he said, kissing his way up her thighs.

Even though Lisa had initially worried about inviting another man into her husband's bed, any guilt she may have felt was crumbling with the warmth of Jerry's sensitive touch. She laid back on the soft pillows to surrender to his tender expression of physical love. Like a fountain of plentiful affection, she couldn't contain the brimming pleasure she was experiencing and she began to coo like a lovebird.

Suddenly Lisa bolted upright. "Oh my god! Stop, Jerry!" she gasped. "It sounds like someone's opening the front door. I've got to go look." Lisa jumped up and ran to the not quite closed bedroom door.

"Jesus, Jerry, grab your clothes and get out of here. David's home! He's home!" Lisa stuttered in a fast, barely audible tone of distress as she watched her husband with his suitcase in hand walking through and closing the front door.

"And where am I supposed to go?" Jerry asked as he jumped out of bed and started grabbing his clothes that were scattered about.

"Oh my God, quick-get into my closet" Lisa said throwing his shirt at him and pulling up the bed covers. As fast as a bolt of lightning, she pulled his hand and dragged him with her to the closet, turned on its light, and closed the door. Lisa then ripped off her garter and slinky black hose, threw her sexy bodice behind some jackets, and grabbed a plush pink teddy bear nightgown from a clothes hook to put on as fast as she could possibly move. Staring wildly at Jerry, she grimaced and made a sad expression with her face to communicate her disappointment. Then she put her finger to her lips to signal no more talking, pointed to a corner for Jerry to sit and hide, and quickly turned off the light and walked out. Ever so quietly, she closed the closet door before running on tiptoes to jump into her bed. She quickly smoothed the crumbled covers so that the bed looked nearly undisturbed, and pulled the sheets over her head and pretended to be sound asleep.

Lisa was relieved to hear the sounds of silence coming from her closet, but she couldn't stop her heart from pounding like a drum being played in a ritualistic frenzy. She tried to calm her breath and told herself that everything would be all right. Within seconds she heard her bedroom door open and David's soft footsteps thumping toward the

bathroom. Lisa could hear the water gurgling in the sink and the toilet flush. She reminded herself that she didn't have anything to worry about as she listened to his steps coming into the bedroom. "God help me!" Lisa thought once again trying to calm her pounding heart.

Slowly, David made his way to their bed. He turned back the neatly folded covers and climbed in. He moved close to Lisa and embraced her with his body. "Honey, are you awake?" he asked. "Lisa, I need to talk with you," He said gently tapping her on the shoulder and encouraging her to awaken. "Sweetie, sweetie….I'm home. Please, I need to talk to you. I need you to wake up."

Lisa rolled toward her husband and sat up. "David!" she said, pretending to be startled. "What are you doing home?"

"Honey, I need to be home with you. I talked for a long time on the phone with my dad, and my mom's going to be okay. My dad told me that he didn't think I needed to come to the hospital since I wouldn't be able to do anything to help her. She's on so many meds that she wouldn't know or remember if I was there or not. He knows how busy I am at work, so it wasn't hard for him to convince me to turn around and come back home. I changed my ticket when I was sitting in the Chicago airport and got the first available flight back to you."

"David, that's great. I'm happy to hear that your mom's going to be okay. Welcome home, sweetie."

"While I was waiting at the airport I saw this beautiful necklace in a store window. It was so beautiful that it made me think of you and how beautiful you are. I had to buy it. Is it okay if I turn on the light so that I can show it to you?"

"Um…sure, but not the overhead light. I'm still groggy. Can you can just turn on the light on the night table?" Lisa answered feeling a troubled knot of guilt tighten in her neck.

Jerry watched David through the slight opening of the closet door. As if he was a shadow moving in the dark, he could see him get out of bed and walk to Lisa's nightstand to turn on the light. He reached toward Lisa and gave her a kiss on her forehead. "Are you awake enough to see what I've brought you?" David asked, sitting next to her on the bed with a big smile on his face.

Lisa sat up and made an attempt to act like she was just waking up, and rubbed her eyes and yawned. "I guess so."

"While I was on the plane and waiting at the airport I had time alone to think about my life and our lives together. I thought about my dad and mom and how grief stricken my dad was at the thought of losing her. I realized that I have a fear of losing you too. I know that I'm not always

available to you and I don't give you as much attention as you deserve. I'm sorry, baby. I want you to know how much you mean to me and how much I love you. This diamond is a symbol of how I feel." David opened a small box and handed it to Lisa.

Lisa's eyes opened wide. "Oh my God, David! What did you buy? I can't believe it," she exclaimed excitedly after looking into the small box.

"It's a two carat stone, and it's surrounded by six small blue sapphires. The jeweler told me that blue sapphire has a magical property that acts as a talisman to guard the purity of love. I don't know if that's true, but I do know I couldn't resist it, just like I can't resist you, and I want to protect our love. This gift comes from my heart, baby, and it's just a small expression of my appreciation of you."

"I don't know what to say," Lisa mumbled wishing she could erase the script of the recent events in their bedroom. "I'm in shock."

"Good. I want to make you happy. This gift comes with a promise to you, Lisa. I'm going to start putting our relationship before my other commitments. Yes, I'm dedicated to work, but I can start setting more boundaries there, and make our relationship my priority. I make the company enough money for them to know my value. I don't want to be married to my career. I want to be married to you. I love you so much."

"I'm stunned," Lisa replied while resisting the urge to look toward the closet.

"Good. I wanted to surprise you. That's why I didn't let you know that my plans had changed and that I was returning home earlier than planned. Let me help you put on your necklace." David took his present out of the box and fumbled a bit while putting it around Lisa's neck.

"It looks so beautiful on you, but I bet it will look even better if you weren't wearing your nightie. How about if you let me help you take that off so I can see your beautiful curves?" David murmured reaching to pull off Lisa's gown. "Yes, it's so much more beautiful against your bare skin." He started passionately kissing his wife, and began to tenderly stroke her breasts. Soon, he turned off the light. Climbing back into his bed as quick as a bunny, he held Lisa's warm body closely against his own. "I don't care if you're sleepy, I just want to make love to you."

"No, David." Lisa replied jumping up and turning on the light. "First I want to get up and look at your gift in the mirror." Naked, she walked to the full-length mirror on the closet door, looked at her reflection, and closed the door tight. "Wow! This stone is amazing," she remarked looking toward her husband. She walked slowly back to her bed trying to hold her composure intact, and climbed back in.

"Remember the night we first met, and the first time we made love?" David asked Lisa who was unusually quiet.

"Yes," she answered, inwardly trembling with fear of Jerry's discovery.

"I'm sorry that I've been too busy to express gratitude for our time together. I want you like crazy, and I'm going to make love to you with more passion than you've ever felt," David said as he started to feverishly kiss Lisa and gently stoke her between her legs. "Oh my, you're so juicy."

Lisa was thankful that their foreplay didn't last too long. But she was surprised that David immediately started keeping his promise to be more present for her, and made love to her with greater enthusiasm than she had experienced for a long time. He explored every inch of her body, took his time, did everything he could to drive her crazy with pleasure. The resounding moans of her pleasure reverberated loudly, letting David know he hadn't lost his spark.

As the intimate enjoyment of the loving couple became more and more apparent through the closed closet door, Jerry, sitting on the floor behind heaps of expensive shoes, felt his heart becoming heavier. As he heard Lisa moaning with pleasure, he wanted to scream out in agony from his pain. Every time he heard Lisa's expression of delight, it felt as if she was throwing a grenade into the core of his very being. He didn't know how to contain his emotions. His eyes were filled with tears. *Damn her*, he thought, feeling trapped in an intolerable situation. He sat there quietly, not wanting to listen or to be a voyeur; not wanting to make noise and blow Lisa's cover, and not wanting to be stuck in a closet of the woman whom he had given a piece of his heart. Soon, emotions turned to anger. He was angry with himself for being caught in this horrible situation, and he was angry with Lisa for placing him in a trap which he could not spring.

To distract his mind from the sounds of the erotic melody being played on the body of the woman he had falsely imagined was his soul mate, he began to think about Carmella and how sweet she was. Why couldn't he find someone as nice as her to be with? And then he began to think about Jodi and how much pain she must have been experiencing before she shot herself. Why couldn't he have had more compassion for her? Why couldn't he have felt her pain, and prevented her from committing a hideous crime against herself? Why didn't he, who was known in psychic circles as "the best intuitive in the city," see the tumult of her pain and her impending doom? Jerry wanted to vomit. Even Norman sitting in jail must be having an easier time than I am, Jerry thought.

Instead of giving in to more jabbing pains of jealousy and anger, Jerry took hold of his emotions and shifted his focus. Sitting as still as stone, he recalled a lecture on morals that his mother had given him when he was a teenager and he was caught sneaking out the window late at night to see Destiny. "You're only hurting yourself when you lie. Dishonesty blocks you from perceiving the interconnectedness of life. To hear the song of your soul, you need to be honest." As much as he had hated his mother for blocking his attempt to go out that night and for disciplining him by grounding him for a month, he found that her words had helped him to listen to his reigning higher self in this merciless moment.

Kicking himself for ignoring his own integrity, and not seeing what should have been clear as the light of day, he knew he was living a lie. He missed his wife. Stella was a good woman. When she wanted to be with another lover, she didn't lie or hide her desires; she had told him what was going on in her mind. Sitting alone in the dark, he realized that he actually respected Stella for being honest, even if her truth had stung deeply and had changed his idyllic perception of love. And now he was treating her like dirt. He was making sure that she would pay for hurting him with ignoring her and her attempt to make amends even though they were living together. By refusing to talk with her, he felt his power over her, and could repay the suffering she had inflicted on him. Right now, all he wanted was to hold Stella, and to be with her again.

And he was stuck in the closet. He decided to try and distract his mind from the revolting moans and shrieks of love, and listen to the secret wisdom of his soul. He carefully moved into a crossed leg, yogic sitting position, and decided that perhaps the reason he was in this mess was that he was placing too much attention on chasing an unsustainable dream. Listening inwardly, he followed the somber trail of voices in his mind that reminded him that joy and sorrow, love and hate, and forgiveness and blame were all a part of life. *Once I get out of here, I never want to see Lisa again*, he said to himself, feeling his libido completely flat line.

Focusing his attention on his breath, Jerry started to deeply meditate and calm his emotions. He listened to the voice of his sorrow and tried to calm its intensity by visualizing unconditional love erupting from his heart like molten lava steaming from a volcano. Then he made a commitment to himself that he would buy a plane ticket and leave behind all this craziness and fly to somewhere he could see a real volcano. He imagined watching the lava flow into the sea on the big island of Hawaii, and for a moment almost forgot that he was sitting in a dark closet.

Sitting motionless, Jerry played with thoughts of alchemy and subtle vibrations. He called upon the Angel of Temperance to guide him in quieting the igniting fire of anger that continued to erupt each time he heard amorous sounds coming from the bedroom. He imagined angel wings fluttering a cool breeze to help him find his equilibrium, and that a celestial being was pouring him a cup filled with soothing waters of eternal love. He heard his inner voice spark a dialogue with The Angel and began to commune about moderation being a godly virtue.

Suddenly his thinking was interrupted by a sound that he hadn't previously heard. Someone, he assumed it was David, was beginning to snore as loud as a chainsaw cutting apart a tree. Jerry's mind jumped to the possibility of escape. He moved into a walking-on-all fours position and crawled to the closet door and opened it just a crack. As the sounds of snoring were continuous and unending, Jerry pushed it open widely enough to look into the room. He could barely see inside the dimly lit room, but almost immediately saw the way out. Lisa's hand silently waved to him, but he ignored making any contact with her. His escape route toward the bedroom door was finally clear.

Thinking of himself as a courageous lion, and following the rhythm of David's snoring, Jerry began to move quietly yet swiftly out of the closet toward his freedom. Crawling beast-like, he was soon outside the bedroom hastening down the dark hallway with considerable speed. With all of his yogic strength, he stood-up, and while trying not to make a sound, started slowly walking toward the front of the house. When he got to the large wooden door, the heavily sprung double bolts made his hope fall like a boulder. It was not going to be easy to leave without waking the household.

He turned and walked silently toward the kitchen. Earlier in the evening he had seen a small porch with a fire escape at the back end of the building. He imagined that being farther from the bedroom, the back door would make less noise when opened, and he was right.

Carefully, he felt in the darkness for a doorknob. His heart lightened when he found it, unlocked the double bolt, and let himself outside. The cool mist that touched his face made his confidence soar with renewal, and he felt that luck was finally on his side. He carefully made his way down the fire escape. Once on the ground, however, Jerry found himself trapped in a backyard jungle, cluttered with piled up yard furniture and entangled vines. It was hard to see much in the dark of the cloud-covered night, but fortunately his night vision helped him see the outline of a garden wall that his fingers followed all the way to the front of the house. When it came to an abrupt end, Jerry heard a car going by and knew

he had reached the street. He struggled to move a large, potted plant so that it could serve as a stepladder to help hoist himself up and over the wall.

Once on the other side of the fence, he was relieved to see that no one was there to witness his escape. Jerry had avoided being seen by David and was free at last. He rushed to his car, feeling a tremendous sense of relief. He fumbled for his car key, and even though he couldn't move fast enough, he soon opened the door. Shouting out his happiness like a man freed from disgrace, he jumped into the driver's seat and started the ignition with a burst of renewed energy. He let his shaking hands rest on the smoothness of the steering wheel to calm his nerves before he moved smoothly out of the parking place, and began to drive. The fog was so thick it was like steering through a tunnel, but whatever was happening outside didn't bother Jerry. Everything felt better now that he was going home.

Fifteen: The Devil

XV. CHIMÆRA

Chains of Fire

Norman sat in his jail cell on the one-inch thick mattress that was a poor excuse for a bed. His mind, body, and spirit were in the utter horror of withdrawal, and if he could, he would be willing to do almost anything to get a fix. His aching muscles twitched violently, forcing him into a fetal position of consuming despair. Cramping and hardly able to move, he groped his way across the mattress toward the rimless steel toilet to vomit the contents of his already nearly empty stomach. What the hell did I do? he asked himself over and over as he tried to rub an ever-present, phantom itch that couldn't be soothed no matter how much he scratched. He fell to the floor just in time to see a metal barred window slide open and an eye peek into his cell.

"Obviously whatever he's on didn't kill him." Norman heard a voice say. "I wonder how much he's enjoying getting high now!" Then the window slid closed with a clang that echoed endlessly in Norman's delirious mind.

Feeling as if he was about to be disemboweled, Norman could hardly string words together coherently enough to complete a thought. In his body a tremendous pain was rising up, increasing with every breath, with no visible remedy anywhere in sight. Surely death would be better than this horrific suffering!

Out of the jumbled confusion of his mind, his thoughts staggered together without much meaning. He realized that he hadn't known how high he had been until this moment when he was falling helplessly into a hopeless abyss. The upset circuitry of his nerves sent his body into intermittent spasms as if he had lost control over his physical senses. His mind raced to find answers, but his thoughts were like ants crawling through soft glue. Through the mental haze he searched for answers to what had happened that brought him into this cell. He barely recalled police banging on his door and Jodi bleeding on his bed. Surely the small dose of crystal meth he had given her wouldn't have been enough to cause an overdose. What had happened to her?

His gut-piercing dry heaving subsided, then finally stilled. With intense effort, he turned away from the contents of the toilet in disgust, dragged his body to the metal door, and attempted to pull himself up on its horizontal cross bar. He screamed into the dimly lit space. "Hey man, I'm sick. I'm not high. I want a lawyer. I have rights." Minutes seemed like hours. No one answered. Norman could not bear the pure hell of his pain, and he started yelling with as much force as he could muster. Finally, a gruff voice answered from somewhere in the distance, "Shut the fuck up. I'm trying to sleep!"

Startled, Norman fell silent. His mind was on fire, and while going in and out of his mental maze he thought that perhaps he had died and was experiencing the flames of hell. Even so, he could feel drops of cool water falling from his closed eyes, and for a moment he imagined that he was standing beneath a pounding waterfall. But as he opened his eyes and saw the metal bars, he had to work hard to push away the fear. He started grinding his teeth together inside his tightly locked jaws while feeling his mood turn into a violent self-condemning anger. Moaning like a wounded dog, he told himself that he was a powerful man, and men don't cry. If only he could call Jerry, his mind-over-matter buddy. Without doubt, Jerry could wake him from this unearthly dream, chase away the devil, and wave a magical wand to pull him from the depths

of hell and make everything all right. And where was Carmella, his hot friend who was always pulling tarot cards? She and Jerry would come any moment and help him get back home, he was sure of it.

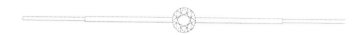

Fat chance. At that moment in a prison of his own making, Jerry was busy licking his own wounds caused by the unpredictable fallout with Lisa, and he was lost somewhere beyond Pluto in the solar system of his mind. Even though he was not the kind of person who normally feels sorry for himself, Jerry was sure he could hear a violin playing a soulful tune of lost love as he turned the key to open the door to his apartment.

Quietly, he walked into the front room, turned on the light, and started to tiptoe toward his private room. To his surprise, Stella walked out of what had once been their bedroom and met him in the hall.

"Where have you been? You look like you've been in a cat fight," Stella said, looking directly into his eyes.

Jerry gazed unresponsively at Stella, whose dark hair fell in picture perfect waves on her bare shoulders. Then he noticed what she was wearing and went into a panic. She was dressed in a black lace teddy nearly identical to the one that Lisa had been wearing earlier in the evening. Even though Stella looked deliciously invitingly, Jerry's libido went limp.

"What are you doing up? I figured you'd be asleep." Jerry managed to reply as he tried not to think about how he had removed Lisa's lingerie just seconds before the mind-numbing experience of jumping nearly naked from her bed to hide in her stuffy closet.

"Well, truthfully, I've been waiting for you. I've been hoping for a little time to talk with you."

"At this time of night? You were waiting to talk with me? What about?" Jerry couldn't believe his bad luck that Stella chose this night of all nights to want to talk.

"I'm about to go crazy because of what's happening to our relationship. I can't stand it that you won't talk with me. I want to tell you how horrible I feel about what's happened between us."

"It's been awful for me too, but please, can we talk about this some other time? I'm exhausted," Jerry replied while avoiding eye contact.

"Please, if I can just explain," Stella said.

"Stella, are you hearing me? I'm beat. I'll be glad to talk with you about what's happening in our relationship, but another time. Right now I need to crash. Please!"

"Okay, Jerry, I can wait a little longer. By the way, I made you an apple pie. It's in the kitchen. Can I bring you a piece?" Stella felt her heart beating with the faint beginnings of renewed hope because for the first time in what seemed to her to be an eternity, Jerry wasn't avoiding her. Yet, even so, he didn't comment on her lingerie that she had put on to attract his attention. Honesty, she wasn't sure how to read his shocked expression. However, she did feel herself breathe a little easier since he wasn't shunning her.

For the first time since they were talking Jerry's eyes met hers. "Apple pie? What happened, Stella? I must be dreaming. You've never been the baking type. You must be going through some pretty big changes to start making pies. After I get some sleep I'll be happy to try your pie. Right now, it's too late at night and I'm not feeling that well," Jerry confessed as he started moving down the hall.

"Jerry, maybe I can give you a back rub to help you feel better."

"Stella, what's going on with you? No, don't tell me. Let's wait until tomorrow to talk. Right now I'm struggling to stay awake and I'm on my way to bed. I'm so tired that I'll fall asleep standing up if I don't hurry to bed." Jerry couldn't bear the thought of talking with anyone right now, and especially didn't want Stella to get a sense of his painful emotional predicament. Turning away, he stumbled down the hall toward his room without giving much thought to their brief interaction.

Stella followed him down the hall. "Sweetie, can we sleep together tonight?" she asked. "I've been missing you so much."

"What's up with you, Stella?" Jerry said feeling a murky mixture of surprise and annoyance. Once again, it was obvious that she was not listening to him, but he was too tired to confront her about this weird behavior. Not waiting for her answer, he went into his study, closed the door, and turned on the light.

In the privacy of his room, he tried to relax, but the inner voice of his overwhelmed emotions seemed louder than ever. Sleep would be the best remedy to block out the pain from his aching heart. As he started to undress, he realized that he was too tired to even look for pajamas, and climbed naked under the covers draped over his futon bed.

Eager to enter the world of his dreams, Jerry closed his eyes. Just as he was beginning to fall asleep, he heard the door gently open, and footsteps slowly walking toward his bed.

I must be imagining things, he thought, right before he heard Stella whisper, "You didn't say that I couldn't give you a rub."

Jerry, too tired to resist, didn't reply. Instinctively, he felt that he and his wife would soon be having an emotionally charged conversation if

he pushed her away. Right now, he couldn't deal with any more chatting, and decided that it would be easier to pretend to have already fallen asleep.

Stella's hands slid under the covers, found his bare shoulders, and began to knead the knots buried in his neck. Her soothing touch made Jerry realize just how stressed he was. He could feel her warm breath on his skin and smell the sweet lavender scent of her perfume. His wall of defense melted as her hands lovingly caressed his back, helping him to relax. Soon, Jerry felt Stella crawl into his bed and lay her naked body next to his. He held his body in check so that he didn't make even the slightest movement. He didn't want Stella to feel the nervous tension that he had in response to her body touching his. He struggled to ignore her explicit signals giving him an invitation to make love. After the erratic events earlier in the evening, Jerry didn't even want to think about the possibility of having sex, above all with his wife who had created an oceanic wave of distance between them with her demand for an open relationship.

Perhaps he was already dreaming and his subconscious imagination was playing tricks with him, he told himself. Maybe in his present state of mind, he was hallucinating and Stella wasn't really in his bed wrapping her legs around him. Whatever the illusion or reality of the present moment, he was too stressed to be emotionally or physically accessible for making love. Truthfully, Stella and the rest of the world would have to wait for him to get some sleep before he would be available for anything.

At the same time Jerry was finally getting to sleep, Carmella was across town, once again awakening from her fretful sleep. She was nervous in a way that made her feel like crying. Turning on her light, with one eye open and one eye half closed, she looked at her clock and saw that it was four thirty.

Norman's nothing but a dope fiend! Why did I have to get involved with an idiot? she thought, feeling her anger rise. Making a mental list of why she didn't need Norman in her life any longer made her feel less like crying. Stoically, step by mental step, she tried to detach from her emotions. Torn between feelings of compassion and annoyance, her inner voice was too loud to ignore. She sadly realized without any doubts that he had proven himself to be an unlikely candidate for her love. If Norman hadn't been such a party animal, she wouldn't have left

his house last night, and maybe Jodi wouldn't have had an opportunity to shoot herself in the head.

Reaching toward her nightstand, she switched off the light, and rolled over in her bed to go back to sleep. Luckily Rambo, her beloved dog, was still asleep at her feet. Her throbbing ankle, wrapped in its temporary support, jerked painfully from accidentally getting tangled in the sheets. Maybe Norman needs to be in jail to get his head in order, she thought. To compound her confusion, at the same time she was feeling angry toward Norman, she was feeling equally bad that she didn't know what she could do to rescue him. After all, perhaps it wasn't Norman's fault. Maybe the invisible Seega had caused the peculiar events at his house. She'd have to ask Jerry if it was possible for that shapeless evil force to come into the house and lure Jodi into trying to commit suicide. Just the thought of the Seega made her reach for Rambo and hold him close to her chest for comfort. "Oh, Rambo, I love you so much," she said, giving her pet a squeeze.

Still unable to fall asleep, she got out of bed, turned on the light again to find her tarot cards that she kept in a crushed velvet drawstring pouch. As she opened her bag, the stone she had found in the haunted house seemed to jump into her hand by its own volition. If she hadn't previously believed in magic, feeling the stone grow hot to the touch, she now knew that it had to exist. A tremor of fear went through her and she grew anxious. It was obvious from the intensity of heat in her hand that this stone had some kind of power. Summoning her courage, she quickly put it back in her tarot pouch and out of sight.

There were so many things to occupy her mind. Earlier in the day at the unemployment office, she had accidentally run into Mary, Jerry's dad's friend who she had briefly met in his apartment. Mary had told her in a shaking voice about her impending eviction. She was putting her meager savings into fixing her car as she was fairly resigned that it would soon become her mobile home. Carmella, feeling empathetic to the discouraged woman and her sad situation, offered to let her take showers in her apartment until she could find a job and afford to pay rent again. Hopefully, this idea will work out, Carmella thought, wondering who would come to her rescue if she couldn't pay her rent.

Still not able to sleep, Carmella started thinking about what she needed to do when she got out of bed in the morning. Because of her injured ankle, she couldn't do yoga, her usual morning routine. As soon as it was business hours she would call the prison and talk with Norman to find out what she could do for him, and then she would go to the ICU at Marin General Hospital to visit Jodi. Tossing and turning, beating her

pillow frantically, she tried to put everyone and all of their problems out of her mind.

Surrendering to her insomnia, Carmella continued making her mental to-do list and putting the events of the coming day in order. She let herself get excited as she thought about her one p.m. interview with Mr. Stalsburg, the movie producer. Her mind started going over the most pertinent questions she could ask to create a gripping news story before she finally fell back to sleep.

Her alarm startled her when it awoke her from a dream. Looking around to find her clock, she sat up quickly in bed, knocking Rambo to the floor just in time to realize that the alarm was actually her phone ringing. Half asleep, she reached for the receiver. "Hello," she said feeling her mind jump hesitatingly into wakefulness.

"Will you accept a collect call from Norman?" the operator asked with a robotic tone.

"Yes, of course," Carmella answered excitedly. "Norman! Hello! Are you okay?"

"No, baby, I'm not okay. Can you get me out of here?" Norman sounded as though he was a five-year-old pleading for a favor from his mother.

"I'll try. What can I do?"

"Come down here and talk with these assholes. Maybe you can find out why I'm here. I don't even know, but I do know I want to get out right now!"

"Okay, Norman, but will they let me see you?"

"I've been told I can see one person for fifteen minutes today. Can you get over here quick? Maybe they'll tell you more than they're telling me, and I can find out what's going on and when I can get out. All I keep hearing is that I've endangered the life of a young woman."

Carmella could hear Norman moaning in pain and a disheartening desperation in his voice. Suddenly the phone went dead.

Alarmed, she looked at her clock. It was seven in the morning. Jolting into wakefulness, she realized that she didn't even know where he was. She imagined that most likely her friend was in Marin County jail.

After fixing herself a cup of coffee, she started making phone calls to inquire about Norman's whereabouts. It didn't take long to find where he had been taken after his arrest, and within a few calls she was talking with the receptionist at the county jail, an infamous holding tank for wrongdoers, addicts, and drunks. Norman wasn't a criminal, she told the police officer on the phone before asking what could she could do to help him get out.

"I'm not allowed to disclose information," he replied gruffly. "It's better if you visit during visiting hours and talk with him yourself. That will be this afternoon."

"I'm working this afternoon," Carmella replied. "Can't I come earlier?"

"Your friend isn't well enough to see anyone this morning. Perhaps you should come tomorrow," the indifferent voice answered before abruptly hanging up.

Carmella felt helpless. Her day was getting off to a rough start. Perhaps, later in the morning, she could call Jerry and ask him to help. Presently, the only thing she could do was dial Marin General Hospital.

The phone rang ten times before someone answered and she could ask for Jodi in the ICU. Carmella sighed deeply with relief when the receptionist told her that Jodi was still alive. When asked if she could visit Jodi, the woman replied that Carmella could only go into her room if she were a relative. Carmella quickly responded that she was her sister and that she would be there as soon as possible.

Carmella jumped out of bed, mindful of her ankle, got dressed, and decided against her better judgment to take Rambo with her for moral support. Soon she and her dog were in her car, and Carmella was driving down the highway with lightning speed to check on Jodi. She needed to know what to tell Norman about Jodi's condition. Perhaps, if Jodi was going to be okay, maybe Norman could be released. Since her morning was packed full of important errands she didn't waste any time getting to the hospital.

Shortly after Carmella parked, she gave Rambo a quick goodbye kiss on the nose, left him in the car with the window cracked, and was soon riding the elevator to the second floor of west wing in the hospital. The nurse at the reception desk asked Carmella a long list of questions about herself and her relation to Jodi. Seeming satisfied with her earnest answers that Jodi needed Medi-Cal because her family was poor and didn't have health insurance, the nurse said, "She's in a coma. The bullet missed going into her brain by about a sixteenth of an inch. She's very lucky that she had such bad aim. Since she missed her target, hopefully she will recover to live a normal life."

Carmella's heart throbbed with a current of hope. "Jodi's not going to die?" she asked.

"Hopefully, she'll be okay." The nurse pointed down the hall to Jodi's room, and said, "Go to Room 203 and pay her a visit. She's still at serious risk, but if her will to live is strong, she has a good chance of coming back to join us in this world. By the way, do you know a Jerry?"

"Yes, he's a good friend of the family," Carmella lied.

"She had a letter in her pocket. It's addressed to him," the nurse replied, pulling it out of Jodi's file.

Carmella reached for the letter. "I'll be happy to take it to him." She smiled once it was in her hand, and then she turned and walked quickly down the hall toward Jodi's room.

The door to Room 203 looked like all the other doors in the white-walled sterile hall. Carmella took a deep breath, turned the knob, and walked in the room.

When she saw Jodi's pale appearance, she was afraid that she could be dead. The young woman reminded her of a ceramic doll, lying still as stone under white covers, with a drip line going into her arm. Carmella looked at the heart monitor with its blinking lights and her stomach tightened with worry.

Moving closer to Jodi, she reached to take her tiny limp hand and held it between her own. "Jodi, I'm sorry we didn't get along. I'll be nicer to you in the future. Please come back to us. We'll have fun hanging out with each other."

Carmella bent down and gave Jodi a kiss on her white-bandaged head. After standing there quietly and saying a prayer to call on healing angels, she whispered, "I have my dog in the car with me, so I can't stay long. It's not so easy, seeing you like this. And later I have to go see Norman. He's in a mess, too," she said. Releasing Jodi's hand, she wiped the tears from her eyes and turned to walk away. "I'll be back to see you soon," she said, looking over her shoulder while she moved quietly out the door, trying to dodge a sense of mounting sadness.

Once outside the hospital, she moved slowly toward her car as if she was sleep walking. Wishing that she could wake up to a different reality, she closed her eyes, and stood still to feel the cool morning breeze. If she didn't worry about her friends she could improve her attitude and unwind from her state of panic. Without question, she needed to get out of her negative mood.

Looking at her watch she realized that she had enough time to pull a tarot card before starting her drive to the jailhouse to visit Norman. Before she did anything else, Carmella was sure that life would feel better if she took a moment to consult her oracle.

She reached for her cards in her purse, unwrapped them from their silk cloth, and began to shuffle. What is my card for today, she questioned. Within seconds she pulled the card, The Devil. Oh great, she thought, Norman's been catting around too much and has gotten caught in a web of negative forces. And Jodi has taken a nasty fall in the karmic

Chutes and Ladders game of life. If only we could protect ourselves from troubles, our life would be so much easier. Carmella sighed deeply.

Just as quickly as she had taken her cards from her purse, she put them back, and hurried to her car. After visiting with Norman, she wouldn't have much time before she needed to be at her afternoon interview. This is a busy day, she thought while getting into her car and starting her ignition.

After a short drive anxiously zooming down Marin County roadways, she pulled into the jailhouse parking lot, She felt a little guilty because she needed once again to leave Rambo alone in the car. Actually, she felt a little bad that she had brought him on this hapless journey in the first place, but her dog offered her the cheerful company that she so desperately needed to take her mind off of her multitude of problems. Her personal challenge was remaining optimistic about her plan to make a living by selling her writing. Even though she had a verbal contract for the sale of her magazine article on modern practices of witchcraft, she hadn't gotten written confirmation about its acceptance. As a freelance writer, the payment for the sale of her story would certainly pay a few of the bills that sat on her desk waiting to be paid. Be absolutely positive and remain confident, she told herself trying to pry her concerns from her mind.

Getting out of her car, she hurried to the jailhouse so she could talk with prison officials and find out about Norman's release. If only her tarot cards could tell her what was going to happen, she would be better prepared for this sudden mission of mercy. Trying not to stress, she hurried to the visitor reception room and walked inside. The large room filled with wood benches crowded with pregnant women, crying mothers or nervous friends, intimidated Carmella with its sterile unfriendliness.

"No, you can't see the prisoner, and no, we can't tell you anything," said the impassive man in dark blue uniform who sat looking like he was hiding behind his big desk. "When he's feeling better, he can talk with you and tell you whatever he wants to tell you."

"But doesn't he get to see his visitors?" Carmella asked, feeling desperate.

"Yeah, but he's too sick right now to see anyone. Maybe he'll be okay enough tomorrow to talk with his friends," the man replied indifferently fixing his badge to make sure it was straight.

"What is wrong with him? Does he need a doctor? I'm really concerned because he called me and asked me to come here and see him today," Carmella responded. She felt like running past the guard to look for her friend behind locked doors.

"We're taking good care of him. Don't worry. He needs a little time to sober up before he can visit with you." A phone rang and the man picked up the receiver. "Hello. Just a minute." He looked up at Carmella, offered a tight-lipped phony smile and said once more. "You can come back tomorrow to see him. Sorry, but there's nothing you can do here. You'll have to excuse me now; I need to take this call." He looked away, and started talking as if no one was standing in front of his desk.

Dejected, Carmella turned and walked out of the dismal room. She couldn't wait to be outside in the fresh air. When she passed through security into the warmth of the sunlight, she realized what having freedom really meant.

Forcing her mind to remain calm, she rushed to her car, and opened the door for Rambo who licked her on the face and excitedly jumped out the door. She let him take a pee and walk around her parking space before he eagerly jumped back into her car. Once again she slid into the driver's seat. "This is a beautiful sunny day," she said trying to convince herself there was reason to be happy. Soon, she was joining the speeding traffic weaving in and out on Highway 101. Tightly gripping the wheel, she took a deep breath to reduce her accumulating stress as she rushed to get to her highly valued interview on time.

Sixteen: The Tower

XVI. PHOENIX

Twisted Truth

Carmella had rushed through the morning with help from her two cups of coffee. Although she'd felt sad when she saw Jodi in a coma, her visit to the hospital and encouraging talk with the nurses had inspired hope that most likely Jodi would recover. Her trip to see Norman had been much more frustrating, since she was denied access to visiting him. It had been heart-rending, but she figured denial of his visitation rights because of a debilitating sickness could only mean one thing. Most likely, Norman was coming down from his addictions cold turkey.

Driving on Highway 101 now, she had to be alert to the cars speeding around her and didn't want to dwell on her suspicions about what might be happening to Norman. Weaving in and out of all the traffic with her

beloved Rambo sitting like an honored guest in the front passenger seat, Carmella was relieved when she could finally exit the freeway and take the frontage road toward her destination. She could hardly believe her good timing when she pulled into the asphalt movie set parking lot five minutes early. After turning off her ignition, she gave Rambo a goodbye kiss between his ears. Quickly she got out of the car, and walked to building number five that was nestled inside an oasis of large buildings surrounded by blazing gardens in full bloom with natural river rock water fountains and koi-filled ponds. In front of her destination, a Chinese red barn-like building, a large white tent created a makeshift reception office for what appeared to be a hectic day at the studio. Out of breath, she tried to relax her nerves before approaching the receptionist.

"My name's Carmella and I'm here to interview Mr. Stalsburg," she said politely.

The woman looked Carmella up and down with narrowed critical eyes.

"Yes, you're on the appointment calendar. Unfortunately, he needs to finish an important project before he's free to talk with you. He'll be busy for at least another hour or perhaps even longer. Do you still want to wait?"

Carmella didn't have to think twice. It was important for her professional credibility to get this interview and she was willing to stay as long as needed.

"Yes, I can wait," she said, "but is it okay if I walk around with my dog? He's in my car. Normally, I don't mind leaving him sit in the car for an hour, but if I'm to be gone longer than I expected, he's going to need to stretch his legs."

"No problem," the woman said with a smile. "I like dogs. Just don't let him pee in here."

"Don't worry about that. Rambo's well trained," Carmella replied as she turned to walk outside to the parking lot. The bright afternoon sun and a garden of three-lobed fleur-de-lis greeted her as she walked outside the door. Smiling with anticipation of what was to come, she moved down the path to get her dog.

Within minutes, Carmella was back in the large tent sitting in the makeshift waiting room with a happy Rambo wriggling in her lap. Her scheduled interview had the potential to turn into a large paycheck. It was also a sign from the gods letting her know that she could be successfully self-employed. With focused determination, she had made more than seven phone calls to set the date for this important meeting. Writing made her happy, and since she'd spent so many hours seeking out her

present opportunity, she didn't mind spending a little time waiting for this interview. Besides, life always improves when her little dog is by her side.

After some time of happy tail wagging, little Rambo jumped from her lap and started checking out the environment. A steady stream of people passing by stopped to say a word or two about her "White Fluff Ball." Rambo was becoming the center of attention.

In a short while, two young women came up to Carmella.

"What a totally cool, little dog! He looks like a Maltese. Is he yours?" the taller of the two girls asked.

"Yes. His name is Rambo."

"He's so cute. Can we take him to show our friend? She's right outside the tent." the other girl asked.

The girl's friendly manner made it apparent to Carmella that Rambo would be in safe hands. Rambo obviously enjoyed the affection he was getting, and willingly jumped into the girl's arms. A dog sitter couldn't come at a better moment for Carmella. She agreed with a smile. She needed a little undistracted time to rethink her interview questions. A little break from Rambo could come in handy right now.

After about twenty minutes, Carmella looked up from her writing and surveyed the room. Even though earlier she had been able to see Rambo near the front door, she felt a shiver of alarm when she realized that her dog had not yet been returned and was nowhere in sight. Putting down her pen, she went outside to look for the girls who had taken Rambo. She walked in the direction she had seen them go, and made her way along the path outside the tent.

"Rambo! Rambo!" she called. Neither her dog nor the young women were anywhere in sight. Carmella began to feel an ache in her heart. As her sense of dread began to increase, she ran to the parking lot. Without seeing her dog, she then returned to search the outdoor tent area surrounding the blocked off façade of the movie set. She asked a few people walking by if they had seen the girls and her dog, but no one remembered seeing them.

Carmella ran back to the reception room where she had last seen Rambo.

"Did those girls bring my dog back yet?" she asked the receptionist.

"No, I haven't seen the girls or your dog," the woman replied, her fingers hovering over the keyboard. "You just missed Mr. Stalsburg. You weren't here when he left his busy schedule to speak with you. You should know that someone like him doesn't have time to wait. He won't be able to see you any other time today."

Carmella held her stressed emotions in check. Not only was her dog missing, but now she had just lost her chance for an interview that could have easily landed her a paycheck. Panic was surging through her veins. Her logical mind went into battle to control her emotions that were ready to fly out of control.

"What can I do to reconnect with Mr. Salsburg? And I'm concerned about my dog. He isn't here. Do you know those girls who took him?" she asked, trying to appear in control.

The heavy-set woman looked irritated. "I wasn't paying attention to who took your dog, but I'm sure they'll bring him back. I'll send a text message to alert the security folks working on lot to keep an eye out for him. Most likely someone has it sitting on their lap, and they don't realize that you're looking for it. Young people can be so unpredictable," she said, rolling her eyes in disbelief.

"Oh yes, you're probably right," Carmella said, sitting down to wait. She could hardly believe how horrible the afternoon had become. She was reminded of her inability to control her own life, and she felt an overwhelming sense of helplessness. She wanted to scream. Her precious Rambo, her loyal, true love and long time companion, was missing. Anxiety from her building sense of loss began to compound with the thoughts of failure from losing her interview, Norman being in jail, and Jodi near death in the ICU. The dramas of the day were too much for Carmella. She started to cry.

"Here's some tissue," the receptionist said handing her a box. "Maybe you should go back outside and continue to look for your dog." Now appearing to be concerned for Carmella who was in an obvious state of panic, she said, "I can talk with Mr. Salsburg about rescheduling his appointment with you, but he may not be available. I'll let you know, and call you."

"Yes…that's nice of you. I'll go outside and look for those two girls. If they come back with my dog, please ask them to wait for me?"

"Well, I'll be leaving soon, but if I see them before I leave, I can tell them to wait here for you," the woman answered while moving a large stack of papers across her desk. Avoiding Carmella's eyes, she turned away and looked intently at her computer screen.

Trying to hide her tears, Carmella walked outside the door to her search for Rambo. The sun disappeared behind the clouds, hiding its once cheerful glow. Angry at her own naïve trust in strangers, her self-directed criticism resounded like a dirge from Hell.

After some time had passed, Carmella returned to the office. The receptionist had left. Tightly holding her purse and her notebook, she

sat in the nearly empty waiting room, hoping that the girls would bring Rambo back. After watching numerous people come and go who were too busy to pay any attention to her, two hours slowly passed. No one who she stopped to ask about Rambo had any helpful information. Carmella imagined that something terrible must have happened. She decided to call the Humane Society, but no one had called in a report on her missing dog. She called her friend Jerry, but he had just awakened, was eating apple pie, and in an important conversation with Stella. "I'll call you later when we can talk," he told her.

After a long fruitless day and an unsuccessful search for precious Rambo, she was exhausted. Making her situation worse, she had to sneak around to avoid the security guards who had asked her to leave the gated lot. She felt as though she had fallen from her inner tower of strength. Feeling defeated from her miserable experiences, she decided to go home and unwind from the craziness of the day. It would soon be dark and there was nothing more she could think to do at this time to find her pet. No one seemed to notice that there was a young woman whose heart was dying from the pain of losing Rambo. She would certainly not ever give up her search, and she'd be returning to this horrible place early tomorrow.

Far removed from Carmella's plight, Jerry's luck seemed to be coming out from hiding. Although it was late afternoon, Jerry had just climbed out of his futon, and gave thanks that it was the weekend instead of a workday. Remembering his recent dream of being lost while looking for Lisa, he wasn't sure about the strange twists of fate that had been occurring, and he had to take a few minutes to untangle what was real from his imaginings. As he got dressed, he mused that the strange events of last night seemed entwined with the fiery forces of Mars, the planet symbolizing war and power, because his obstacles were so acute, as if he'd gone to battle, and lost control. Reaching for his phone, he listened to his messages, and afterwards decided that it might be better to return to bed. His world of friends seemed to be in mass hysteria. But perhaps things weren't as bad as people made them out to be, he thought as he stumbled into the hallway.

Trying to shake a sense of gloom, he followed the sweet fragrance of cinnamon into the sunlit kitchen. Standing there Venus, the goddess of love and seduction, seemed to be welcoming him as he looked across the

room and saw Stella cutting him a piece of her delicious-looking apple pie.

"Hi, Sweetie! I've been waiting for you to wake up," she said. "I've saved you a cup of coffee to go with my homemade pie."

Jerry seated himself at the table, feeling glad for a change to be at home with Stella. Despite his friends' disturbing phone messages, it was a new day, and he could take a few minutes to enjoy it. He was ready to start fresh and leave the events of last night far behind.

"Hi, Stella," he said with a smile as he eagerly reached for the piece of pie and took a bite. With the taste of warm cinnamon on his lips, it was hard to remember why he had spent these last few months ignoring his wife. Today she seemed lovelier than ever in her snug black lace blouse that tantalizingly revealed her beautiful curves.

"Do you like my pie, Jerry?" Stella asked, looking at him as if he were her prince.

"It's amazing! I didn't know that you knew how to bake a homemade apple pie."

"While we've been too busy for each other, I've been taking cooking lessons. Someone told me that making you a pie might help you understand how much I care for you."

"And who told you that?" Jerry questioned.

"A lady friend." Stella replied coyly.

"Do I know her?"

"I don't think so." Stella crossed her fingers behind her back and smiled. She couldn't tell him the truth about her visit with Naomi. Certainly, he would be angry with her for paying a bruha to cast a love spell.

"Well, you should thank her for me. This pie is the best thing I've had to eat all week. Will you cut me another piece?" He asked after finishing the rather large piece that she had previously placed on his plate.

"Are you sure, Jerry? You've already eaten plenty. I don't want you to get sick from eating too much." Stella said with a false concern that hid her sense of delight.

"You don't need to worry about that. I love your pie. And I didn't have any dinner last night."

Stella looked at Jerry, her smile fading. "What were you doing last night that you came home so late?"

"I was out with friends. Why do you care, anyway? Isn't your new boyfriend keeping you distracted enough that you don't have time to worry about where I've been going?"

"Jerry, let's not talk about any of that," Stella said, looking down while mumbling something inaudible.

"Why? How are things going with him anyway?" Jerry looked intently at her. He noticed that her cheeks had grown red.

Stella looked deeply into Jerry's eyes. "He isn't my lover anymore," Stella blurted out. "It's finished!" She hoped that Jerry wouldn't say something to make her feel worse than she already did. The warm glow of just minutes before had faded, and in its place a sudden gust of cool wind was blowing through their conversation.

Jerry dropped his fork loudly.

"Stella, is this what you wanted to talk with me about last night? I might have known there was an underlying reason why you'd be making me a pie. Do you think a pie is going to make me forget how much you hurt me when you told me that you wanted to be with someone else?"

"But Jerry..." Stella started to say.

Jerry interrupted her without giving her a moment to continue. "I trusted the love that you gave me. You promised to be my loving wife, and then told me I wasn't enough for you. Am I just supposed to forget that you threw me out of your heart because you'd met your new 'true soul mate'? You can't make enough pies to take away the pain that you caused me."

Suddenly, the pieces of the puzzle fell into place, and Stella's unusual behavior made sense. Jerry had felt that it had seemed like a strange turn about last night when she unexpectedly started playing the seductive she-wolf. If her recent affair had gone up in smoke, as seemed to be the case, then it made sense that she would become interested in him again. Even if his own love life was going poorly, his body contracted as he found himself feeling like Stella's best second choice. His emotional nature wasn't fluid enough to immediately mirror the twists and turns of her feelings for him. He felt as if his next words were floating up from a deep well of sadness.

"Stella, I'm sorry things aren't going well in your romantic world. I wish it could be like a happy-forever-after soap opera and I could eagerly jump in bed with you again. But you made me feel like I was damaged goods. Just because your new boyfriend left you or you're changing your mind once again about what you want, doesn't mean that I can easily forgive and forget."

As Jerry heard his own words, he was surprised that he could be so clear about his thoughts. Ever since their falling out, he had been feeling so confused about his emotions that he couldn't communicate much of anything to her. But now things felt different.

"What is it that you want this time?" he asked.

Stella held back the tears. She sighed deeply as she looked up from the floor to meet his glare.

"Oh, Jerry," she said softly. "I want us to get back together. You're my husband! I'm sure I can make you happy. We can begin our family and make a fresh start together. I'm so sorry for the pain I've caused you."

Her eyes fell to the floor again in a gesture of helplessness. This was not working. One apple pie was not strong enough magic to make up for what she had put Jerry through.

"You're moving a little too fast for me. I haven't had time to adjust to your change of heart. I'm still stuck in your demand for us to have other lovers. Now you want to start a family?"

Stella felt confused and ashamed at the same time as Jerry spoke. They were both young, and it hadn't seemed so wrong to have a little extra adventure at this point in life. But now as she heard Jerry's words and the layer of feelings that were beneath them, she realized how much anguish she had caused him that he had been unwilling to expose to her, how sensitive he was beneath his confident, all-knowing veneer. That sensitivity was part of what had attracted her to him from the very start, an endearing quality that had made her fall in love with him.

In this moment Jerry's voice came back into her consciousness. She realized that he was looking straight into her eyes, something he hadn't done for some time.

"Stella, I don't know what to think or say. Especially right now. I need to breathe some fresh ocean air, and wake up from my nightmare of the last few days. My Dad is freaked out about something he can't talk about on the phone and needs me to hurry on over. I've got a friend who just attempted suicide and is a coma in the ICU in the hospital, and Norman's in jail. Destiny called and left me a message telling me that her sister Angel is in grave danger and wants me to do something. And another friend called several times, crying about her dog being stolen. I'm starting to panic just thinking about all the calls I need to make to find out what's happening. My head is in too many places right now to make decisions about our relationship. For the past three months my mind has been rehashing your harsh remarks that shut me out of your life. I just can't dismiss all that and pretend like nothing happened. I need some time to figure out my feelings."

Jerry's laundry list of problems, grave though they sounded, was the wrong thing to say to Stella at that moment. She felt invisible. Had he heard anything she said? Her inner window on her own sorrow for the wounded feelings she'd caused Jerry slammed shut and her own feeling

of being unheard moved into the foreground. "Can't you just get out of your head for once and listen to my feelings?"

"That's not fair, Stella! I have listened to your feelings. How rude of you to say that!" He wished he could tell her that he felt like an emotional train wreck, but he couldn't. The soul-destroying truth was that the anger he felt toward Lisa was now merging with the memory of Stella's betrayal.

"Stella," he said, "do you want me to suddenly respond to your needs when you didn't respect mine? You couldn't wait to stop sleeping with me because of another guy, and now you can't wait to sleep with me again. Like I said, I need to go out for some fresh air, think about all this, and go see my Dad."

"Okay, Jerry," Stella said. An edge had crept into her voice.

"Don't worry about our relationship. Go rush to help your friends. I can wait to talk to you when you're ready! I can keep waiting and waiting for you, just like I've been doing for the past couple of months."

"Haven't you heard anything I've said? This conversation is getting too crazy for me. I've got to go!"

Stella's voice rose. "Damn it, Jerry, I love you. Will you at least hear that?" Then her voice fell into a whisper. "Can we please kiss and make up? Other couples have conflicts. It doesn't have to be the end of our relationship. We can make our life together better now than what we had before."

Jerry was feeling numb. No matter what Stella said, her words were like messages painted on panes of glass that went sliding past him without making contact.

"Stella, I'm serious. I just woke up, the day is almost gone, and I've got to find out what's happening with my friends who are suddenly all calling for help. Please, give me just a little time." He got up and put on his jacket.

"Well, if you truly need to go, you might as well take a piece of the pie with you, just in case you get hungry. I did make it especially for you."

"Thanks, but no thanks. Save some for yourself." Jerry turned to look at his wife before walking out the door. The sight of her made him soften. "Stella, don't worry. We'll figure all this out," he said as he started to walk away.

"Wait!" Stella moved toward him. "Can I at least have a hug?"

"Yes," Jerry replied, giving her a loving embrace. But he didn't feel it in his heart. All he wanted was to find his car keys and get out the front door.

Seventeen: The Star

XVII. THE GRAIL

Illuminating Hope

The rhythmic click-clacking of the cable car hurrying down the hill soothed Jerry's frazzled nerves as he walked to his parked car. Once inside, he stretched in his seat to get comfortable and then hurried to call Destiny, who had left a frantic message on his voicemail.

"Hi, Destiny. What's the matter?" Jerry asked when she answered her phone.

Destiny was obviously distraught. "My Dad just told me that Angel is acting so crazy that she needs to be under heavy sedation or be put in a mental hospital."

"What? He actually said that? That doesn't sound like the Taylor I know. Listen, calm down. I'm guessing that he's willing to give my Dad

more information about your sister than he'd give to either of us. He and my Dad are always talking together in their secret brotherhood code language. And my Dad must know what's happening because earlier today I received a message from him telling me that something terrible is going on with your sister. Is there any chance you can meet me at my Dad's house so we can ask him what he knows about Angel? I'm on my way to visit him now."

"Yes, you're right. Mark and my Dad are always sharing secrets. I'll go right now," Destiny said without a good-bye.

Jerry began making his way to his father's home in Twin Peaks. He was relieved that it was Saturday and didn't have to worry about work. There seemed to be enough to do in his life without worrying about deadlines.

Lost in thought, the trip to his father's seemed timeless, but then it took him the customary fifteen minutes to find a parking space. Feeling a momentary sense of freedom from his concerns as he got out of his car, he was happy to feel the refreshing chill of the cool air and didn't mind walking up the steep hill. He couldn't help but smile as he saw Destiny sitting on the steps waiting for him in front of his Dad's apartment. Jerry helped her stand and gave her a welcoming embrace.

"I can't believe that my little sister has lost her mind because some demonic spirit has taken over her body. That can't be true, can it?" Destiny asked with a panicked look. "Just hearing things like that coming out of my Dad's mouth makes me want to scream."

"Well, it does sound pretty crazy. Jodi told me that she saw your sister involved in a séance and those can get pretty weird. But at this point, try not to worry. Let's see what my Dad knows about her," Jerry said, trying to invoke his faith in divine providence as he knocked on his father's door.

Mark opened the door and ushered them inside. "Destiny, I haven't seen you in a while. Nice to see you again. You're certainly becoming a beautiful woman," he commented.

"Dad," Jerry started, "earlier today both you and Destiny called me about Angel. I invited her here because she's hoping you can help solve whatever problem Angel's facing."

"I've never heard my Dad sound so hopeless," Destiny said, breathing a heavy sigh. "He told me that Angel's possessed and that he doesn't know what to do. He's says I can't help her and doesn't want me to come over."

"You should be talking with your father about this, not me," Mark answered with a somber look.

"Dad," Jerry said, "Taylor isn't answering his phone, and yesterday when he did talk with Destiny, he refused to talk about Angel except to say that she's out of her mind. He didn't want to scare Destiny with 'gloomy' details. Unfortunately, now she's more worried than if he'd told her what's going on."

Mark walked to the bar at the other end of living room and poured himself a double shot of scotch. Then, he sat in the chair across from Jerry and Destiny and downed his drink in one gulp.

"Look," Mark said, "I don't know how much you know, Destiny, but when I saw Angel the other day, she looked like a pawn of Satan caught in the grip of Hell's fury. It felt dangerous to be near her. That's why your Dad doesn't want you to visit. He's afraid for your safety."

"But maybe I can help her," Destiny replied in a wavering voice.

"Or maybe, you'll attract the same dark energy to you. I'm sure your Dad is trying to protect you from hostile forces. Taylor's going crazy watching Angel and not being able to help her."

"Dad," Jerry interrupted, "I think I can help. At least, I'm willing to try."

"And how are you going to do that?" Mark asked.

"I need to talk with Taylor and Angel, and ask some questions. I've helped with other similarly strange situations," Jerry said calmly.

"Jerry," his Dad continued, "Angel is obviously stuck in some subterranean plane. She had been practicing astral traveling. Taylor said that he taught her to disengage her spirit from her physical body and fly to faraway places in her ethereal, light body. At the day of the séance, he instructed her to astral travel on a mission to visit a sacred etheric temple, but when she was out of her physical body, a phantom entered it. We saw her struggle to reclaim her body, but whatever entered her vacant body is stronger than Angel and it's blocking her return. It quickly became obvious that her body is possessed by a ghoul who enjoys violence and lack of restraint."

"If it's truly an evil force that has taken possession of her, I can get rid of it," Jerry said confidently as he reached for Destiny's hand to give her emotional support.

"My poor sister," Destiny said. "She needs me."

"No, you need to listen to your father and keep a safe distance from your sister," Jerry replied. "It's better for me to try and help her."

"Well, both of you should talk with Taylor before you try to do anything. And you know, she's not the only person in trouble," said Mark. "Earlier today, I got a call from that friend of yours, Carmella. She asked me if I could bail Norman out of jail. Do you know what's going on?"

Jerry nodded. "Norman's having criminal charges filed against him. He's been charged with endangering the life of a teenage girl as well as with growing and possession of drugs for sale. He might even be charged with statutory rape, but that hasn't been determined yet."

Mark's face contracted into a frown. "Damn! I feel sorry for him. It's always something with Norman. I've tried to tell him that he needs to slow down, to be more careful, but Norman always laughs it off," Mark said. "And that Jodi, the silent one, it was easy to see that she's trouble. But it's his own bad karma that got him busted."

"He wouldn't be in this mess if Jodi hadn't tried to commit suicide at his house," Jerry explained. "After the paramedics responded to the 911 call two times from his home in one week, and found his place smelling like a marijuana farm, it wasn't long before the police arrived with a search warrant."

Mark shook his head. "Two times?"

"Yes, Carmella got hurt in his driveway earlier in the week and called 911."

Destiny shook her head in disbelief, got up and moved toward the door. She turned to look at the two men.

"It sounds like Norman's got big problems, but I'm focusing on my sister. I've got to go. Mark, thanks for telling me what you know about Angel. At least now I have a better sense of what I'm going to be dealing with at my dad's. Bye, guys."

"Destiny, you shouldn't go," Jerry responded, growing concerned. He hadn't seen Destiny this upset in a long time.

"I'll talk to you later, Jerry," Destiny said as she rushed to open the door.

Jerry was torn. Should he go with her or not? He consulted his intuition and understood with an inner awareness that it would be better not to leave with her. Since his romance with Destiny had ended, Taylor took delight in refusing to let him be part of his family's social gatherings even though he and Destiny had remained good friends. He had a better chance of not stressing Taylor if he warned him of his own arrival instead of coming in the door unexpectedly.

"Okay. Call me later and tell me what happens," he said. "Tell your Dad that I'm willing to help, and I'll be coming to visit Angel soon."

"Thanks, Jerry. Will do. I'll call you." Destiny hurried out the door and quietly closed it behind her.

Jerry turned to Mark, "What about Angel's mother, Naomi? Was she involved in the ritual too?"

"No," Mark answered. "A few years ago she vowed never to attend his rituals because she wasn't willing to watch Taylor's 'ego on steroids.' And right now she's so mad at Taylor that she's moved out of the house and told him she's never coming back. I think she's staying with her sister. They're probably lighting candles for Angel and sticking pins in a voodoo doll that looks like Taylor."

"That would almost be funny, if Angel wasn't in serious trouble," Jerry responded.

"Everyone's got big problems, it seems," ranted Mark. "I'm getting phone calls from collection agencies all the time telling me that I owe them money. I'm afraid to answer the phone and they're leaving threatening messages on my answering machine. You can't talk with those idiots. And to make things worse, now I've got my Lodge brothers calling me and blaming me for setting a disaster in motion the other night at the initiate's rite of passage. As the Master of Ceremonies, I'm supposed to be the man to fix everything, and I'm the one who's getting blamed and facing the threat of a lawsuit. Where's your mother when I need her? Even though we're divorced, she's the one person in the world who's always been strong enough to help me when I need it."

Jerry had never seen his father appear so shaken. "Mom's camped out in some redwood grove working to help save an ancient forest. Her cell phone doesn't have reception in the woods, so you can't reach her."

Jerry was like a pot full of boiling water that needed to be moved from the burner. It seemed lately as though his father was always having financial challenges, and Jerry knew that he didn't want to listen any longer to his list of problems. He'd heard weird stories too many times before, but his potential lawsuit story seemed to top the list. The only thing Jerry knew for sure at this point was that Mark's analysis of what might happen to him was based on fear instead of fact.

Jerry's cell phone rang just then. Happy for the distraction, he answered his phone. "Hello."

Instantly Jerry heard panic in Carmella's voice. Upon hearing her crying about Rambo's disappearance, he turned and walked away from his father to continue his conversation in private.

"Oh, Carmella," he said sympathetically. "I'm sorry about Rambo. Do you really think it was a dognapper or could he have just wandered off? Please stop crying. We'll find your dog."

Jerry was quiet as he continued listening to Carmella's unfolding story about how Rambo mysteriously vanished. He sadly wished he knew how to calm things down and then he heard something that made his mood lift like the fog in the morning sun, "What? You have a letter

for me from Jodi? I can't believe it. I'll come over to get it as soon as I leave my Dad's."

When Jerry hung up from his phone call with Carmella, he turned and walked toward his father.

"Dad, you'll be okay. Pull yourself together. I've got to go. A friend has something for me, and I need to get it before she goes to bed."

Mark sneered at him. "I hope it's something between her legs."

Jerry wouldn't listen to any crude remarks from his Dad. He had spent so much of his life supportively listening to his father's traumas and most of what he had received in return from his father was insensitive, abrasive comments. He felt lucky to have had his mother's warm-hearted empathy to offset his father's surreal twisted take on life and love.

"I'm outta here," Jerry responded.

"Don't blow me off. I'm your father," Mark replied.

"Dad, I've got so much to do," Jerry answered reaching for his jacket and edging toward the door. Sometimes it seemed like his father was more a child than adult. At times like these, Jerry didn't want to be around him, and have to play the role of the concerned parent. "We'll talk again later. Don't worry so much. This stuff will all go away sooner or later. Right now, I'm sorting through my own problems, but I'll be back before too long to check on how things are going for you."

Concerned about how weary Mark looked, Jerry walked back to his dad and gave him a hug. And then he quickly left. The day was almost over and he needed to visit one more friend. He was saving the best for last. At least he hoped his next meeting would be better than what had transpired earlier in the day.

By the time Jerry got to Carmella's apartment on Green Street, it had started to rain, and he realized that not only did he not have an umbrella, but he was also emotionally spent. The day had been one long series of highs and lows, with nothing in between. He knocked gingerly on the door, looking forward to being with her more than he wanted to admit.

"Jerry, I'm so happy to see you," Carmella said as she opened her door inviting him inside. "Do you want some coffee or tea?"

"You forgot to say 'me.' 'Do you want coffee, tea, or me?' That's how the saying goes." Jerry smiled as he saw her blush. He wondered if he had been too forward. "Sure, I'll have some tea," he said looking around her brightly illuminated room.

"Okay. Follow me into my kitchen and I'll heat some water." Carmella gestured him inside and Jerry followed, feeling himself relax in her presence. The more time he spent getting to know Carmella, the more drawn he felt toward her.

"Have a seat," Carmella said as she poured water into her tea kettle and set it on the stove. "I'm sorry about the frantic phone calls. I hate to dump on you, but I'm going nuts. Besides feeling devastated about Jodi trying to commit suicide, and that Norman's locked up in jail, now I'm going crazy worrying about Rambo."

"You're not dumping on me. I'm happy to listen," Jerry replied. "You've got a lot to deal with. And how's your leg?"

"It's getting better, but I'm really upset about Rambo. He's like my child. I've had him since he was a puppy. I can't stop thinking about him. I'm going back to the movie set tomorrow to continue my search."

Jerry stood and took her in his arms before he knew what he was doing.

"I'm sure Rambo will find his way home," he said huskily. "My intuition tells me that you'll find him."

Carmella easily made her way into Jerry's arms, felt the warmth of his embrace, and smelled the musk of his wavy hair. For the first time all day, she relaxed for a brief moment. She wished that the teapot hadn't started whistling, but it had, and she needed to turn off the fire. She kissed Jerry on the cheek, pulled herself out of his arms, and walked to the stove.

Jerry noticed that even though she was slightly limping her body moved gracefully as she moved about the kitchen and reached in the cupboard to get the teabags. Jerry felt his heart pounding. He wasn't supposed to be feeling good right now, but there was something about being near Carmella that made him happy. He didn't want to resist his happy feelings, especially since they seemed to occur so infrequently. He smiled despite all that was going on in his chaotic life. He couldn't be sure, but he thought that he saw Carmella smile for just a moment as she poured water into his empty cup, and then sat in a chair close to his.

"I know you feel scared, but you've got to stop thinking about Rambo so that you can get some sleep tonight," Jerry said in a soothing tone. "Tomorrow you can begin your search for him all over again." He moved his body so that his shoulders would be touching hers. They were both silent for a while.

"You're so right, Jerry," Carmella said, breaking the silence. "I so badly needed to talk with someone who understands. I really appreciate that you took time to come here and listen to me."

Jerry put his arm around Carmella and gently said, "You've got to be strong so that you can find Rambo. And we've got to trust that our friends will make their way out of their crazy predicaments and be okay."

"Thanks for your encouragement," Carmella said, turning to look at him. "Before I forget, the nurse at the ICU found a letter in Jodi's pocket. It's addressed to you." She took the crumbled envelope from her purse that sat on a nearby chair and gave it to Jerry.

"I don't know if I can handle any more surprises today," Jerry said. "I think I'm going to open it after I get some sleep. I might start to lose my sanity otherwise. Please forgive me for drinking your tea and running out the door, but I've got to go home and sort out some stuff with Stella. It's a difficult time, and I feel like I'm at a test point to find out if I'm I the master of my fate, or if I'm just a puppet who is playing a part in a drama that can't be rewritten. You understand, don't you?" Jerry asked.

"I think so. I'm still trying to understand my fate in relation to Rambo, but I feel better since talking with you. Can we talk again tomorrow? Hopefully, I'll get more news regarding Norman and Jodi."

"Of course. And if I hear anything, I'll call you too." Jerry reached over and gave Carmella a kiss on her cheek before he made his way to the door. "Good dreams, sweet Carmella. If you start to worry again, just remember that my intuition sees you finding your dog," Jerry repeated as he left.

Although Jerry was glad to have spent a little time with Carmella, he was happy to be going home again, and happy that the rain had stopped. He needed some time with Stella to help him get more clarity about the choices he was facing.

When he finally unlocked the door to his apartment and walked inside, it was quiet as a church. Stella was nowhere to be seen. As he heaved a sigh of relief, he realized that he was happy to be alone. He felt exhausted from listening to the myriad complications of life that were weighing on the shoulders of his wife, friends, and family. Even his own mind seemed to be whirling. Should he reconcile with Stella? Could he find a way to heal the craziness that was going on between them? And what about Lisa? He felt his blood start to boil when he remembered what had happened last night, and it even got hotter when he realized that the day was almost over and he hadn't heard a peep of an apology from her.

After going into the kitchen and getting a soda from the refrigerator, he walked back to his private room congratulating himself for having the willpower to resist eating another piece of Stella's tempting apple pie. He sat at his desk, turned on his reading light, and though he knew he should wait, pulled out the crumpled letter from Jodi. Even though the paper was crinkled, the words were clear. *Jerry,* Jodi had written. *You are my one true friend. I've written you a poem to thank you.*

Night Time Stars
A glowing sun
Sets over a hill:
Caught in reflections of light,
As the earth stands still.
Now begins the glory of night
And the sky begins to fill
As a million stars
Sparkle and shine bright.
A deepening calm sweeps over the land
When the moon dominates the sky.
The dark horizon is moved
By the hand of night:
Stars shine bright.

Jerry reread her poem several times. He thought about her feisty nature, how real she was, and how much he really liked her. For someone so young, she was so bright. Like a star herself, he thought, while sliding her poem into a book sitting on his desk. Her inspiring words made him feel better. If he could only have cured her problems, he would truly be happy. He envisioned himself sending Jodi healing rays of Reiki energy just as he was falling asleep.

Early the next day, Carmella returned to the makeshift reception office. Less friendly than yesterday, the receptionist appeared weary of her repeated requests for information about the lost dog. Carmella had a knack for reading people and sensed that she would help find him. When her instincts were too loud to ignore, she knew she should listen.

Carmella was happily surprised when she recognized the man who walked into the office as the producer she had hoped to interview. Hoping that her timing had improved, she jumped and stood in front of him.

"Sorry to bother you, Mr. Stalsburg. I'm the woman who was going to interview you yesterday. My dog disappeared while I was here waiting for my appointment with you, and I went to find him and I missed seeing you."

"Well. I hope you found him. It's upsetting to lose a pet." Then, appearing to be in too much of a hurry to wait for a response, he made a dash for the exit.

Carmella was dumbfounded by his coldness. Needing fresh air to relieve her sense of panic, she walked outside. In the distance she could hear a dog barking. She listened to locate the source of the barking. It was coming from inside a nearby building that was marked with a sign that read: "Off-limits to the general public." Ignoring the sign, she stepped into the industrial building and walked past several rooms where people appeared to be working as she hurriedly went down the hall following the seemingly familiar sounds. Cautiously, she peeked inside the room where she could hear barking. Her mind couldn't believe what she was seeing so she pressed her face against the wood of the door to open it wider. A young woman had secured the dog in place, and another was using henna to tattoo an upside down pentacle on its butt. The little dog looked nearly identical to Rambo except that it was shaven to its shiny pink buffed skin. The only fur that remained was a tuff between the ears trailing down its shoulders fashioned in a rainbow colored mohawk.

"Is this my dog?" Carmella yelled incredulously, as she let herself into the room. "What?" said the woman who was holding the tattoo brush. Both she and the other woman instantly busied themselves trying to relax the yelping mutt that was becoming agitated in response to Carmella's sharp, loud voice.

Just at that moment, another girl walked into the room holding what looked to Carmella like a cake made of ground meat molded into a shape of a cat. Carmella could smell ground liver as she walked by. The young girl obviously knew how to distract the dog from noticing that its butt was being used as an art canvas. Pulling free from the woman who was holding him, the little dog forgot about being the center of attention and lunged for the plate. Apparently hungry, it could hardly care about anything in the room except for the appearance of its tasty treat.

"This isn't your dog," the girl said. "It's Roland's dog and he's paying us to get him ready for a role in a movie."

"But, it looks just like my dog without its hair!"

At that moment the door opened and the producer walked in. Not acting surprised to see her there, he looked directly at Carmella and said, "Do you know that you're trespassing?"

Carmella tried to choke back her frustration. "I couldn't help but come here when I heard this dog barking."

As if he was lost in thought, Mr. Stalsburg said, "Isn't he an interesting looking mutt?"

"This dog looks just like my Rambo without its hair!" Carmella said with alarm. "You stole my dog and you've shaved off his fur," she screamed, no longer able to hold back her emotions. "You're heartless monsters!"

"Not only are you wrong, but you're also insulting," Mr. Stalsburg hissed. "Girls, didn't you get this dog from a trainer who's in contract with our studio?"

The young women whispered with each other before one said, "Yes, we picked up the dog from the on-set trainer."

Carmella couldn't believe what she'd just heard. As she hurriedly walked toward the table and reached to grab the jewel studded collar of the excited dog, the younger of the two women assertively pushed her away.

"I've spent half a day getting this mutt ready to play a role in a movie. You can't come here and just grab it."

"I want to have a closer look at him." Carmella was outraged.

One of the other two women quickly pulled out her cell phone to make a call to security. The henna artist grabbed the dog and started to leave the room.

"Just let me look at him for a couple minutes," Carmella begged once again.

"Do you know what Terra Linda means?" asked Mr. Stalsburg calmly.

"Yes, it means beautiful earth," Carmella responded, trying to get a closer look at the dog that was being quickly escorted toward the door.

As if they had been waiting on cue, several security guards appeared. The young woman holding the dog ducked behind one of them and bolted out the door. Two of the broad, towering men stopped Carmella in motion, grabbed her, and assertively started to escort her toward the exit.

Just when Carmella thought that this day was becoming her worst nightmare, she heard the producer say, "Just a minute! Let her go. Your look is perfect for the part, Carmella. That's your name, isn't it?"

"Yes," she answered. The men that had been holding her arms released her.

"I could have the girls write up a report that details how you broke into our "off limits" building, and charge you with trespassing, but, you're such a beautiful woman, and I feel bad that you've lost your dog.

I understand how sad you must feel. To show my sincerity, I will have one of my assistants find the contractual papers that were signed by the owner to temporarily release this dog to us, and if it will make you feel any better, you can see them. But more importantly, I'm excited. I can't stop thinking that you have the perfect look, your slight limp and all, to play the role of a witch that gets burned at the stake in the production of my documentary. Your image makes such a strong statement. Seriously, would you be interested in being an extra in my movie? The woman we initially hired for this role is out of commission with a broken leg, and I'm looking for a replacement."

Carmella was in shock. She was sure that the dog she had just seen was Rambo, but couldn't prove it. The offer of a part in a movie sounded great, and the thought of getting a paycheck would ease her concern of having enough money to pay her bills. She looked at the producer who had a large smile on his face. She pinched herself to make sure that she wasn't dreaming before saying, "Are you serious? I would love to be in your film."

"Great. I never suggest that someone play a role unless I feel it is absolutely right. There's too much at risk if I make a mistake," Mr. Stalsburg replied while dismissing the security guards with a wave of his hand.

"I'm flattered, and it sounds fun to play a part in a movie," Carmella spoke with calm reserve. "But I'm still hoping that you will let me do an interview with you."

"Sure. We can find time to do that in the next week when my schedule isn't so tight. We can talk about your interview later. Right now, you need to go back to the office where I first met you, and talk with the receptionist about filling out the paperwork. Tell her that I want you to play the role of Sybil. She also needs to give you directions to the costume department, and the dates and times for when we need you for filming."

"I can't believe this is happening, Mr. Stalsburg," Carmella said feeling like she wanted to give him a hug. Except for not finding Rambo, this day was turning out to be much better than she had imagined.

Eighteen: The Moon

XVIII. LA LUNE

Spiraling Emotions

As Carmella was driving back to San Francisco, she decided to stop at the Marin County Jail. She was still in time for limited visiting hours and she knew it would help her sleep better if she could see Norman and hear from his own mouth that he was alright.

Once in the visitor reception room, she warily strolled toward the attendant who was sitting behind a large glass partition, and asked to visit Norman. Without changing his sour expression, he gave her a required legal form to fill out that would allow her a fifteen-minute meeting.

Quickly, she wrote her information in the blank spaces and handed it back to the attendant who said, "Have a seat. Someone will call you when it's time to see your friend."

Although his monotone voice didn't sound very welcoming, Carmella was excited that she would soon get to see Norman. Even though he'd only been locked up for a few days, it felt like an enormous luxury to be allowed to see him. With her heart beating like a drum, she walked to an empty seat on a wooden bench, sat down, and while she waited, tried to think of what she should say to him.

Twenty minutes crept slowly by. She heard the metallic clang of keys, looked up, and saw an officer open a locked door that lead to the interior of the building. Reading from a list, he called her name along with several others. Anxiously getting up, she walked to where the officer was standing. With what felt like a brutally officious air, he first required her and the others who had gathered to show their identification and walk through a metal detector security gate before he led them through another locked door. In a robotic tone, he voiced instructions to them. "Go down the corridor and then turn left into the waiting room."

Carmella went down the windowless hall and into the waiting room and instantly smelled the dry, stale air. Feeling like she couldn't breathe, she tried in vain to calm her sense of panic that was flooding over her. Tears started to fall on her cheek when she saw two men in orange jumpsuits and shackles walk past the entranceway accompanied by an armed guard. Taking a wooden seat, she pulled her shoulders up towards her ears in an attempt to get rid of the stress triggering the onset of what she knew would become a migraine headache.

Another ten minutes passed before she heard her name called again. This time she was led to a private room that had a single chair placed in front of a thick pane glass window. A few minutes later, Norman walked through a door into the room on the other side of the partition and sat on a chair positioned directly across from her own.

"Norman, I miss you," Carmella confessed, blowing him a kiss. "Do you have any news about your situation?"

"No sweetie. It's so nasty in here," His voice seemed to shake with uncertainty. "All anyone talks about, if they talk with you at all, is getting a court date, felonies, and their attorney. I'm bored out of my mind, and I want out of here. It's like time is standing still, and I'm going crazy. This ain't no vacation, that's for sure."

Norman felt as if a swarm of snakes was wiggling through his body. Images of past drug experiences streamed through his mind. There was the opium parlor in Chinatown where he was led through a maze of alleyways until he had no idea where he was. Stepping through a low, ancient wooden door, he found himself in a room with low-lying beds lining the walls that were covered with ancient newspapers that bore

headlines of events such as World War I, newspapers that had yellowed from the smoke of countless years and long thin pipes. Almost all the beds were filled with old Chinese men lying quietly amid their smoky dreams. The small man who was in charge led Norman to an empty cot and motioned for him to lie down. Then he brought a filled pipe and offered it to Norman, who inhaled the bitter sweet smoke with several deep breaths and even several more after the pipe-bearer had indicated that he should stop. Obviously he was too greedy, for instead of disappearing into dreams like the others present, he quickly became violently ill, and fell into a wretched state that bore more than a little resemblance to what he was experiencing now.

"Norman, can you hear me? What are they saying about when you can get out?" Carmella asked, concerned about her friend's temporary silence.

"My situation is very confusing," Norman said. "My bond's set at a hundred grand, and who's got that much money sitting around? If I'm lucky, my dad might pay for a bail bondsman to put it up, but in the meantime I'm playing the waiting game, and wondering if that's going to happen or not."

Norman stopped talking and put his head down between his knees for a couple of minutes. He sat back up, shook his head sadly before continuing.

"Talking with the old man is like talking to the Inquisition, and he keeps threatening me by telling me that I have to go into residential rehab or he won't help me. He's bullying me, like always, but I haven't got anyone else who's willing to front the money and get me out of here."

"Do you have a lawyer?"

"Yes, my dad hired a lawyer, but he hasn't been here and I don't know anything about what he's doing to help me. Like I'm going to get justice when I can't even talk with a lawyer. I want out of this shit hole. My head feels all groggy, and I don't even know why I'm here, except that it has something to do with Jodi. The one thing I know is that I was just trying to help her."

"You know she tried to commit suicide, don't you?"

"She did? She isn't dead, is she?" Norman asked, putting his hand flat on the glass as if he could touch Carmella.

Carmella could see the tracks of scar tissue that covered Norman's veins all the way up and down his arm as it shook uncontrollably. She put her hand on the glass directly across from Normans trying to comfort him.

"No, but she's in a coma. I told the nurses at the hospital that I was her big sister, and they let me see her. She looked so lifeless, but the doctors are supposedly hopeful."

"That's bizarre. Try to find out more of what you can about her, and hopefully things don't get any worse. I feel bad for her, but I feel really, really bad for myself too. I'm in a rotten mood and can hardly hold myself together. I've been sick ever since I've been here, and I can't sleep. I need some meds, but I can't get anything. I'm about ready to go crazy. I just want to get out of here. Hey, you'll remember to water my cactus plants on your balcony, won't you?"

"Yes, I'm happy to do that for you. I'll go home later and water them." Carmella stopped talking when she heard a buzzer ring loudly signaling that their visitation time was growing short. "Is there anything else I can do for you?"

"Just help me get out of here." Norman started to sob like a baby.

"I don't know how to do that," Carmella sadly replied, trying not to become too emotional herself. "But if you can tell me what to do…." She stopped talking when she heard a buzzer ring loudly signaling that their visitation time was over.

Carmella gazed silently through the glass at Norman who looked older than she had ever seen him look. A guard came in to escort him out of the room. Feeling frustrated, sad, and lonely all at the same time, she got up to leave.

Walking out the door, she realized that it wasn't fate, it was Norman's addiction to drugs that was to blame for his current situation. As much as she wanted him to believe that she could have a relationship with him, she knew in her heart that she didn't really love him; she was angry with him. He was totally out of touch with her reality. Perhaps if he had asked her even a single little question about her life or shown some interest in her she wouldn't feel so upset, but he hadn't asked about her feelings or about anything that was going on with her, not even once.

Later in the evening across the Golden Gate, Carmella's fortune appeared to take a turn for the better. As she gingerly walked up the steps to Luna's apartment door, her energy was surging. She made a commitment not to let the recent events get her down, and even if she didn't have her dog, she had her new rock in her pocket that in some strange way gave her strength. She had tried to call Jerry to tell him about her recent visit with Norman, but he hadn't answered her calls. Because

he had talked with her about his challenges with his wife, she knew from their conversations that he was beginning to spend time with her again. Dismissing a fleeting sense of jealousy, she wondered if perhaps they were trying to repair their damaged relationship. She imagined that if Jerry were her man, she'd be a happy woman.

Knocking on Luna's door made Carmella feel hopeful—hopeful that she would find her dog, hopeful that she would stop being mad at Norman, and confident that taking this novel opportunity to talk with an authentic high priestess of a coven would polish off her nearly completed article called "The Revolving Wheel of a Sacred Circle."

To overcome her nervousness, she applauded herself for taking the initiative and calling Luna to ask her about the practical uses of magic and ritual in everyday modern society. As she waited outside a door decorated with a garland of woven oat straw, she mentally recounted the benefits of why she'd accepted an invitation to Luna's woman's empowerment ritual, but more than anything, she was happy for distractions from her present turmoil.

Luna met her at the door with a big hug, and invited her inside her cozy living room. After offering her some mead, she began briefing her on what to expect as more women arrived. Luna wondered if Carmella had any idea that she had received a special invitation to her normally closed-to-newcomers ritual to celebrate the goddess in all women. Sensing her lack of knowledge of the craft, she supposed that she needed to give Carmella a basic introduction to witchcraft, and decided to proclaim to all the women who had already gathered, "We'll be performing our ritual tonight to give thanks to Gaia for fertilizing the gardens of our lives. We'll also be invoking Artemis, the great goddess who is the protector of the feminine and the mystic arts. We'll call on her to bless us with her healing guidance so that we do our work to benefit Mother Earth."

Luna looked at Carmella, and although directing her conversation toward her, spoke loudly enough for the assembled group of women to hear.

"My prayers to the Great Spirit of Light involve meditation, breath work, and invocations. Often, before starting the ceremony, we chant together. Chanting is a way to synchronize everyone's energy with our magical intention.

"But before we begin, I don't want to overlook the real immediate needs of any person in this moment. Do any of you have any problem or situation that you would like to work on in our healing circle?"

Intrigued by the offer, Carmella spoke softly but directly, "I'm fighting going in and out of a fabulous pity party that I keep throwing for myself. Within the last week, I've lost my dog and my boyfriend."

Luna looked at Carmella's striking face and figure, and thought that of all the problems the young woman standing in front of her would announce, losing a man would not be one of them. She shook her head and smiled at Carmella before saying, "All I can say is look inward. How you handle the situation becomes the situation."

"What do you mean?" Carmella asked.

Luna became aware that she needed to divide her attention between all the women and not focus solely on Carmella. "I don't have the time to explain right now, but if you think about it long enough, you'll figure it out," Luna replied before being interrupted by a woman who had just finished placing flowers on an altar against the back wall of the long rectangular room.

While putting on her sparkling crescent moon crown, the woman said, "Situations always change, and you might want to use our circle to pray to the goddess that it changes in your favor. Really though, most of us here feel sorry for you losing your dog, but as far as we're concerned, you can celebrate losing your man. Men want to use women and take control of their manna, their innate power. Seriously, you'll feel better once you realize that you can do just fine without that man in your life. In the past, we invited men to join in our rituals, but time and time again, they'd get into their egos and forget the true work we're doing. We don't need men to tell us what lies hidden beyond the veil."

Her words were almost drowned in the women echoing their agreement. Another woman giggled before she began to tell her story.

"You all know that we choose to be sky clad and take off our clothes for our rituals," the woman said. "More than once I've seen some man's penis rise as he walked near a naked woman—even when we weren't even doing sex magic. Strangely, I always find myself becoming embarrassed even though I'm one of the women in the circle who doesn't cause a rise in the passing Lord of the Circle. Men, without even trying, can be so crude and insensitive!"

"It's not just men who are insensitive," Luna broke into the conversation. "My parents are the worst. I can give them a big share of the credit for why I don't have men at my rituals."

"Why?" several women asked.

"Earlier in my life," she continued, "my dad and mom had a key to my apartment. Once they let themselves into my place while I wasn't home, and friend of mine who'd needed a place to stay was sleeping in

my bed. He didn't let them know he was there and he overheard them talking about me. While they were going through all my stuff, checking it to see if I had any drugs in the apartment, they had a conversation about whether I was a lesbian or not. They even said that if I wasn't gay, I was probably suppressing my latent tendencies, and that it would be better for me if I was queer because then they wouldn't have to worry about me getting pregnant. How's that for being sensitive?" Luna asked sarcastically. "When they finally strolled into my bedroom and found a man in my bed, my friend acted as though he had been sleeping the entire time of their visit and didn't hear what they said about me.

"But I decided to interpret their tactless conversation as a sign from the gods that it would be okay to let the world know that I prefer the smell of a woman to the stink of a man. Women are so much more attractive to me than men."

Carmella's eyes opened wide to Luna's admission that she was gay.

"Are all the women who come to your rituals gay?" Carmella asked, starting to feel a little intimidated.

"Women are women. Gay or straight, they're always welcome at my rituals. Large or slim, young or old, we are all Daughters of the Goddess. What's important is that we come together as sisters and share our desire to honor the Goddess. But, what about you, Carmella? Have you ever made love to a woman?"

"Well, honestly, I'm a man's woman."

"That sounds limiting. Be honest, haven't you ever thought about making love to a woman?"

"Sure," said Carmella. "You've heard the song lyrics, 'I kissed a girl and I liked it,' haven't you? It's a hot song that makes me think about kissing girls, but I've always had a boyfriend."

"Where is he? You said you lost him," one of the other women asked.

Another woman also broke into the conversation: "Where's any man when you need him?"

Carmella was quick to reply. "Honestly, he's in jail, and he's being so weird. I really don't know what's going on between us at this point. He's too stoned too much of the time and I feel betrayed by his connection with another girl, and that's why I feel like I'm not really with him anymore."

"Sounds like he's a loser," said the woman who had been clearing the room to create space to make a circle. "However, I've got a really good spell that will help you find your dog. Are you interested?" the woman asked.

Carmella was relieved at the change of subject. "Yes, of course," she replied.

"What's your dog's name?" the woman asked.

"Rambo."

"If you choose to do this spell, you must do it in moonlight for it to work. First, you must focus your emotions and attune your energy with Rambo. Let yourself express your feelings toward him, just like he was standing in front of you. Then, take Rambo's leash and tie it into a noose and wrap it around a hand held mirror. Stick the mirror with the attached noose into the earth near the place where you last saw Rambo. That will help you locate your dog."

"I can add to that spell," another woman chimed in. "It's similar to making a voodoo doll in order to affect someone's energy. While chanting Rambo's name, visualize him having all the furiousness he needs to bite free of his situation. It might help to cut out a picture of a pit bull, and place it where he sleeps. The cut out image will cause Rambo, who is psychically connected to you and his bed, to feel the energy of what you are thinking. If he's lost, he'll have the strength to find his way home. If he's been stolen, whoever has your dog will get a big surprise when Rambo summons his inner pit bull."

Luna added, "It won't take too long for you to get some sense of a response from the energy you put into these spells. If the Goddess knows your intention is pure, the power of magic will bring fast results."

"Thank you so much," Carmella spoke from her heart, wondering if she could handle doing spells, yet happy to have some guidance in what she might do to find Rambo.

"We're glad to help you," Luna replied. "Everything will work out if you stay even-minded. And our ritual will work better if we take some time to think about what we're trying to effect with our energy. Doing a ritual with people who share a singular purpose is very powerful. Let's have a minute of silence to harness our healing forces and meditate on our group intention. Does someone have The Moon tarot card to place on our altar?"

A chubby woman stepped forward. "I was planning on doing that before I got distracted by all the talk about magic spells to find a missing pet," the woman said. She walked to an ornate table covered with various sizes and shapes of crystals and placed a large Moon card in the center of the altar near a large silver pentacle sitting inside a crescent moon.

Another woman called out, "The Moon is our Mother. Magic come alive!"

A few more women filtered in through the door and Carmella could feel the room filling with silent anticipation. She was becoming familiar with the expectation that she become sky clad and remove her clothes, and knew when she saw the other women starting to disrobe, it was nearing the time for the ritual to begin.

"Who will take the lead to invoke the elements so we can amplify our power and shut out the negativity of the world?" Luna bellowed above the chatter while raising a dragon claw crystal wand above her head.

The woman with the crescent moon crown shouted loudly in a rhythmic chord, "Yod, He, Va, He, earth, air, fire, and water."

From the deepest part of her inner self, Carmella surrendered to the alluring voice of what she imagined could actually be the Goddess herself. The circle of women felt so familiar that she wondered if in some past life, her spirit had participated in this ceremony many moons—or for that matter, many centuries ago.

But even though she found this all very amazing, and good material for the article she was writing, she couldn't help but wonder whether it would really help her find Rambo.

Raising a jeweled goblet above her head, Luna looked upward and smiled as she affirmed to the group, "We are one, we are all! Look to your right, look to your left and see the goddess! She is one, she is all. Isis, Demeter, Diana, Artemis, Persephone, Sohia, Athena, Freya, Yemana, Kuan Yin, Tara, Oshun, Lakshmi, Shakti, Bhavani, Devi, Durga, Kali...."

That same night while tormented Norman was tossing and turning on a thin facsimile of mattress shouting for a fix, and Carmella was chanting to the goddess, Jerry was softly awakened by Stella stroking his thighs.

"Jerry, love of my life, wake up," she whispered. "I have a present for you."

Jerry, who had just recently fallen into a deep sleep, stirred half awake from a dream of walking on the beach with Carmella when he heard Stella's soft voice and felt her warm naked body. The lavender smell of her hair and the touch of fiery energy from her hands on his thighs jolted his body into unexpected wakefulness. "Stella! You've climbed in my bed for two days in a row. What's happening with you?"

"I want us to get back to how we were when we slept together in our bed and told each other before going to sleep every night that we loved one another. I can't stand being without you anymore, Jerry. I love you so

very much," Stella murmured in his ear. She started to gently nibble on his ear. Her hands slid to his legs and she rubbed him in ways that were like matches lighting the tinder for a fire.

Jerry's body couldn't ignore Stella's gentle touch. His body didn't care that he hadn't resolved the issue of what to do about their problematic marriage. Their bodies were talking to each other and mental defenses drifted off with the fleeting clouds of the night sky. His passions were hungry, and she was offering him a delicious feast.

Stella opened her lips so that her tongue could deliver a moist kiss on his neck. She started biting his skin ever so softly, and continued tenderly kissing his bare chest. She knew what turned Jerry on in bed and she wasn't going to wait for him to tell her whether he was ready for her or not.

Nineteen: The Sun

XIX. THE SUN

Unexpected Surprises

After the previous night of being with Jerry, Stella wasn't about to let him sleep late in the morning. She wasn't going to hold her feelings back. Maybe she could entice him into making love again. She knew that if she waited much longer, he would wake up and make some lame excuse about needing to go somewhere or do some alchemical thing to save the world. Even after several years of marriage she wasn't sure about his self-proclaimed visits to other dimensions, and wasn't even sure that she liked the part of Jerry that she called the Spirit Walker. It seemed sane enough when he was talking about visiting other worlds, but when she thought about it, it didn't quite fit her perception of reality.

For now, the best thing she could do would be to use her own form of magic and decide how to successfully continue yesterday's conversation. Summoning her courage, she walked down the hallway, pushed open the door to his room and peeked inside. "Jerry? Are you awake? It's time to wake up."

"Do I have to?" replied sleep deprived Jerry, who hid his head under the pillow.

Stella walked into his room and sat down on his bed. "No, of course not," she said, gently rubbing his head. "You can choose to sleep the day away, but I can think of nicer things to do. Did you enjoy last night?"

Jerry rolled over and looked at his wife. "Yes, that was delicious," Jerry answered, his body feeling a tingling contentment. He smiled as he realized that his dilemma of what direction to go with Stella had been happily resolved as their bodies became one in heated ecstasy the previous night.

"Jerry, I want to talk with you about something important. I'm at a crossroads and I need you to hear me out. You agreed to marry me for better or worse, right?" she asked softly, her voice shaky and child-like.

Jerry jolted into concerned wakefulness when he heard her question. Even though the sweetness of her lavender scent made him want to move closer to her, he steadied himself. He could sense something intense coming next, and wished that he was still asleep and the present conversation was part of a dream from which he would awaken.

"Stella, I married you because we loved one another. For the past three months we've hardly spoken so we're already been weathering 'the worse.'"

"I need you not to judge me or think me to be a bad person when I tell you what I'm about to say."

Jerry sensed a tightening in his chest and his emotions immediately became heavy, but seeing the look of panic on Stella's face, he gently asked, "How can I be judgmental about you when you're deep in my heart?"

"Jerry, it's because you are the love of my life that I want us to be together," Stella said.

Jerry could hear the panic in her voice. "Well, I'm happy to hear that, since we're married. Before I fell asleep last night I was thinking about my love for you. Even when I felt like I wanted to die after you said you wanted to date someone new I knew I wouldn't be hurting so damn much if I didn't love you. I didn't give up on us. I'm here with you now."

During the preceding months she had closed the door on him emotionally in order for her to have her adventures, and in return he

had done the same. Now he was remembering those waves of discordant feelings and trying to put them out of his mind. He told himself to relax, breathe, and to be grateful for the present moment.

Stella took his hand and placed it on her belly. "Jerry," she said, "I'm pregnant."

"This is a joke," Jerry said, yanking his hand from her stomach.

Stella looked afraid. "No. I'm serious," she whispered.

"How many months pregnant are you, for god's sake? Until last night, we hadn't slept together for three months," Jerry replied in a fiery burst of emotion.

"Jerry, I'm not sure how pregnant I am. Honestly," she answered.

Jerry sat up in bed and moved to create distance from her. "What do you mean, you're not sure? Who's the father of this baby, Stella?"

In her sweetest voice she said, "Sweetie, I want you to be the father." Stella began to plead her case. "As much as you are my husband, and the ground beneath my feet, I'm counting on you to do what's right for us. It's only reasonable to have a child together."

Jerry's mind was quickly jumping to an unsettling conclusion as he questioned, "What do you mean, 'you want me to be the father'? Who is the father? How many months pregnant are you?"

Stella lowered her eyes. This conversation wasn't going as she had hoped. She wasn't sure if she should just run out of the room or keep trying to talk to Jerry, who had a wild, crazy look on his face.

"Did you know you were pregnant when you made me apple pie? Why didn't you tell me yesterday when you crawled into bed with me?" Jerry asked.

Stella found herself feeling aghast with the terror of her self-disclosure.

"I just found out that I was pregnant this morning. Jerry, please, I need you to hear me out. I want our relationship to work and I want us to have a family. You said you wouldn't judge me."

"Okay, well…I'm not judging you. I'm happy for you," he quickly replied with a bitter tone of disdain. "It only makes sense that when we were talking yesterday you must have also been questioning whether you might be pregnant. And if you just found out today, that means you can't be very far along, and that also means I can't be your child's father. Didn't you think that I might want to be involved in the decision of having a child? Do you think I will happily go along with anything you ask of me because you're pregnant?"

"Jerry, please don't go there. You just said that you love me. If you truly do, and you just said that you do, you can be my child's - our child's - father."

"Are you crazy? I can't be your child's father if we haven't been sleeping together for the last three months," Jerry said, jumping out of bed and starting to get dressed.

"But, Jerry, please listen to me! We can look at this child as a gift from God and our love can continue to grow. Our relationship can become stronger than before."

Sick and angry, Jerry looked away. He didn't know what to think anymore. Stella was making his life very difficult.

"Thanks for trusting me enough to share your thoughts with me, and letting me know what you're planning for our future," he said sarcastically. "Maybe I'll think differently after I have some time to think about this, but right now I don't see myself jumping into the role of being father to another man's child. How can you so easily forget that you recently kicked me out of your life to run off with someone else? Now you expect me to simply overlook the pain you caused me and that you're causing me this very instant? I can't believe that last night I was thinking we could renew our love and make our relationship work, and this morning you're asking me to be the father to a child that isn't even mine. If this is the outcome of your foolish choices, what can I expect from you next?"

"Jerry, have faith in our relationship. You said you would love me for better or worse. I've always been honest with you. I'm sorry that I hurt you. I didn't realize you would get so upset. Truly, I only slept with someone else one time. It was an experiment that turned into a mistake, and it didn't mean anything."

"I'm glad you're able to clear your conscience and get your thoughts out in the open Stella. And thanks for not lying."

Jerry couldn't put his clothes on fast enough. And then ran out of his room, wanting nothing more than to be away from Stella. He couldn't believe the nightmare he was living. He left the apartment, slamming the door shut on his way out. As he walked down the stairs, his heart felt so heavy that it seemed like it had dropped into a pit of misery. The fog in his mind loomed overhead like a blanket of doom as he walked down the sidewalk toward his car. He wanted to drive away, to flee his tortured emotions, in hopes of finding some remnant of his departed sanity.

Meanwhile in the apartment, Stella sat as if paralyzed on Jerry's bed. Why hadn't her love spell worked? After paying Naomi, the reputed real-deal bruha, so much money, and lighting so many candles that she almost burned down her home while making the magic spell apple pie, she had

expected Jerry's love to withstand this test of their commitment. As her assurance in Jerry's positive response waned, beads of sweat streamed down her face and her body began to shake.

Jerry was wishing that he were on a sun-drenched island far, far away from the windy San Francisco Bay. Once in his car, he kicked over the engine, pulled out from the curb, and drove down the street like a reckless race car driver.

Sadly he realized that he had lost all faith in Stella. How could he continue to allow himself to be manipulated by Stella's thoughtless choices for his future? He needed to make a change and would start making plans to walk off the stage of a drama in which he no longer saw himself playing a part.

Perhaps right now if he focused on someone else's problems he could forget about his own. Remembering the heart-touching poem that he had recently been given by Jodi, he decided that once he got to the beach and could clear his mind, it would be a good time to use his Reiki skills and do a long-distance healing for her. As for his own healing, that would have to wait.

With every city block he drove past on the way to the ocean, he repeatedly told himself to breathe deeply and release his stress. Once he got to the long stretch of beach that bordered the western edge of San Francisco and parked his car, he sat quietly willing himself not to cry. Trying to steady his shaken nerves, he made a vow to never let Stella make him feel this way again.

And he had to stop himself from feeling upset that Lisa hadn't called. Why was he being so stupid to think that Lisa would be kind enough to say she was sorry for what happened the other night? He rolled down the car window to smell the fresh salty air, and tried to put his problems out of his mind. He needed to clear his mind in order to do Jodi's long distance healing. Jodi hadn't placed any demands on him at all, and knowing how her innocence had been victimized, she was one person who truly deserved help. She had always been straightforward with him and he respected that. It was a perfect opportunity to do an act of random kindness and use his energy to send Jodi a spiritual stream of healing energy.

Going into a concentrative meditation, he sat inwardly still, and focused on sending healing thoughts and prayers to Jodi. Psychically, he

envisioned sending angels of light to surround her with love and health-giving rays of illumination to encourage her ability to heal.

Just as he was getting deeply into it, his phone rang and interrupted his train of thought. He saw from the caller display that it was Destiny. As soon as she spoke he could hear a tone of intense panic in her voice.

"I've talked with my Dad about you coming over to visit with Angel," Destiny told him. "At first, he said no, but then I told him that one time you rescued some woman who had been practicing Lobsang Rama's astral traveling techniques and had gotten stuck in the fourth dimension. You brought her back from near death, and if you can do that for a stranger, I'm sure you can help my sister, who's almost like your family. I need to warn you, though, that my Dad said that Angel isn't in her physical body and the ghoul who is inhabiting it is dangerously vicious. She's growling like a mad dog and trying to tear apart anyone who comes near her. Do you think you can help her?"

Jerry left the healing vibrations for Jodi to travel on their own for the moment. He was glad to do everything he could to take his mind away from his own problems, and often he felt more at home diving into the spirit realm than walking into his own apartment. It was one place he could get away from the worldly cares and complexities of his own life.

"Yes, I think I might be able to help Angel," he replied, wondering what had triggered her possession.

"Do you have time to visit with her today?" Destiny asked. "The sooner you can help, the better!"

"Yes. I've got some free time, and will be happy to try and help. Are you going to be at your Dad's house? I'll feel better around him if you're there too."

"Yes, I can be there. What time is good with you?"

"Can we meet there after lunch, around 1:30? I don't like involving myself in dark spirit activities on an empty stomach. I need physical strength to be as grounded as much as I can be and shut out the hubbub of logic."

"Thank you ever so much, Jerry. I feel better just knowing that you're willing to help. I'll plan to arrive at my Dad's before you get there."

Jerry ended the call and looked out the car window at the gray clouds that were floating by. How much of what was happening with Angel was fact and how much fiction, he wondered while watching the surfers riding the waves. Then he returned his attention to sending healing energy to Jodi.

Before he left the beach to get some lunch, he decided he wanted, or rather needed to pull a tarot card, and find out if the fates would offer

any good advice. Without hesitation, he picked up his cell phone, and called Carmella. Realizing that she was the last person who had made his heart smile, he felt relieved to hear her voice again.

"Carmella, will you do me a favor and pull a tarot card for me? I just need a quick, one card reading to help me understand what kind of joke the gods are playing on me."

"Jerry, are you okay? You sound a little shaky."

"I'm a little more stressed than normal, but I'm okay," Jerry said not wanting her to know how shredded and vulnerable he was feeling.

"Sure. I'll pull a card for you," Carmella answered . "Do you want to ask me a question?" she asked.

"No. Just pull one card for me."

"Okay. I'm shuffling my cards right now," she told him. "Tell me when to stop shuffling and I'll pull the top card in the deck to represent what's happening with you."

Jerry closed his eyes, and envisioned the spectrum of recent events in his life. When he thought about everything that he had recently gone through, he imagined that he was lucky his head didn't explode. Was this really a good time to visit with Angel who could be in seriously deep waters? Switching subjects, he tried to focus on Stella, then Lisa, and then Angel, and then his present commitment to make a change in his life. He imagined Carmella holding the cards.

"Okay, Carmella, stop shuffling and pull my card," he asked.

"Jerry. It's The Sun card. It indicates that positive vibrations will clear the storms of life and attachments to painful past memories. Whatever you're doing will turn out to be okay. Visualize yourself being healed by the radiance of the Sun. Get in touch with a sunny attitude to adapt to evolving circumstance."

"Yes, you're right. Even though I'm not feeling very sunny, I need to be more in touch with positive energy…and I need to spend more time doing my magical work to connect with the invisible healing masters."

"Are you okay, Jerry?" she asked.

Without revealing his circumstance, Jerry replied, "I don't know, Carmella, but I appreciate your time and support, that's for sure."

"Do you want to come over?"

Jerry was silent for a minute before he replied, "If you want company, I think I'll be free tonight. I can call later to let you know what's happening. This afternoon I'm going to see if I can help a friend who may be possessed."

"That sounds scary. How do you work with that?" Carmella asked.

"You just do it, and see what happens."

"Oh! That makes me a little nervous, but since I pulled the Sun card for you and it symbolizes success, I won't worry. Be careful, and give me a call when you can to let me know how everything went and when you can come over. Bye, Jerry. Good luck!"

"Bye." He turned off his cell phone and started his engine. He was ready to find something to eat and then go over to Taylor's to meet with Angel and the spirit who possessed her.

Twenty: Judgment

XX. AWAKENING

Trapped in The Shadows

Jerry was lost in his thoughts when Destiny opened Taylor's front door and greeted him. She looked like she had been crying. Jerry gave her a little hug as he walked in and then his eyes settled on the pitiful sight of Taylor. The man was slouching over a table pouring him self a shot of rum. He was obviously in the middle of disagreement with Destiny, and when he spoke, his words were slurred.

"We're not going to call 911!" Taylor said. "Just forget that stupid idea. Besides, your old boyfriend is here to save the day. Right, Jerry?" Taylor said sarcastically.

"Yes, sir," he said respectfully to his old nemesis, remembering how much time they'd spent arguing about the future of Jerry's relationship

with Destiny. In his present state, Taylor seemed less like the stubborn, bull-headed Taurus that Jerry knew him to be, and more like a worn down circus clown pretending to stay calm while losing control of untamed forces in the animal ring. What a strange transformation, Jerry thought, wondering if he would still have to endure any of the interrogations that were a typical part of Taylor's communications.

"I'm here because Destiny asked me to check on Angel," Jerry continued. He knew that in the past Taylor had spread nasty rumors in the community about his manhood after he broke up with his daughter. He had made a point of not being in the same room as Taylor ever since. Even now, Jerry didn't feel comfortable standing in the same room with Taylor.

"I know why you're here," Taylor answered, slurring his words. "You don't have to act so formal. I'm impressed that you've volunteered to help. Hopefully, the curious stories I've heard about how you can exorcise spirits are true. Your skills will need to be sharp if you're going to be able to help our Angel."

Jerry tried not to respond to the intimidating look in Taylor's eyes or the dread he sensed in Taylor's words. He looked at Destiny, who was wringing her hands with despair.

"Where's your sister?" he asked her. "Is she doing any better?"

"I'll let you make your own judgment call when you see her," Destiny responded, exhaling loudly.

"Okay," Jerry answered, trying to diminish his growing sense of dread. "Taylor, it's better for you to stay here. I'll let Destiny take me to see Angel. I know you're concerned about her, but when I'm talking with her, I need the energy around her to be undisturbed so that I can do an unbiased reading of what's going on."

"Undisturbed energy around her," Taylor said mockingly. "You're in for a big surprise, little man. I thought that you had experience with possessions. How can you possibly think that the energy around her is undisturbed?"

Jerry held himself back from responding to Taylor's insult. He nodded and quietly said, "Okay, I get your point, but for now, I need you to trust me enough to be alone with her."

Destiny wanted to avoid any further banter between the two men. She hadn't forgotten how they both could argue endlessly about nothing, trying to prove who was smart enough to speak the last clever word, and she didn't want to waste this moment on a senseless power struggle.

"Jerry," Destiny said, "Let's go. I'll take you to Angel's room, and Dad, you can wait here for us. If we need you, I'll call you."

Destiny led Jerry down the hall. They stopped in front of Angel's bedroom. "Do you need anything before I unlock the door?"

"No, I'm fine," Jerry answered. "Just don't act nervous once we're in the room with Angel. That's the worst thing that either of us can do." He braced himself for the worst and steadied his nerves to override his rising impulse to go in the opposite direction. After Destiny unlocked the door, he slowly opened it and peeked inside the dimly lit room.

Jerry took a deep breath, exhaled, and said, "Okay, let's go see your sister."

Jerry went inside Angel's room first, and Destiny followed right behind him. The room had an unpleasant order that couldn't be masked by the cedar incense that was burning right outside the bedroom door.

Jerry looked at the room, which had been torn apart from floor to ceiling so that it appeared as if a herd of jackals had recently run through in a chaotic rampage. Uneaten dishes of food lay scattered and broken everywhere. Shredded and soiled bedclothes lay in a tangled mess on the floor entwined in the cord of a shattered lamp.

Angel's head was at the foot of the bed, covered in vomit, and her hair was a matted nest. Jerry assumed that Angel disapproved of their presence, because she jumped up on the bed and began urinating on the torn mattress. Seconds later, Angel lunged at Jerry, but he deftly moved out of her way, and she fell to the floor wailing as if someone was stabbing her.

Jerry quickly moved behind Angel, whose nose was now bleeding from the impact with the floor. He grabbed her arms from behind while she was disoriented from her fall, assertively turned her, picked her up and then threw her back up onto the mattress.

"Do you want to fuck me?" Angel snarled.

"No, Angel. Try not to move," Jerry commanded, his adrenaline surging. "Just stay in bed. We'll be leaving and won't bother you anymore."

Angel's swollen, blistered tongue hissed and then she spit at Jerry. She turned to Destiny and said with a smirk, "Sister, pretty sister, do you want to get in bed with me? We can cuddle together, and I'll make you feel so fine."

Jerry reached for Destiny's shaking hand and pulled her to leave. "Don't answer her. Let's go. We can't do anything for her right now."

"I love you, Angel," Destiny whimpered while Jerry pulled her from the room.

Once outside, Jerry closed the door, looked at Destiny, and held her close to try and to stop her body from trembling.

"It will be okay. Don't worry. That's not really your sister in there," Jerry said trying to give reassurance.

Destiny spoke through her tears. "How is any of this going to be okay? Did you see what was going on in that room?"

"Listen to me. Don't give any energy to that ghoul by reacting so strongly. Obviously, it wants to tear everyone apart and it will do a good job of it if you give it any power. You must appear strong, calm, and self-controlled when you go into Angel's room," Jerry asserted.

"That sounds easy when you say it, but I've been in that room enough to know that I can't be calm, cool, and collected when I'm in there," Destiny answered. Jerry noticed her fingers trembling as she relocked the double bolt on Angel's door.

"Okay, okay. Just do your best." Jerry stepped back to breathe some fresh air. "If I'm going to visit Angel, it's not going to be in her room. Right now, I need to go somewhere quiet where I can be undisturbed for a short while. Then, I can astral travel to find Angel, and find out what is happening to her from another dimension," Jerry said. He consciously slowed his breathing as the first step in calming his mind to prepare for going into an altered state of consciousness.

Destiny took his hand and led him down the hall to her old bedroom that had been transformed into an office. The door was wide open, welcoming them into a normal world. Jerry sat down in a comfortable chair and made himself at home. He looked at Destiny who was still visibly upset.

"You've got to leave me in here by myself," he told her. "I need to be alone, completely alone. I'm going to go into a trance and I don't want anyone to disturb me. If I'm going to be able to help your sister, you and your dad can't bother me while I'm in here. Promise me that once you leave this room, you won't open the door until I say that it's okay."

"Are you sure about what you're doing?" Destiny questioned with a note of alarm.

"No guarantees. I'm going to try to contact your sister from within the astral planes. I'm not sure what will happen, but if she was astral traveling when this happened, her spirit has to be out flying around somewhere. I might be able to help find her." Jerry gestured toward the door. "And, you promise not to open the closed door, right?"

"Yes, I promise not to disturb you as long as you come out of this room before it gets too late."

"Okay, fair enough. Now, go." He watched Destiny slip out of the room like a gentle wind and close the door shut.

Jerry lit a candle on the desk. He stood up, shook the tension out of his body, and sat back down on the soft cushioned chair and closed his eyes. He started humming and his humming turned into a chant that was as low and quiet as the murmur of a well-oiled wheel spinning down a highway. His magical sound grew louder and louder until it was like a beating drum, and then he was silent.

In the total quiet, all Jerry could hear was his breath, going in and out, in and out. His mind was slowing, going deeper and deeper into inner space. From within his mind, he saw his subtle body rise and float above him. His inner spirit began to speak.

"I call on St. Germaine, Michael the archangel, Thoth the Mighty, Mercury bearer of the caduceus, and all the other healing masters to accompany me on my journey. Soul of my soul, fire of my mind, beating heart of the seventh ray answer my prayers, hear my chants, protect my spirit, and merge our collective dreams to raise God's window for Angel's healing. Let my spirit be a channel for your work."

Jerry felt energy rushing through him. He heard a voice calling somewhere in deep space beyond the threshold of time.

"Call on your soul guide to help you find her," the voice said.

Jerry sensed his spirit detach from his body and float away while still being tied to an umbilical cord of light attached to his body. He started to fly through the clouds of mist in the inner heavens in a space without time. He felt himself being lifted by a magnetic force that he was powerless to resist, and his spirit soared in spirals through cosmic windstorms. After seemingly timeless flight, he dropped downward until he landed on a soft, receptive solid matter. He opened his eyes wide to look through the pervasive, unfamiliar hues of light.

In the distance the sand dunes glimmered. Were they near, or were they far? Mesmerized by their beauty, he couldn't tell whether they were a mirage or real.

Just looking at the fluorescent sun that glistened like volcanic fire made Jerry feel parched, but he couldn't take time to think about that. Pulled solely by the will of his stubborn determination, he began searching for Angel, knowing that the longer he lingered in this peculiar place, the more difficult it would become to locate her. He called out to her in the echoing emptiness. He scanned the distance, but the sand appeared to dissolve and mysteriously reappear in a far, more distant place, making him feel disoriented. He willed himself to continue his search, but as he went along, he realized that he was in an endless maze of shifting cliff-like sandbanks, and his hope began to dwindle.

Again, his eyes swept the horizon searching the volatile dunes that appeared and disappeared in the blink of an eye. His refocused his vision and summoned his courage to move forward. The ubiquitous, ethereal heat that was moving within the multihued clouds of his dream-like state made him sweat until he was drenched in his own body's water. He saw shadows in veiled shapes dancing in the otherworldly desert landscape that took the seductive forms of Lisa and Stella, and watched them play their parts in the drama of his life.

Jerry remembered his promise to find Angel, but at this dreary moment his aloneness in this god-forsaken place seemed so foreboding. His heart was aching from an overwhelming sense of betrayal by these two women he had trusted with his love. He could see Lisa's face laughing at him, and that made his heart beat with a rhythmic madness that drove his consciousness toward the point of snapping. He screamed in an anguish that echoed through endless chambers in his mind, making him even more aware of being lost in an unfamiliar astral space. He wasn't even sure if he was going forward or backward, or standing still, and he desperately needed water to quench his thirst.

As if his scream swung open a new doorway in his mind, he finally saw Angel standing in the near distance confined in an encircling ring of molten fire. Momentarily his hope soared. Renewed by her sight, he quickened his steps to reach her, but then suddenly she seemed much farther away. What was that looming shadow that stood near her? The moments that it took to reach her seemed like hours, making him more conscious of the burning heat enshrouding him.

From somewhere in the distance he heard devilish laugher.

"She is mine," a voice thundered all around him. "My sweet innocent belongs to me and me alone!"

Jerry refused to acknowledge the bellowing voice. He knew better than to activate a power struggle with an invisible force. With an intensified sense of urgency, he held on to the purpose of his quest, and willed his spirit to move forward.

"Light conquers darkness," he repeated over and over in his mind, as he sensed that he was trespassing into an unknown predator's domain.

After what seemed an eternity, Jerry moved through the illusion and delusion of superficial space to reach Angel, who was now chained to a stake buried deep within a mountain of metallic stone. Using his hands as a tool, he began pulling the chain attempting to remove it from her wrist.

"Angel, what happened? Who did this to you?" he asked her.

"I don't know," Angel responded. "The last thing I remember is taking part in Dad's ritual, and astral traveling to visit our ancestral temple. Then I saw these large, red slanted eyes staring at me. Soon I was immobilized, tied with these heavy chains. Every so often, I hear a voice that tells me to do what I am told or I will die. Jerry, I'm so afraid. Can you get me out of here?" Angel pleaded.

"Yes," Jerry replied, "but you must free your mind from your fear. Completely ignore every command of whoever has been speaking to you. Your will must be strong to free yourself from this. I'm certain that we must be in the lower astral planes where chaotic forces fight to reign. If you give your power to dark forces, they will use it against you. Don't let them have your power, and they won't have it to use against you."

Angel started crying. "I don't know how I arrived here or how long I've been here, and I don't know how to set myself free. How do I keep my power when this force already took it?"

"We don't have time to waste talking. You have to trust me...." Jerry began to say, but then he was startled into silence by the rattling of chains behind Angel. He jumped back as he began to hear a high-pitched screech echoing in reverberating circles that penetrated the rational walls of his sanity.

A bodiless voice began to speak. "And what do you think you're doing? No one invited you here. Innocent Purity is staying with me. I've seen enough of you in Norman's parking lot to know I don't like you, and right now, I'm not the least bit amused. However, since you've crossed over to my side of reality, I might as well make your visit useful. Perhaps you won't mind letting me eat your heart for dinner, your poor, betrayed, worthless heart."

If the situation weren't already strange enough, Jerry was taken aback at facing the Seega head on. Jerry already knew that between the extreme heat in this place and chains molded to Angel's wrist, they were both in severe danger. But knowing that he was facing a powerful threat, his mind went into survival mode.

"You don't scare me," he replied, willing his voice to sound calm. "This is the inner planes and the experience of reality is only a delusion. You're not really of this moment."

"Oh, really?" the voice answered. "Then experience this reality, you dimwit."

In an instant, Jerry felt himself being lifted into the air and turned upside down and shaken like a doll. He started to scream from a pressure inside his head that made his mind want to explode. Then he heard the shattering of glass and felt a glass-like shard penetrate into his heart.

Jerry grasped from the pain and frantically tried to free himself, but the Seega's grip became tighter and tighter, intensifying the pain.

"Put me down!" Jerry yelled as he pulled his torso upward and started punching the invisible hands that were holding his ankles.

Suddenly the colors of the surrounding mists changed. In an instant the extreme heat cooled, and Jerry felt his spirit being gently lifted and placed next to Angel. A commanding feminine voice spoke to him.

"Okay, Jerry, do what you need to do….and get the two of you out of here," the voice told him.

Jerry could hardly believe it. It sounded like—of all people—Jodi.

"Is that you, Jodi? It can't be you."

"And why can't it? I heard you screaming. At first I thought the sound was coming from hell and I was having a bad dream, but then I recognized your voice. I started looking for you and you quickly came into view. You were jerking upside down. I knew you needed help, so I came to help you deal with the spook, but honestly, you're acting like a child and you obviously shouldn't be here." Jodi spoke with a strong voice of authority. "In this place nothing is predictable, and the hot wind never stops blowing across the void."

"I need to free Angel so she can go home," Jerry announced.

"It looks like you gave your power over to the spook who you saw in Norman's driveway. Anyway, he's not as bad as he wants you to believe. He enjoys giving you a hard time. Since I've been here a while, I've had some time to figure out how to deal with his ghoulish outbursts and we've become friends. You know I don't put up with shit from anyone, and I didn't let any headless spook tell me what to do either. He's name isn't Seega, He likes to be called Zakar or Zak for short. You clearly haven't had as much magical training as you make out, or you would have been controlling Zak instead of him controlling you. I always suspected you were just full of hot air. Anyway, now is a good time to take your friend and make your way out of this timeless warp. You can't exist here for too long without it getting the best of you."

"But what about you, Jodi?" Jerry asked. "Can't we all get out of here, the three of us? And I don't know how to free Angel. Can you help undo those etheric chains?"

"Easy said and easy done. It's mind over matter. I thought you knew that. You need me to tell you how to work in the astral planes? This is hysterical!" Jodi laughed.

"It's not funny," Angel yelled. "Get me out of these chains!"

"Yeah, yeah, I know it's not funny," the voice of Jodi said. "Okay. On the count of three, I want to see your hands hanging free. On the count of three your chains are gone!" Jodi ordered.

As invisible Jodi spoke, Jerry began to see the transparency of her thoughts turn into astral actions. He saw Angel's chains dissolve and turn into butterflies. He sighed in relief. He had witnessed an imprisoned soul being miraculously released from bondage.

"Jodi," he said quickly, "if we can leave, so can you. Come back with us."

"I don't think so. Except for occasional swarms of black holes, I like it here just fine. By the way, the spirit that's taken over Angel's physical body murdered children when he was alive. He's one mean bastard. He makes Zak look like a saint in comparison. You have to make him leave her body or she'll be vulnerable to bigger problems than you or I can ever solve," Jodi warned.

Jerry couldn't believe that Jodi was so knowledgeable.

"Thanks for telling us all of this. And you need to come back, too," he repeated.

"I don't have anywhere to go," Jodi answered. All of a sudden, Jerry felt Angel move close to him.

"My hands are free! Jodi, you've rescued me!" Angel said into the ether. "You're welcome to stay with me. We have an extra room in my home. You don't want to stay here. Please come with us."

"That's a nice thought. But I don't want to leave this world. By the way, if you wear garlic earrings and a cross, that can help get rid of the spook who is haunting your body," Jodi advised.

Jerry moved to where he could feel Jodi's electrical heat. From his heart he sent a telepathic thought telling her soul that he would do whatever he could to help her.

"Stop sending those thoughts. You know I can hear them." Jodi replied boldly.

Jerry wanted her to know that he cared. "You've got to come back. You don't want to leave your body half-dead with cords plugged into your arms while you lay in a cold hospital room."

"No matter what you say to me, I do what I want," she answered him coldly.

"Yes, I know. I just want you to know that it's important to leave this place of shadows and illusions," Jerry said rubbing his chest where not too long ago it felt like it had been pierced.

"I'll think about it." Jodi replied as her voice got fainter and fainter, until Jerry could no longer hear it.

"Jodi, Jodi, are you still here?" Jerry cried.

"Where did she go?" Angel asked.

"I don't know, but what I do know is that you and I need to leave. We've got to get back and you have to be strong enough to force the entity to leave your body. Your body belongs to you and even your DNA will help you reclaim it. You get back in your body by pulling your astral umbilical cord. So start pulling on it, and keep chanting for God's grace while you move back into the center of your body."

"Aren't you going to help me?" Angel asked sounding unsure.

Jerry knew that if they were going to be able to leave, he needed to open her mind to using its innate power and summon the strength of her inner spirit. He spoke silently with a gentle, yet dominating tone. "If we keep in fear, it weakens our spirit and diminishes the power of our thought forms. Whatever we think expands, so you need to see your strength. You don't have to let the negative play out in your life. And I'll help you even if I have to engage in telepathic Aikido."

"Well," Angel said, "I want to go home and I want my body back."

"Yes, we both need to go home," Jerry answered as he began to chant his protective mantra.

He reached out to touch Angel's hand and together they instantly floated through a spiraling universe on their way toward home. Soon their astral bodies were hovering over Angel's physical form that looked bruised, unkempt, and misshapen.

"It's time to reenter," Jerry reassured Angel. "Remember, I'll be helping you rid the entity from above your body. Don't give in to fear. Ask your guides to manifest love and healing."

Jerry watched Angel's spirit hover motionless for a few minutes and then dive toward her physical form. From where he was positioned, he drew an imaginary Star of David in the air and used it like a fly fisherman casting his fishing line. Soon the six-pointed star was being used like a hook to catch the darkness and yank the entity out of its new home. Beady, red slanted eyes of fire floated from Angel's body, and slowly rose, to look Jerry directly in his eyes. Jerry psychically drew back and used his finger to draw an aerial image of a Celtic knotted dragon. Instantly, the entity dissolved in air, and Jerry could hear it screaming angrily as it drifted farther and farther away.

He looked down from above and watched Angel's body transform from being hard and rigid into a soft supple peacefulness. Once he knew Angel had safely reclaimed her body, Jerry willed his astral spirit to return to his own physical body.

"Anyone in there?" he yelled to his body before diving into its welcoming form.

Jerry woke up to Destiny and Taylor standing over him covering him with warm blankets.

"Jerry, are you all right?" Destiny was asking with obvious concern.

"Breathe, Jerry, come on, breathe deep, come back to us," Taylor chanted.

"What happened?" Jerry asked, coming out of his sleep-like haze.

"Well, it looks like you went to the Illuminati's playground," Taylor answered. "What a trip you must have been on. All the mirrors in the house were breaking and you were screaming so loud that I thought the neighbors would be calling the police. We came into the room and your body was frozen like ice."

"Wow," Jerry said, squirming under the heavy blankets. "There's enough blankets on me now to cook me to death. You need to go check on Angel!" Jerry sputtered, trying to get his mind back into earthly time and space. "She didn't know her way out of the fourth dimension, so I had to show her the way. She's back in her body now."

Destiny and Taylor looked at each other and then ran out of the room, leaving Jerry to take care of himself. Trying to steady himself, Jerry sat up and stared around the room. He shuddered when he saw the shattered mirrors and took a deep breath. Doubts about his recent sojourn flooded his mind, and he started to worry about Angel. Just then, down the hall he heard Destiny and Taylor talking excitedly with her. Jerry relaxed as it became more and more apparent that Angel had safely returned.

Although he felt groggy, he happily remembered his commitment to call Carmella. Willing his mind to jump back into normal reality, he slowly pulled his cell phone out of his pocket to ring her number.

"Carmella, do you still want company tonight?" Jerry asked when she answered the phone.

"Yes, I'd love for you to come over," Carmella told him. "But I've got to tell you, Norman's father bailed him out of jail and he's coming here tonight." Her voice was filled with uncertainty. "I'd really like you to be here to give me some support. When I last saw him in jail, he was acting so strange."

"He can't be acting any more strange than the people I've talked with lately," Jerry said with a laugh. "I have a lot to tell you. If you want my company, I'll be happy to come over."

"Good! I'll order some pizza for dinner. See you soon," Carmella replied enthusiastically.

Twenty-One: The World

XXI. THE WORLD

Do You Believe In Magic?

As Jerry drove across town, he could hardly believe that it was still daylight. His mind was still occupied with the shadows of darkness that he had recently encountered during his sojourn into the astral planes, and he had completely lost awareness of time. His most immediate reminder that it would soon to be evening was his stomach growling loudly. Thank goodness Carmella had invited him for pizza. His favorite!

Happily, he drove across town, feeling deeply relieved that he had been able to find Angel even though she had been trapped in what appeared to be a fiery well of negativity in the astral planes. And even now the gods were obviously looking out for him, as he had no trouble finding a parking place on Green Street - where it was usually impossible

to find parking. His car fit in the space exactly in front of Carmella's apartment building with several inches to spare. He turned off the motor, looked at himself in the rearview mirror, and tried to smooth his wild-looking hair. Before opening his door, he took a deep breath and mentally released his stress that had accumulated earlier in the day. Diving into his inner calmness, he felt the cool ocean air revive his senses as he stepped onto the curb and began the short walk toward Carmella's.

Knocking on her apartment door felt strangely comforting, as if he was going to be united with a long-lost friend. Even before she opened the door, Jerry intuited her sense of welcome.

"Hi, Jerry," Carmella said, opening the door. "I'm so glad you're here. Come on in. The pizza just arrived. Norman's already here."

Jerry walked into the living room and couldn't believe his eyes. Norman was sitting on the couch in a near fetal position, sucking on his bong as if he were a baby with a bottle.

"Hey, buddy," Norman said, blowing puffs of smoke through a crooked smile. "It's been a while since I've heard from you, but it looks like you and Carmella have been getting along pretty well."

Jerry tried to sound nonchalant.

"Life keeps going on, even when you're in the pokey," he told Norman. "I've been working really hard today, and luckily Carmella invited me for dinner. She told me you'd be here. I hope I'm not disturbing your plans."

"Heck no, you're not in my way. Not now anyway. I just stopped by on my way downtown. I've got to get something to help with my headaches before my old man makes me go to rehab again. Luckily, I've got my man in the Tenderloin picking me up a prescription of my favorite drugs. Once he calls to let me know that he's got what I want, I'm out of here." Norman replied as he sat up, extending his long thin legs to show off his shiny red leather boots.

"Jerry, have a seat," Carmella suggested, giving him a welcoming look.

"Thanks. I hope you don't mind that I didn't pick up anything to help with dinner. I'm so spaced out." Sensing something different about the tone of her voice, Jerry looked deeply into Carmella's eyes.

"What?" Norman said gruffly. "Don't you two sound lovey-dovey? I'm locked out of sight for a week and you two have become best friends."

"Norman, you're out of line," Carmella said with a frown.

"Oh, really? And now you're even talking for him. Something smells like dead fish around here."

"Norman, you're acting paranoid," Jerry said defensively. "Maybe you can thank Carmella for making us dinner instead of insulting her with your insinuations."

"And maybe you're full of shit. I may be a stoner, but I'm not blind."

"Nothing's going on between us," Carmella replied with fire in her voice. "We're becoming better friends. But to keep our communication clear, I need to tell you, whoever I invite to my home is my concern, not yours."

"I don't need to listen to this shit," Norman spit out the words. "I've got better things to do. I'm getting out of here and doing what's really important. Besides, I don't have time to socialize. I've got business to take care of."

"Norman, what about the charges against you?" Jerry asked, trying to stay calm and undisturbed by Norman's aggressive words. "If you get caught buying drugs, you're going to have bigger problems to deal with."

"Don't worry, buddy," Norman said coyly. "I'll beat my drug-related charges. And this Jodi mess is on hold. I've been told that she could come out of her coma any minute and when that happens, I'll be free from pending charges of her endangerment. Besides, I know that her old pimp is still looking for her to get back some of his investment he put into building her career. I can prove that Jodi ain't so innocent. She's a hooker!"

Jerry tightened his arms and clenched his teeth to hold his emotions in check. He felt like grabbing Norman by the neck, but he willed his body not to move and remained motionless.

"Okay, if you've got to go and get your drugs, then just leave," Carmella said with obvious disgust. "I can't handle it that you've just got out of jail and you're in my home calling your buddies to get you high."

"Aren't you sweet? I get the message. I guess you won't want to be getting high with me later on tonight, right?" Norman replied, visibly annoyed.

"No, I don't want to be getting high with you, and you shouldn't be getting high either. Your drug habit makes you look like you're sinking in quick sand."

"Okay, Mom. You and Dad have a good night watching the telly and eating pizza. I'm going out to have some fun," Norman said sourly as he got up and went to the door. "Bye, my friends. I'll catch ya soon, but not too soon," he said walking out and slamming the door behind him.

"Jerry, are you all right?" Carmella asked. Jerry realized that he had been nearly holding his breath and loudly exhaled.

"Don't worry about me. I've got more important things to worry about than Norman." He smiled. "Like when can I have some pizza?" He'd had enough stress this afternoon to last him a long time. He was more than ready to focus on something light-hearted.

Carmella returned his smile and walked to the kitchen, pulling Jerry by his hand so that he had to follow her. The table was already set.

"You must be psychic. You set the table for two."

"I had a strange feeling that we would be the only two people sitting down for dinner. I just knew."

"Well, next time I'm not sure what might happen, I'll call you to get your intuitive scoop," Jerry said, pulling out a chair and sitting down at the table. "If you're still looking for work, you can call a psychic hotline and ask if they need any extra help."

"You're funny. But it's so stressful lately that I would like to pull a card right now. Let's ask the tarot muses about our fate. We can just pull one card," Carmella said pulling out her deck of cards and fanning them face downward. "Okay, Jerry, pick one card to represent our future direction."

Smiling, Jerry closed his eyes and let his hand float over her cards until he felt intuitively drawn to pick one. After pulling it from her deck, he looked to see the name of the card he chose.

"It's The World card. Crowley calls it The Universe, the birth of the daughter of Babylon, 'the Virgin of Eternity,'" he said, studying its picture before giving it back.

"You sound as if you're reading from Crowley's *Book of Thoth*. But if I look at the card in relation to what's happening now, I see it as sign to trust in the richness of life. Let's hope it means that we'll find resolutions to our challenges. That would be a relief," replied Carmella, putting away her cards. "By the way, can you tell me what happened to you this afternoon?"

"I had to take a little trip into the astral planes. A long-time friend had been separated from her body by a phantom who had moved into it while she was out and about flying around in her astral form. I had no recourse except to dive into inner dimensional space to try and find her. This girl had vanished beyond her worldly existence, but thankfully, I found her and brought her spirit back to reconnect her with her body. She wasn't mentally strong enough to get the phantom out of her body, so I helped get him out and her back in."

"Wow! You can really do that?" Carmella asked incredulously.

"There's infinite power in your thoughts if you link them to the right energy. To help her, I had to surround myself with faith in overcoming the dark forces that blocked her return. Even when I thought I might fail,

and in spite of my runaway doubts, my unseen guides helped me stay on course. It was like finding a missing child in the dark. In all honesty, if I hadn't found her, she might never have made her way back home and into her body."

"Okay, now I know who to call when I'm lost in space," Carmella joked.

"While I was out of my body, I lost complete sense of myself. I lacked any awareness of time and place. Much to my surprise, when I thought I was doomed because of hostile forces, Jodi unexpectedly came from out of nowhere to rescue me. Just like we have weird energy in this world, there's so much strange, unpredictable energy in that invisible nonmaterial realm."

"You saw Jodi! She was there?" Carmella was obviously taken aback.

"I don't know how she found me, but she did. It's obvious her inner spirit is journeying through the etheric realms. She found us and easily defeated our hostile rival."

"I wonder how's she's doing," Carmella said. She was silent for a moment before speaking again. "How did you learn to astral travel? Do you think you can teach me so that I can go where you went and find Jodi?"

"I learned in an occult school, and no I won't teach you, but let's change the subject. I'm so glad to be here right now. I don't want to think about that strange world anymore today. Where's the pizza? I'm hungry!" Jerry said, his mouth making a childlike pout.

Carmella walked to the stove and took out a steaming pizza. Humming, she cut the pizza and brought it to the table, and then poured them both a glass of wine.

She lit a candle, gave thanks to the Cosmic Mother, and then said, "I'm so happy that you're here. For some reason, I didn't want to be alone with Norman."

"No wonder. Norman looks like he's on a bad trip. I can understand why his intensity is a bit of challenge. And you've been his lover."

"Yes, he loves me so much that when I overwatered and killed his peyote plants, he went into a fiery rage. I was afraid he was going to kill me, too."

"That is an odd brand of love, and it doesn't sound too pleasant. Maybe our meal will taste better if we don't talk about him anymore."

"I agree. What would you like to talk about?" Carmella took a sip of her wine.

"Has anyone called you about Rambo yet?" Jerry asked.

"No. But this afternoon Luna came over and we practiced some magic that her coven suggested I do to find him. I'm hoping her spell really works, because so far, trying to find Rambo by putting up lost dog signs hasn't been very helpful. I feel so sad and violated that someone would just walk away with him."

"What kind of magic did you do?" Jerry said looking slightly uncomfortable.

"We faced the noonday Sun and put a mirror with a spiked collar on his pillow where he sleeps to reflect the light of an all-knowing Sun God, Amun Ra. Then we sprinkled some dust on it that Luna said came from a hidden temple chamber of an ancient Egyptian pyramid," Carmella replied with an air of confidence,

"It might be simpler to walk around the site where you lost him and call his name," Jerry said.

"I did that most of yesterday and the day before, too. Actually, I know this sounds crazy, but I think I saw Rambo being groomed on the movie set where I went to do my interview. There was a dog that looked similar to mine except it had much of his hair shaved off, and was taken away before I could get close enough to be sure of its identity. Despite all the weirdness, I had some good luck while I was looking for him at the studio. I had an unexpected chance to talk with the producer, and he hired me as an extra to work on a documentary he's filming about the Inquisition. Tomorrow, I'm going back to the set to star as a witch who's about to be burned at the stake. Although the main reason I want to go back there is to have more time to look for Rambo."

"Maybe you should call Luna and get some tips on how to be a witch," Jerry said in a sarcastic tone.

"What? You're joking, right?" Carmella asked in obvious disbelief.

"Well, I remember how she looked at you when we met her. I'm sure she'd be happy to have an excuse to talk with you again."

"Jerry, you're sounding like a jealous boyfriend. If you want to know about Luna's interest in me, she's already opened the door for me to join her coven."

"Wow! She wants you to join her coven?" Jerry asked remembering the howling of aspirant she wolves that he heard when they first met Luna.

"Yes, but she's offered me more than what I can honestly accept. Her group is doing a private ritual and she asked me if I would be willing to be trained to take a priestess role and play the part of the goddess Persephone. She told me that there would be some surprises and she couldn't tell me all the details of her group's secret workings. Since she

said they were doing sex magic, I was afraid that I might be encouraged to have sex with Hades, or something. I wasn't sure about how I could set personal boundaries in a magic circle. I just can't put myself into a situation where I'm totally unsure of what's expected of me. I'm not that open-minded."

Jerry looked at Carmella with surprise. For someone who was supposed to be an uptown writer, she certainly had more than her fair share of interactions with the occult underworld. Jerry took a bite of his pizza and chewed slowly while looking at his friend, trying to get a better sense of who she really was. After a long silence he asked, "You didn't accept Luna's invitation?"

"No, but if I change my mind, I don't think I would have a problem joining her moon circle."

Jerry was surprised at his emotional reaction to Carmella's story. He felt relieved that she had said no to Luna. He wasn't sure exactly why, but he became a little uneasy around Luna. Perhaps it was because he had an uncanny sense that she was a little moon struck over Carmella.

"Well, I'm happy you're here with me instead of dancing around a circle with a group of goddess-obsessed women," he told her. "Besides, you're already a tarot reader, and that's considered by many to be witchy, and tomorrow you'll be acting the role of a witch for a movie. How much more practice do you need before you become one? You'd better be careful or you'll be cooking your meals in a cauldron," Jerry cautioned with a smile.

Carmella laughed. "You're right. But you're forgetting the most important thing. Hanging around you automatically makes me a witch's apprentice."

"I'm not a witch, maybe a wizard, but definitely not a witch. Did you know that when angels lose their wings, they fly on brooms?"

"No, I didn't know that, Jerry, but I'm glad to have that very valuable piece of information," Carmella replied with a coy smile while reaching for his hand. "Also, I need to tell you that I showed Luna my magical stone. She sensed that it's an enchanted shaman's stone and told me that I need to return it to where I found it as soon as possible. She compared its energy to a witch's injured familiar that had suffered from being forced to do too much magic."

"Carmella, will you show me the stone?"

"No. I don't want to take it out of its bag anymore. It makes me feel strong, yet renders me weak, and it's beginning to freak me out. But I want you to take me to the old house so that I can return it. I'm too afraid to go there on my own," she said, letting go of his hand.

"Sure. I'll take you back. The other day I talked with a realtor about that place, and it turns out that it was built over an Indian burial ground."

"Oh, great," she said sarcastically.

Jerry couldn't help but grin when he saw the pitiable expression on her face.

"It has an unpleasant history. No one has ever been known to be able to live in the house for very long, and the last man who lived in it committed suicide in the room upstairs where we felt the presence of departed spirits. For adventure's sake, I'm happy to have an excuse to go back inside." He was quiet for a moment before speaking again. "Honestly, it's more of a treat that you invited me to be here to be with you tonight."

"For me, too," she answered. Even though she spoke in earnest, Carmella didn't tell Jerry the complete story about her afternoon with Luna. In spite of her mind instinctively closing to Luna's invitation, her curiosity was attracted to the idea of playing the role of a goddess in a ritual. When she had refused Luna's invitation, she laughed and told Carmella to stop holding herself in check like a shy schoolgirl. The energy around her seemed electrically charged as Luna said, "Let me teach you how to intensify your senses and develop your psychic abilities. I can initiate you into the mystery of the phoenix and the dragon and show you how to use alchemical formulas to tap into celestial power. With more knowledge, during a heated moment of sexual rapture you can harness the power in your stone for your own benefit." Perhaps if I hadn't lost my dog, I wouldn't feel attracted by her invitation, Carmella reflected. Jerry's beautiful eyes seemed to pierce the veil of her soul. She smiled at him and reached for another piece of pizza.

"It's funny, Carmella, because sometimes people say I'm hard to talk to, but it feels easy to talk with you," Jerry confessed. "What do you think?"

"It feels like we've known each other a long time and I'm really comfortable being here with you, but both of our lives are so complicated."

"Yeah. I know. I do my best to communicate with Stella, but we keep not being able to hear one another. She thinks on a different wave-length. I'm seriously asking myself if I can be married to her anymore. I've been willing to work on our relationship, but she keeps driving me crazy with her unilateral choices for our life."

"Maybe we should ask Luna to do a spell to help your relationship," Carmella said in earnest. "Honestly, I know how painful it is to separate from someone and I wouldn't wish it on anyone."

"Oh, no, thank you very much. That's already being taken care of. I found out from my friend Destiny that her mother, the wise witch of the west, Naomi-Know-Me, was hired by my beloved wife to do a spell to weave our lives back together. If the spell worked at all, its magic backfired because Stella's pregnant with some other man's baby. I just have no idea of how to be with her at this point in our relationship. I've lost all positive feelings toward her. Reconciling with her doesn't feel like it's in the cards."

"That does sound a bit challenging to deal with. But whatever you decide to do, I'll support your decision and help you in any way I can."

"I appreciate that a lot," Jerry said. Looking at her, he couldn't ignore what he was feeling. Made more confident by the wine, he asked, "And what about us, Carmella? What direction is our relationship going?"

"I don't know, and honestly I'm surprised to hear your question," Carmella answered. "You're so much fun to be with, and I appreciate you as a friend. I know you've been having a difficult time in your relationship with your wife, so I've been trying to be respectful and not take time away from Stella. I've been learning from you. You know more about magic than anyone else I've ever met. Well, except for Luna, who also seems to know more than most people."

Jerry's was thinking about how to respond, when his cell phone rang and he looked at the number.

"I need to answer that," Jerry told Carmella. "It's my Mom, and I haven't been able to get a hold of her for a while. She's been in the woods up north without phone reception."

He picked up his cell phone and answered.

"Hi, Mom," he said, getting up and walking to the living room so that he could talk in private. "You left a message on my phone telling me that you're on your way to the rain forest in Brazil! What's happening? I thought you were fighting to save the redwoods in Sonoma County."

"Jerry, I don't have time to explain everything, but in this world, this global village, everything's connected. Yes, I'm still supporting our mission to stop the loggers, but things are happening with the new man I met. He wants me to go with him to Brazil next week. He's so cool, and he's helping me become more aware of my higher purpose, something I feel really good doing. I want to give my life to protect Mother Nature. The Amazon contains the lungs of our planet. If they keep cutting down the forest, we won't have any air to breathe." Jerry's mother sounded like she needed more air to breathe at that very moment.

"Mom, what about your pregnant daughter?"

"I'm on a mission to become more alive than I've ever been in my past. Julie is old enough to take care of herself. If she can get pregnant, she can learn to be an adult and take care of herself. Besides, she's moving in with your father and he can watch her."

"Mom, if you're going to the Amazon who's going to look after your house?" Jerry asked.

"Why do you ask?"

"Because I'm going through a rough time with Stella and I'd love to have some place to get away and clear my head so I can figure out what I'm wanting in my life in relation to my marriage. That woman is driving me crazy," Jerry confessed.

"Sorry about you and Stella, but right now there seems to be an epidemic of troubled relationships. My friend Moe refuses to talk to me. Last time I talked with him, he mumbled something about my lack of integrity, before he said he never wanted to see me again. After that I had the surprise of my life when your father called me crying about his problems. He said he'd crawl on his knees to beg me to come back into his life if I would have him. He sounds like he's half crazy," Rowan said.

"Yes, I know Dad's under scrutiny because of something with his secret fraternity. He might be sued by an initiate who got hurt during some ceremony that went out of control."

"Well, his group has enough lawyers in it to sink the Titanic. Your father won't have any trouble doing some counter-suit or mediating his way into being the helpless victim. Like they do for everyone in their group, his buddies will help him find a way to squirm out of any trouble."

"Mom, how can you sound so cold hearted about Dad?"

"Oh right! I forgot," she said with obvious sarcasm. "I'm not supposed to say anything bad to you about your father. Okay, well in answer to your earlier question…if you want to make my home your home, that will actually help me out because I was wondering who I could find to feed my animals and water my plants. You'll have to walk my dog and get her groomed as part of the deal, oh, and obviously keep an eye on your sister," Rowan said, quickly changing her tone.

"No problem. I'll be glad to do all that. How long are you going to be gone?"

"We'll stay as long as we can to fulfill our mission to help save the trees in the Amazon. I'm told that we might be gone as long as four or five months. Would you be able to stay that long?"

"Yes, Mom, I think that it will work out well for both of us. I'll take good care of everything. Are you going to be home tonight? Can I come by and get instructions?"

"Yes, I'll be home in about an hour. Come on over, but I'm frantic about needing to pack and get everything in order. I have so much to do."

"Don't worry. I promise not to take too much of your time. I'll be over later. Bye, Mom." Jerry said and hung up.

As he walked back toward the kitchen, Jerry realized that one of the stresses in his mind had eased because he had made the decision to move out of his apartment. Now he had a plan and an escape route from his life with Stella.

His thoughts were disrupted when he walked into the room and saw Carmella putting a piece of pie on his plate. He sadly remembered Stella's apple pie and her betrayal.

"That was my mom," he said, gathering his thoughts. "She's becoming a tree hugger with a vengeance. She's getting ready to go to Brazil to help save the rainforest. I'm going to house sit for her while she's gone. Just the thought of having a different space to live makes me feel relieved."

"Darn. I was hoping you'd ask to move in with me," Carmella said with a big chuckle. It was obvious that she had continued drinking wine while Jerry was in the other room.

Jerry laughed.

"Sure, that sounds good, too. It wouldn't complicate things much, would it?" He felt his heart lighten just from hearing her suggest such a possibility.

He was about to reach for Carmella's hand again when he was jolted by an unexpected sound. Someone was pounding on the door like thunder. They both jumped up and went running toward the front room. Carmella looked through the door's peek hole.

"It's Norman," she said before slightly opening the door.

"Hi, Carmella," Norman said, obviously in a daze. "I thought I'd come over and see if you were missing me. I need you to come over to my house 'cause I'm going to have a party tonight. I've invited this totally cool Jewish shaman with connections to the other world to come over and play drums to send the ghost in my drive back to wherever it came from. Jerry, you can come over too. Maybe you and my shaman friend can drum together and get the bogey man out of my space. I'm hoping if I get rid of the ghosts, things won't be so weird around my house. Can you let me in? It's cold out here."

Carmella opened the door wider and Norman walked in. His eyes looked wild and wasted at the same time. Jerry watched him walk and realized that he was so stoned that his feet didn't seem to move as he walked. Norman got to the couch and fell down. Jerry looked at Carmella.

"Are you going to be okay?" he whispered to her so that Norman wouldn't hear.

"Yes. It isn't like I haven't seen him like this before. I know what to expect," she replied. She turned to Norman. "Do you want me to drive you home? You look like you need a chauffeur."

"Yes, baby, that'll be great, but I'm not wanting to move right now. Maybe I can just sit here with you 'til my head clears enough to get in my car and go home," Norman answered with a slur.

"Well, if you've invited a shaman to your house, you should be going home soon to meet him," Jerry interjected.

"Don't worry, my man. I've already given him permission to be in my space and do his thing. You jealous? I've got my woman by my side and a shaman who knows how to get rid of bogeys instead of run from them… like some people around here do. If you're lucky, you might learn a few lessons from this dude," Norman said condescendingly.

"Sure, maybe I'll come by to meet him," Jerry answered, feeling his blood begin to boil. "Carmella, it's time for me to go. I've got some errands to run before I can come to Norman's later. Thanks for the pizza."

Jerry wasn't happy to see Norman grabbing for Carmella and was even less happy to hear that he was getting her to drive him back to his home for the night. The only reason he accepted the invitation to visit Norman's home later in the evening was to check on her safety.

"Carmella," Jerry said, "I've got to get going, but it sounds like I'll be seeing you at Norman's later. By the way, if you hear anything about Rambo, call me. I've got a gut instinct that he's coming home."

"Thanks. I hope you're right," Carmella said, opening the door for Jerry so that he could leave. She walked him outside to say good-bye. "Thanks, Jerry, for being here with me. I feel happy spending time with you."

Jerry looked at her. She appeared vulnerable and strong at the same time. He was becoming more aware of his attraction for her, and felt a soulful sense of longing.

He reached over and awkwardly gave her a kiss. "I'll see you soon," he said, "but it feels completely wrong to be leaving you with Norman when he's acting like an erupting volcano."

"I'll take him home. He's had a rough week. Don't worry," Carmella said.

"And what if I do worry?"

"It will be a waste of your time. Besides I thought you said you were coming to his place later. I'll be waiting for you there. I'll even bring your

slice of pie that you're leaving behind," she said, giving him a quick kiss on the cheek and a gentle push toward his car.

"I've sworn off of pie lately, but I'll be happy to have a little more of you."

"Only a little more?" Carmella said playfully.

"Okay...a lot more of you." Jerry looked at Carmella and felt an unfamiliar sense of joy.

Twenty-Two: The Fool

0. THE FOOL

The Cauldron of Consciousness

Surrounded by darkness, Jodi kept searching through the veil of shadows trying to find the source of the voices she heard calling her name. For a fleeting moment, she glimpsed a ray of light, but then it vanished as suddenly as it appeared. From challenging mishaps during her out of body journey and her accidental arrival at the crossroads of alpha and omega she had been tested to the point where she knew the sound of truth from lies; she recognized the voices of the light from those lost in darkness; and no spirit or worldly presence would ever be able to lie to her again without her hearing the falsehood.

Submerged in subconscious vortexes, it had been a struggle to learn to the decipher the differences between illusion and reality in the fourth

dimension to make sense of what she was witnessing, especially since the reality she knew did not exist here, and the strange world around her was constantly shifting like sand in windblown dunes. Through trial and error, she came to understand that for her own survival she had to make a choice between forming an alliance with her higher self and her light body consciousness, or stumble and tumble into an alignment with fear and terror. Like opening an unexpected gift, she used her intuition to play her part well in what she named the Theater of Karma, and had learned to recognize the magical forces that exist beyond reason.

She felt the pulse of her life force and realized she was near physical death. In vain, she tried to do away with the foreboding sense of her own demise. With every turn, her awareness told her that she needed to balance her perspective, find the center of her spiritual gravity, and make peace with the transformative forces of death and rebirth.

Somewhere on her journey—she didn't remember when or where—she made a pledge never to let anyone talk her into following a path that led away from her true self, but now that distant voices were calling to her, her spirit wanted to follow them to hear what they were saying. She listened with her heart to the meaning behind the words she was hearing, and continued to search the emptiness to find where the voices were loudest.

"Jodi, please come to us, please!" she heard someone say. Electrical shivers ran through her. She hadn't heard anyone calling her name for so long it was shocking to hear a voice calling her now.

"We see you in the light and we want you to come home to us. Call on your angels to guide and protect you."

Jodi looked around and didn't see any angels, but the pinpoint of light she had seen earlier was gradually becoming larger and brighter. The Angel who she had watched falter and fall into a trap set by Zak's fiendish strength wouldn't be able to help her; she was certain of that, but now she was afraid that she was losing what was left of her own power.

Oh my God, am I going to die?

She tried to consciously hold on to what remained of her astral form and willed it to stop moving, but it was as if she was in a whirlpool being twirled in a flurry of dazzling electrical currents. Then she sensed a tunnel and felt herself being hurled by some invisible force toward the light.

"I'm scared," she cried out in a loud voice. "I don't want to die."

Another voice answered her and she knew it to be the soothing familiar voice of her mother.

"Don't let your heart be troubled," her mother said. "Your spirit is pure and protected by the light. Please forgive me for the harm I've mistakenly caused you. Fear not, for I am always with you, as I am in God's house."

Now Jodi knew for sure that she was dying, as her spirit was caught in the whirlpool of motion beyond happiness or sadness that was carrying her to realms unknown. She stopped trying to speak. So this is what death is like, she thought as she struggled to open her eyes.

Everything was blurry and she couldn't quite make out the forms that were slowly coming into focus.

Someone said excitedly, "She's opened her eyes! She's come back to us!"

Jodi felt her physical body, the pain frozen in her head, the annoying vibration of loud voices, and the shock of being in a bed in a hospital room with tubes running into her veins. Jerry and Carmella were standing next to the bed. Carmella ran out of the room calling for a nurse.

Jerry held her hand and bent over her to give her a gentle kiss on the cheek. "I'm here for you, Jodi. I'm going to make sure that your life gets better," he said, squeezing her hand. His voice, appearing as a light wave entering her mind, spoke silently with a gentle, humble tone. "Do you remember rescuing me and Angel while we were stuck in the inner dimensions? One good turn deserves another. When you get out of here, it's my turn to rescue you and make sure you are safe. My mom is giving me her house while she's out of town. You can stay there in my sister's empty room. It's comfy and secure, and this time I promise not to let you down.

The shock was too much for Jodi. Was this real? The sharp pain in her head prevented her from speaking even though she wanted to answer her friend. Just then, Carmella and a nurse entered the room. Jodi closed her eyes to pretend she was asleep.

"It's better to let Jodi rest. You both need to leave now," the nurse told Jerry and Carmella as she checked Jodi's vital signs. "You can come back tomorrow to see how she's doing."

Carmella and Jerry each gave Jodi a kiss on the forehead before they left her side. Walking to the parking lot, Jerry wanted to hold Carmella's hand but stopped himself. Even though he was drawn to her, he had made a silent commitment not to disrespect her relationship with Norman, and he would keep it, even if it was becoming more difficult.

After they reached the hospital parking lot, they climbed into his car. Jerry looked at his cell phone messages, and was surprised to see that

Lisa had called and left a message. I'll never again listen to anything that woman has to say, he thought to himself as he erased her message.

Focusing on Carmella, he said, "I'm glad you agreed to meet me here today after the craziness at Norman's last night. I'm looking forward to his rehab treatment. Hopefully I won't feel the need to check on your safety after he becomes clean and sober." Even when Jerry heard himself say this to Carmella, he wasn't sure he believed it. His heart would be happy to see her whatever the reason.

"You don't have to worry about me. Norman is a friend and nothing more. If I did have any lingering doubts about our relationship, Norman doomed any chance for it last night when he took out a syringe, pulled down his pants, and dosed himself with a shot of speed in the vein next to his balls. " Carmella answered. "He's too crazy for me."

"Yikes! Maybe it's better not to think about Norman. My ears are still ringing from listening to his mojo friend drumming in the parking lot last night to scare away the Seega. Perhaps it wouldn't have been so hard on the ears if that guy would have taken a drum lesson somewhere along his shamanic path. But when I'm here right now in this moment everything improves. Today's a brand new day, the weather's great, and we get to drive up the coast together. I'm feeling good."

"I'm happy too, and glad to leave thoughts of Norman behind in the parking lot," Carmella said.

"Truthfully, I'm feeling so much better after seeing Jodi open her eyes. My raven guides came to me last night in a dream and soared in a serene, unbroken circular pattern. When I looked past them I could see the turning of the earth and in the distance I saw a bright light coming from a dark cave. When I woke up, I hoped that my dream symbolized Jodi would be coming out of her unconscious state." Jerry looked at Carmella, then turned his ignition key, and began to drive. He couldn't help but smile when he glanced at Carmella in the soft afternoon light.

"I wish you saw Rambo in your dream and you could tell me that he's going to be alright."

"Have faith in miracles, Carmella. Maybe you'll find him roaming around somewhere today." Jerry reached over to squeeze her hand for support. "And your good fortune is that you've been offered an acting role in a movie."

"I'm not so sure about becoming an actress," she said. "All my life I've been a writer and an introvert. Getting into the acting guild and jumping center stage in front of a camera is a little overwhelming."

"Life always presents new opportunities. My crystal ball tells me that you're perfect for the role because inside your soul lives a magnificent witch wearing an invisibility cloak."

"Thanks a lot for your vote of confidence. I don't know about this witch stuff, and I don't own a black cape or broomstick, and strangely enough, my shoot was canceled today. His secretary called me to say that Mr. Stalsburg had an emergency rush to the hospital, and most likely will be rescheduling his work this week."

"I wonder if he's suffering from a dog bite," Jerry mused.

"If my dog is shaved bare naked with a henna tattoo on his butt, and my spell worked that might be the case. But then again, maybe you have an overactive imagination."

Jerry laughed. "And maybe I believe in magic."

"That's obvious, Mr. Magic Man," Carmella said with a grin.

"It's not a joke, really. It's just that my mind stays open to possibilities and the inner connectedness of all things."

"Really," she asked. "Well, I believe in magic too. It's very magical that I'm here with you right now. I was so certain that your relationship with Stella would prevent us from spending much time together, and I was a hundred percent sure that I would never go to that haunted house again. Yet we're finding time to be together, and we're going back there now."

"Never is a fleeting concept. For instance, my supposedly lifelong bond with Stella is broken. Luckily, when she told her estranged lover that she was she was pregnant with his child, he was ecstatic, and invited her to become part of his polyamorous tribal family. Its six members swap partners within their own group, but shy away from allowing new partners to join their intimate family. Because Stella's pregnant with the patriarch's child, she's being invited into their private circle. It's her good karma that she can explore love with the real father of the child and has an extended family to help with her baby. Her choice sets me free of my commitment with her. As of today, I'm moving out of my apartment with Stella and into my Mom's home to take care of it while she goes to South America."

"Really? Are you sure about all these changes?"

"I don't know. I'm still a bit confused. Ever since several months ago when Stella decided to change the terms of our relationship, I've been analyzing the meaning of love, trying to make sense of my life. Not having clarity about my feelings made it almost impossible to make decisions about what to do. 'Only fools fall in love,' the saying goes, and I've been trying so hard to not let myself be a fool. Love is so mystifying."

Carmella gripped Jerry's hand tightly and took a deep breath. "I'm sure you're making the right choice," she told him. "You're following your heart."

"I hope so. I'm sure we'll find out, but for now I'm feeling relieved. And as far as going back to the haunted house, I'm glad that you're willing to return your strange rock to where you found it."

"That house is scary, but if you feel okay going there again, I'm willing to follow you. I'm hoping that when I return the stone, maybe my luck will improve. Besides, the energy in that stone keeps letting me know that it wants to be somewhere else, and that it's unlucky for me. Since I've been carrying it, I've had one misfortune after another…the car accident with Norman, my ankle nearly breaking, and my dog disappearing, not to mention what happened with Norman and Jodi. When I think that the stone may have something to do with all those things, I feel frightened."

"I'm not surprised. You probably have the invisible legions of the underworld knocking on your door to retrieve their precious rock." When Jerry saw the panicked expression on Carmella's face he said, "I'm kidding, don't worry. Hopefully everything's getting better." Even though he was driving, he turned to look at her, and for a moment their eyes met.

His mind took a detour and became lost in the growing sense of his new-found freedom and the potential direction of their relationship. In the next moment, Jerry had to swiftly return his focus to the road and slam on the brakes, almost passing the driveway that led to their destination. Smiling at Carmella, he turned his wheel and slowly went down the bumpy drive. To ensure an easy exit, he parked his car facing the road before shutting off the engine.

He looked at Carmella and noticed her face turn pale. "We'll be okay. All we have to do is walk inside and return the rock. I won't try to communicate with any ghosts, so don't worry. We'll make it quick."

"I'm scared. I can't help it."

Jerry reached over to hold her hand again. "We'll be safe. Our thought forms are connected to emotion. If we keep focused on fear, it feeds our thoughts and makes the negative grow. As our negative thinking expands, it attracts bad energy, and we get trapped into believing that our fears have more power over us than they really do. Thank goodness, we don't have to let negative forces rule our life."

"But why am I so afraid? This place freaks me out."

"Fears can be past life memories or subconscious phantoms. You can ask your higher self, your spirit guides, or your angels to illuminate your path with a protective light."

"So you're not scared now?"

"Truthfully, I'm more troubled thinking about how Angel got trapped in the astral planes." Jerry admitted.

"But you rescued her." Carmella said.

"Maybe if knew what went wrong I'd feel better. I really wish I had seen her father's ritual where her possession started."

"It's all strange to me. And I don't have a clue about the astral realms," added Carmella. "Regardless of any mistakes, the most important thing is that she's safe now," she replied in a matter-of-fact tone, as if what had happened was completely normal.

"Okay, let's do what we came here to do. We'll go in, you return the stone, and we'll get out of here," Jerry said opening the car door and getting out. Soon he was leading them up the familiar path to the old dwelling. The wind had blown the door off its rotting frame so that it was already open, but even in the middle of the day most of the house was unnervingly dark and lifeless. The stifling smell of mold and decay made it seem older than its wearisome years. He gave Carmella a little smile before they entered the front room.

"Do you want me to help you? I don't want you to worry about being here," he asked.

"Right now I'm testing my courage. I can do this."

"Yes, I know, but I don't mind helping."

"I need to return the stone myself," she said bravely. Then, in a gentle sprint she went to the broken chest of drawers, opened the top drawer, and placed the stone in the exact spot where she had found it. For some reason she had expected chains to rattle or a bolt of lightning to crackle through the sky, but nothing happened.

She looked at Jerry. "It's back in its rightful place. Now, please, please, please, let's get out of here. I just felt something brush past my hurt ankle, and I'm getting scared again. Maybe it's the owner of the rock."

They both dashed outside into the sunlight, and even though the return of the stone seemed anticlimactic, Carmella was happy she would never have to go back into the old house again.

"I'm glad to see your ankle has mostly healed," Jerry commented, noticing how fast Carmella had left the house.

"Yes, it's healing, but that place feels so creepy that even if my ankle was broken in three places, I would have run out of there."

"Well, here we are, and it's a warm sunny day," Jerry said as he opened her car door. He looked back at the house and was sure he saw an unusual shadow move across the door, but he didn't mention it to Carmella.

Jerry got into his car, started the engine, smiled at Carmella, and then looked in his rear view mirror. He took a deep breath and turned off his engine. "Zak, get out of the car. You're not invited to come with us."

Carmella jumped and turned around to look behind her. She saw nothing. "What is it?"

After a couple of minutes of stressed silence, Jerry replied. "It's nothing," and then he started his car again. "We're out of here. I'll drive you back to your car."

"What did you see, Jerry? For a minute I felt like I was in a sci-fi movie."

"An old acquaintance. Don't worry. He's gone."

Just at that moment Carmella's cell phone rang.

"Hello," she answered and became deadly silent. Then she squealed in excitement. "You have Rambo? Thank you, yes, I'll be there as soon as possible! She talked for a few minutes and then turned off the phone before starting to scream with joy.

"Someone has found your dog," Jerry replied with certainty.

"Yes, someone with a bandaged arm brought him to the secretary in the production office. She's sure it's Rambo because his name tag is on his collar, and she recognizes him from the other day when she saw him in her office. I'm so excited!"

"Does she know the person who brought him to her office?"

"A man she didn't recognize dropped him off and left quickly. She said that he was polite, but wouldn't say anything about where he found him. I don't care, though. I'm so happy."

"So far, today is a day to celebrate. I'm very happy for you," Jerry said.

Carmella couldn't contain her happiness and repeatedly asked Jerry to drive faster even though he was already going over the speed limit as he zipped around the curves and wove in and out of the traffic.

"Will I see you later this evening?" Carmella asked as they arrived at her car.

"I was hoping you'd ask. I'll come by after dinner. Right now I'm going home to start packing for my move."

Carmella felt her heart smile as she opened the door to leave.

Later in the evening, Jerry found himself feeling anxious as he knocked on Carmella's door. He made a mental commitment to accept whatever happened between him and Carmella with a positive attitude.

Good or bad, right or wrong, he would welcome whatever this experience would bring.

Carmella invited him in like a long lost friend, and Jerry enjoyed the warm embrace and easy connection that she offered him. After having watched her anxiously fret over her lost dog, it was a relief to see Carmella and Rambo back together again.

"I knew you'd find him. My gut instinct was telling me that he would be found."

"Yes. I'm so excited, and he has all his fur," Carmella said. "You were also right when you said things would be getting better. When I went online after I got home I had an email telling me that my "Revolving Wheel of the Sacred Circle" magazine article sold and is going to be published at the end of next month. I'm getting paid enough for my writing and for my little acting role that I'll be able to pay my bills for a couple months. And I feel so much better knowing that someone appreciates my writing. It was so hard getting fired from my editorial position. I didn't know if I'd ever recover."

"You look like you're recovering just fine," Jerry replied with an expression of unswerving enchantment. "In fact, you're showing all the signs of doing better than if you'd have stayed on with your job in New York. Do you know how many people wish they could get hired at the production studio? Lots! Fortune is obviously on your side. And now you have genuine proof that you're one gorgeous witch!"

Carmella laughed. Jerry felt irresistibly attracted to her.

Her natural warmth touched his heart in a way that made him want to sing a song of gratitude to the gods. A good sign, Jerry thought, but he didn't want to look too deeply into her eyes in case he was deluding himself and might wake up from this dream of happiness. Still, he couldn't deny that his longing for her grew stronger every time they were together, but what if she wasn't feeling the same way?

His uncertainty stirred as he watched her kiss Rambo goodnight and put him into his doggie bed. Almost instantly, his mood turned to excitement as she turned toward him, smiled with her bright, beautiful eyes, and walked to his side to pull him close to her. Holding him tightly, she gave him a kiss that merged their bodies in an unspoken bond of trust. Together they turned and started to walk past the flickering candles toward her bedroom. Jerry began to experience something that had been missing in his life for in a long time: his heart felt the peace of being welcomed home.

About The Author

After graduating from college in Ohio with a teaching credential and then saying "no" to teaching high school English, Kooch followed westward winds to San Francisco. There she pursued her love affair with metaphysics and became a student of the tarot. Early in her career as a reader she did beer foam readings for fun at her favorite night time hot spots, and in the daytime she sat in front of Ghirardelli Square to offer her tarot insights for one dollar a reading.

Kooch claims that her life is stranger than fiction. She returned to school and completed a Master's degree in psychology, but then found her inner voice pulling her into being a professional reader. This included doing readings for twenty-five years at the northern and southern California Renaissance Faires. Hoping to change the perception of the tarot from being a tool for fortune telling into being a guide for life-choices and inner transformation, in recent decades she has done readings in the corporate world for many high profile Fortune 500 companies, uptown private parties, and modest down home suburban gatherings.

Besides spending time with her family, Kooch enjoys hiking in the redwood forest and playing on the beach. But when Kooch is near her desk at home, she loves to write. Besides writing Theater of Karma, she has written The Art and Magic of Palmistry, and with her husband Victor, she has coauthored Tarot D' Amour (Redwheel Weiser 2003.) and Matrix Meditations (Inner Traditions 2009). On the tech side, she has written The Timely Tarot (ASC 1987), a computerized tarot program that divines personal readings, published by Astro Communication Services.